THEY NEVER STOP
LOVING YOU

SAL SANFILIPPO

Publishing Coordinator – Sharon Kizziah-Holmes
Cover Design – Jaycee DeLorenzo

Paperback-Press
an imprint of A & S Publishing
Paperback Press, LLC.
Springfield, Missouri

ISBN -13: 978-1-964559-67-4

DEDICATION

Oh Captain, my Captain
You're everywhere in this story
You're always in my heart
Wherever we go, we two shall never part

ACKNOWLEDGMENTS

To my loving wife Gina, who reads every draft, my son Michael, who inspires me to be the best man I can be, and my daughter Leah, without whose "Can I have a dog?" this story would never have been written.

I

MIRIAM

I stared into the old man's cold, dead eyes. He'd swallowed the last mouthful of tapioca, locked his teeth on the spoon, and appeared to die with a muted gurgle. Well, with those ice-blue eyes staring cross-eyed at the spoon clenched between his ancient yellow teeth, he sure looked dead to me.

I took a deep breath as beads of sweat formed on my upper lip.

Damn. Don't die on my watch.

My hand twisted, shifting the spoon to the side of his mouth, leaving the ninety-two-year-old man looking like some perverse version of Popeye the Sailor Man with the spoon replacing Popeye's ubiquitous pipe. With my heart pounding and struggling to breathe, I hurried out of the room to search for the charge nurse.

My shrink had told me I suffered from the narcissism endemic to the young people of my generation and suggested I do some volunteer work to remind myself what real pain and hardship look like. So rather than joining so-called friends blocking traffic on the 110—as they pumped additional toxins into the air while protesting issues like nuclear power or climate change—I found myself wearing a silly pastel smock and doing community service at this hospital in LA.

"More than three hours left on your shift," the supervising nurse said, looking unimpressed with my performance to this point. "Let's see if you can safely pass them here."

So, there I stood in the hospital waiting room with instructions to grab a stranger and share some of my unique brand of goodwill. Close to a dozen people sat scattered around, most seeming like they wanted to be anywhere but in the gray, fluorescent-lit room with its frayed, coffee-stained chairs. My attempts to engage people in conversation were met with blank stares or indifferent shakes of the head. With a warm December sun shining on garish Christmas decorations, I looked out the window at the palm trees swaying slowly in the breeze. I'd been in Southern California for nearly four years, and the holidays still made me homesick. I sighed as the lyrics of The Trade Winds' "New York's a Lonely Town" played on a loop in my head. Like the palm trees, I'd been pulled out by my roots and taken to a foreign land. I was more out of place in

Southern California than the lonely surfer boy in the song who walked the winter streets of New York.

That's when I saw him.

He stood alone, facing the window, medium-height, with out-of-proportion broad shoulders, a strong jaw, and a full head of curly gray hair. He turned and looked at me like I'd been expected and smiled. His alert, dark eyes met mine, and with a flick of his head, he signaled me to join him.

Moving through a fog, I walked across the room and fell into a chair facing the window, my legs no longer my friend.

"Rough day." It wasn't a question.

"Do I look that bad?"

His smile grew, lighting his weathered face as he lowered himself into the chair beside me.

"Not at all. You're every bit as pretty as my daughters, and God was at his best both those days. You just look like you've had a tough day. But hey, we all have them. It's what we do with them that matters."

"You believe that?" I said, my seventeen-year-old cynicism bubbling over.

"Belief is a powerful thing. And I know you can accomplish almost anything when you believe."

I clenched my jaw, blinking back tears. This old man's guileless smile somehow brought back thoughts of my father: slender, long-necked, with a prodigious nose and the gentlest eyes.

Boy, I missed those eyes. My Bubbe Rachel would always look at me with those same eyes and sadly shake her head, saying I inherited my father's looks and my blue-blood Yankee mother's dour view of life. I always wanted to argue, but she was right. I'd never be pretty, and I didn't need some guy old enough to be my grandfather hitting on me.

"I'm sorry. I've made you uncomfortable." The man offered his outstretched hand. "My friends call me AJ. I'm waiting for someone, and you look like a nice person to talk with while I wait."

He smiled again as I took his hand. It was oversized, with thick calluses, but he had a gentle touch. I could almost imagine these rock-hard hands playing piano or performing surgery. My shoulders relaxed, and I smiled back.

"My name's Miriam," I said. He released my hand, and I felt a pang at the loss of his warmth. Then I jumped as something wet brushed against my open palm. "What the—"

"Sorry," the man said with a laugh. "That's Jules. He's keeping me company while I wait."

I looked down at a dog the size of a small pony as he wiggled out from under the row of chairs where he'd curled up, resting, hidden from view. He nuzzled against me, plopping his big block of a head in my lap. I straightened in my seat and pulled my hand away.

"I didn't see him tucked under there," I said as my body tensed.

"That's all right. Jules likes you," AJ said with a smile. "Actually, he likes almost everybody, but I can tell he especially likes you." Then, with an encouraging bob of the head, the man said, "Go ahead. Pet him. He particularly likes scratches behind his ears."

I'd never had a dog. My mom claimed she was

allergic, and between that and the way she tensed up anytime a dog came within fifty feet of us, I'd developed a healthy mistrust. But a peaceful calm settled over me when Jules's bear-sized head rested in my lap, his unblinking, warm eyes gazing up at me expectantly.

I reached out with an unsteady hand and found my fingers enveloped in the softest tuft of thick fur high up on his shoulders. It felt like coming home on a cold winter's day to find your father holding a cup of cocoa and your favorite book, signaling you to join him by the fire.

Jules leaned into my touch and rubbed his snout against me, welcoming further exploration. I brought both hands under the dog's chin and lifted his head to look into his rich brown eyes. He looked back at me, his gaze inviting and loving. He nuzzled against me, and I let my nails burrow through his thick fur as I scratched his chest.

AJ snorted with glee as Jules's hind leg thumped against its ribcage in rhythm to my rubs. "Oh boy, you found his spot."

I grinned. "I don't think I've ever really stopped to pet a dog before. Does it always feel so good?"

"Well, I like to think Jules is special, but I tend to buy into the old maxim, 'A bad day spent with a dog by your side is better than a good day without one.'"

As if on cue, the dog raised his head and reached out with a long pink tongue, showering me with sloppy, wet attention. I wrapped my arms around his powerful neck, giggling uncontrollably, and buried my face in his furry chest to escape his slobbering show of affection.

"See, even the tough days are better with a dog by your side." AJ reached out and joined me in petting Jules, scratching behind the dog's ear as Jules cocked his head, leaning hard into the touch.

"Special or not, I can't believe they let you hang out in a hospital waiting room with this wooly giant." I leaned forward to study the dog more closely. "Is he a service dog? Is that why he's at the hospital?"

AJ smiled. "Well, in a way. But today, he's helping me pass the time while I wait for someone. But now that I've got you to talk with, Jules can rest."

As if he understood, the dog stepped away and did a series of slow circles in front of us before dropping to the ground with a harrumph.

"So, tell me," AJ said, "why are you so down?"

AJ sat silently as I described my pathetic job performance that day, my crappy home life, and my mother's insistence I enroll in USC's School of Drama in the fall to pursue the career she'd envisioned for me all my life. Of course, she said, not before I get a little work done by *The Magician*, a plastic surgeon my mother swore by in Beverly Hills, who only worked with Hollywood's most elite.

He lost his near-permanent smile at the recap of my sad tale. "Wow, you have your whole life in front of you. How can such an intelligent and pretty girl be so unhappy?"

I bristled. "Please don't do that," I said, waking Jules, who raised an eyebrow.

"Do what?"

"Don't lie to me."

"What did I lie about?"

"Don't tell me I'm pretty. I'm nearly six feet tall, with a big nose and frizzy hair."

"Stop it!" Jules sat up at the change in AJ's tone and cocked his head, looking at him for reassurance. "Listen, I won't feed you the old *you're beautiful on the inside* line. When my daughters were your age, that's the last thing they wanted to hear. But as an old man who's seen true beauty in his life, I'm telling you, you are a damn good-looking kid." AJ stopped and ran his hand under Jules's chin before looking back at me. "Listen, life can seem awfully confusing when you're young, but there's a beautiful world out there. You just have to open your heart and let it in."

I shook my head. "The world's not beautiful. It's cruel and ugly, filled with cruel and ugly people. And those few who aren't, leave you."

"Wow, you don't see the wonders of life." AJ's face took on a special glow, and he turned to look at the dog. "What do you say, Jules? Should I tell her a story?"

The dog jumped up, offered a quick, joyful bark, and spun in a circle several times before sitting back in front of AJ, staring up at him like an expectant first grader.

Strange dog.

AJ laughed. "Okay, Jules has spoken. I've got some time before I have to go. So let me tell you a story."

I exhaled, staring up at the ceiling. I'd failed

every other task I'd been given that day, leaving me forced to listen to this strange old man with his sun-is-always-shining view on life. Sure, I spent all my free time with my nose buried in a book or watching old movies. And my deepest secret remained my dream to write and not be in front of the camera, as my mother insisted. But I wanted my stories to be honest—raw and visceral, talking about the painful underbelly of life that the cowards were all afraid to explore—not some syrupy-sweet view of the world this smiling fool wanted to hand me. I'd read *Silence of the Lambs* and *Blood Meridian*. I knew what true evil people were capable of.

Charge nurse be damned. I had no stomach for this. "Thanks, but I should probably get going."

I put my hands on the arms of my chair and pushed myself up, but a firm tug on my sleeve held me in place. I looked down to find Jules with a mouthful of my blouse clenched between his teeth.

"Jules, behave."

The dog released his grip, and AJ shrugged apologetically.

"Jules thinks you should stay. He recognizes the good in the world and likes it when I share, but you must be ready to let it in. So, what do you say?"

I sat back down, remembering the charge nurse's instruction, and exhaled, looking at the clock on the wall. I still had nearly three hours on my shift. "It looks like I couldn't move if I wanted to," I said with a shake of my head.

"Great." AJ leaned forward, his eyes shining bright. "Now, you have to understand, with every story, you only see or hear a version of the story.

It's like the Buddhist parable of the blind men and the elephant."

"You mean how the men who touch the elephant describe it as being like a tree trunk, a giant leaf, or a snake, depending on which part of the elephant the blind men touched."

"Bingo." AJ's hand flew from his side, like an Old West gunfighter drawing his six-shooter, as he pointed his index finger at me. "I knew you were sharp. So, you have to know the stories *I* tell are filled with the wonder and love surrounding us all."

"Love is a fantasy for the weak."

"Such a gloomy view of life for one so young," AJ said, his expression again making me think of my father. "Loving someone makes life worth living. You don't appreciate the power you possess."

"Power? What power?"

"The power of choosing the life you wish to live and the people you love. Open your heart and follow your dreams, win or lose. Do that, and you'll travel a road you can be proud of and share love with so many along your journey."

"You believe that?" I said, shocked anyone so old could still possess such a childlike view of life.

"I told you before, belief is a powerful thing, and letting go and loving is the greatest power of all. Now, sit and listen. In the end, you decide."

I leaned back in my chair and crossed my arms. "Fine. Tell me a story."

"Excellent." AJ rubbed his hands together, as if preparing to dig into Thanksgiving dinner. "Now, this story takes place in Boston close to sixty years ago. Times were different. Grown-ups knew the kids in the neighborhood nearly as well as they knew their own. In good weather, moms sat on their front steps talking as they watched their kids play and waited for their husbands to get home from work. Kids didn't have cell phones or playdates. They rode their bikes or walked, hanging around playgrounds, the games changing with the seasons: baseball all summer, followed by basketball, football, and street hockey as the weather grew colder.

"This particular story revolves around one kid. Most people found nothing special about this boy. He possessed no unique gifts. But he wanted things out of life and remained annoyingly single-minded in his quest to achieve these goals. This trait helped him on his journey, but it could close his eyes to what mattered most. Yeah, this stubborn streak caused him some trouble along the way. Honestly, some people described him as the most stubborn S.O.B. they'd ever met."

AJ stopped as Jules plopped his head in my lap, gazing up at the man as I mindlessly scratched behind the dog's ears.

"This is one of Jules's favorite stories," he said, smiling, then slapped his hands on his thighs. "Okay, here it is. A story of love and discovering what truly matters in life."

II

The boy stood on the sidewalk, dribbling a basketball, as the United Van Line's truck stopped in front of the house next door. Weeks shy of his fourteenth birthday, the sound of the moving van had caused the boy to lift his head from the small desk in his bedroom, where he'd been working on the document he hoped would finally get him the gift denied him for so long. He'd reverently rolled up the paper, tied it with a red ribbon he'd found in his mother's sewing basket, and raced outside with the basketball under his arm.

Few things ever changed on the busy streets surrounding the boy's home. People were born, lived and died in the old working-class neighborhood in Boston, with the grown children of the dearly departed staying on in the family home. So, having a professional moving truck pull up brought the sleepy neighborhood to life. Mothers feigned cleaning Venetian blinds while old men spread rock salt on already bare sidewalks as they eyed the goings-on.

"Tony, get back in here and put your coat on. You'll catch your death."

"Aw, Ma."

"Don't *aw, Ma* me." His mother stood in the doorway, waving a peacoat. "I've missed enough work this winter staying home with your sister. I don't need you getting sick."

"I never get sick," Tony said, his chest puffing with youthful pride. But his mother stood resolute. Tony's shoulders dropped. *Pick your battles*, his father always said. "All right, but I bet John Havlicek's mother didn't make him wear a coat." Tony kicked at a shrunken snowbank as he walked toward the front door.

"I don't care what Johnny Haversack's mother does. Put the coat on." She handed him the coat as she roughly ran her hand through his thick mop of curly black hair. "Promise you won't take it off." His mother's eyes locked on his. "Promise."

Tony tried to stare into those indomitable eyes but quickly looked down, as if concentrating on bouncing the basketball. Then he turned away, saved by the sound of one of the movers shouting orders. His mother may not have known John Havlicek was the best player on the Celtics now that Bill Russell was getting older. But the woman had an uncanny knack for sniffing out the truth, and Tony remained mindful of his every move under her attentive gaze.

"Promise," he said in surrender as the sound of the movers grew louder.

Maintaining his dribble, Tony shrugged one shoulder into the oversized peacoat and, dribbling deftly, switched hands to slip into the second sleeve. His father's business was always slower with the arrival of the cold weather, so when Tony outgrew his coat halfway through the winter, he inherited his cousin's hand-me-down. Tony didn't mind, but the too-long sleeves wreaked havoc with his dribbling. He glanced over his shoulder at his house as the curtain moved in the family's kitchen.

She doesn't trust me. Tony sighed. *I wouldn't trust me, either.* Ignoring his mother's presence in the window, he performed a series of crossover dribbles, positioning himself behind the moving van and out of view from the kitchen window. He slipped out of his coat, draped it over a fire hydrant, and grimaced as he glanced back toward the now-hidden house. Weekly confession tomorrow, and he'd just added lying to his mother to his ever-growing list of transgressions. Tony shook his head as he stared up at the cloud-filled sky. *It's not my fault. You made me this way.*

Tony's mind drifted back to two summers ago, when he sat open-mouthed in the balcony of the neighborhood movie theater, watching Paul Newman in *Cool Hand Luke*. Newman's character, a man unable to live within society's rules, is sentenced to work on a southern chain gang for the senselessly rebellious act of drunkenly cutting the heads off parking meters. In the movie's closing scene, Newman has once again escaped and is hiding in a small country church as prison guards close in with orders to shoot to kill. Newman, sadly smiling, looks to the church rafters as he challenges God, saying, "You made me this way."

The scene touched Tony as few things ever had, and in his darkest moments, a choking dread blackened his young soul as he feared he, too, might be flawed and doomed, like the uncompromising, ill-fated character in the movie.

The bustling sound of the movers struggling to squeeze an oversized dining room table through the front door pulled Tony from his painful reverie. The movers' profanity-laced argument about how best to maneuver the massive piece lifted the boy's spirits, reminding him God had lots of sinners to keep track of.

With his moment of guilt passed, Tony watched the men's struggles with the huge table. *With a table that big, they gotta have lots of kids.* A hopeful smile lit his young face, and he called out to a third mover inside the truck. "Hey, mister, they got any kids?"

The mover reached a beefy arm into the truck and grabbed a highchair, holding it to the sky to show the boy.

"No, *big* kids," Tony said with a dismissive wave of his hand.

"You mean like you, short stuff?"

"I'm not that short," Tony said, squaring his shoulders. "But yeah, like me."

The mover lowered the highchair to the sidewalk and leaned back into the truck, rummaging before nodding and grabbing a worn Army duffle bag chock-full, with several baseball bats poking through the top. As the man lifted the bag, the electrical tape sealing it shut slowly unraveled and a football dropped to the ground, zigzagging toward Tony. Locking his basketball under his elbow, he bent down and scooped up the ball with his free hand. The John David Crow signature model was genuine leather, not one of those cheap rubber ones found on the shelves of local department stores like Zayres or Bradlees.

Must have cost at least ten bucks, Tony thought, shifting the football in his hand to see written in neat block lettering with a black magic marker:

Property
of
Jo Jo Trocki

"Yes!" he hollered, letting the basketball drop to the ground. He tucked the football tight to his body and leaned forward, simulating a fierce stiff-arm stance in a reasonable facsimile of the famous Heisman Trophy pose.

"Hey, kid," the mover called to him, smiling, his burly fists resting against his hips. "I need the ball back."

"Oh yeah, sorry," Tony said as his fingers found the lacing on the football. He leaned back and, bringing his arm forward, threw a tight spiral to the mover. The man reached out, momentarily bobbling the ball before securing it against his chest.

"Nice throw, Y.A.," the man said as he dropped to one knee, forcing the ball back into the duffle bag. "The Giants could use you. They've been nothin' but crap since Tittle retired."

"I hate the Giants, and Y.A. Tittle's a bum," Tony said with distaste. "I'll be quarterbacking the Pats soon now that Parilli's gone, but thanks."

The sun slipped behind gathering clouds, and a cold wind whipped across Tony's thick hooded sweatshirt. He snuck a look at the house. *Better get my coat back on before Mom spots me.* But even the darkening clouds signaling a nor'easter rushing toward Boston and his mother's potential scolding couldn't dampen his good mood. Spring might come late this year, but along with it would come Jo Jo Trocki. On a street filled with girls his age, at last, there'd be a boy next door.

Shivering against the wind, Tony slipped back into his coat and picked his basketball up from the gutter, where it rested against an exhaust-blackened snowbank. He wiped the ball on the sleeve of his jacket before deftly setting it to spin on the tip of his index finger. With his mind racing, Tony smiled as visions of him and a tall, lean boy trading punches boxing, playing catch, or sneaking into the Pixie Theater to critique the latest films warmed him against the stiff afternoon breeze. Tony's smile grew, imagining other simple pleasures, like sitting on the curb wide-legged in front of the neighborhood variety store, comparing the spit puddles they created while discussing the Sox chances that year and their mutual hatred of the Yankees.

Jo Jo Trocki. . . . Thank you, God. You have been listening.

"So, Sister Mary Catherine said I've been chosen to be this year's Queen of the May Procession." Tony's ten-year-old sister Rosa sat at the kitchen table, animatedly detailing the events of her busy day while their mother circled the table with a large bowl.

"Well, that is big news," his mother said, leaning forward as she grasped a wooden spoon to fill the girl's plate with ziti and a meatball.

"Yes. They had me stay after school, and I tried on the dress Margaret Sullivan wore last year as queen, and it fits perfectly," his sister said triumphantly. "I don't know who they'll choose as the king. I just hope it isn't Billy DePalma. I think he's gross."

"Now, that's not a very nice thing to say." Tony's mother, using her all-too-familiar *I expect more from you* voice, turned to give her daughter the stare both her kids dreaded.

"Yeah, not very nice at all," Tony said, smiling at his opportunity to direct the conversation to more important topics. "And that isn't even the day's big news." He sat back in his chair and folded his arms across his chest. With his sister temporarily silenced, the floor was his, and he waited until all eyes turned to him. Then, satisfied he'd built sufficient drama, he said, "I was talking to one of the guys delivering furniture for the new people next door. They've got a boy my age. . . . *And* they're Italian. Their name's Trocki."

"Trocki?" his father silent until now, furrowed

his brow. "Spell it."

"Let me think." Tony's brow furrowed as he unconsciously mimed his father. "Yeah, they had it written on some boxes and the football. Trocki, T, R, O, C, K, I." Tony paused, doubt creeping across his face. "That's Italian. Isn't it?"

"There's no K in the Italian dictionary. Must be Pollacks. Ahem, I mean Polish," his father said, lowering his eyes. No one was immune to the icy stare of the woman of the house.

"And I'm sure they are very nice," his mother said. Eyes lowered or not, the woman's stare still fell upon any offender.

"Of course, of course." Tony's father reached out and wrapped his right arm around his full-figured wife's waist, pulling her to him. "As always, your mom's right."

His wife nodded her approval. But as she looked away, he slipped Tony a furtive wink, quickly met with an acknowledging nod. The boy understood his father's message. There's nice, and then there's *Italian* nice.

Tony woke in the early morning darkness and jumped out of bed, ignoring the room's cold floor and the chill. He raced to the window, pulled up the long sleeve of the thermal underwear he slept in, and wiped the condensation from the windowpane with an aggressive circular motion. The boy pressed his nose against the glass, steaming the window as he stared at the puddled road glistening under the soft glow of the streetlights.

He shrugged and turned away as the sound of the kitchen radio drifted up to his bedroom. An unsuspected nighttime warming had turned the late-night snowfall into rain, avoiding the predicted snowstorm.

"Sorry, kids," the radio announcer said with a chuckle. "No chance of school cancellations today. So, find your rubbers and your raincoat because it's going to be a wet walk to school. But there's more precipitation and another cold front on the way—"

"Don Kent, wrong again," Tony said, mimicking words he'd heard from his father so many times over the years.

But his thoughts moved quickly to an issue with stakes much bigger than the prospects of an early spring. Barely six o'clock, Rosa wouldn't get up for another hour. He had his parents' undivided attention. Tony walked over to his desk, pulled out the document, careful not to bend it, and headed downstairs to the kitchen.

"Hey, champ, you're up early," his father said with a smile. "Hoping for a school cancellation? I told you, don't trust them, TV weathermen. If you wanna know if it's gonna snow, just ask the old man's knees. And last night, my knees said no."

Tony nodded. His father's meteorologically gifted knees were a common topic of conversation. "I was hoping I could talk to you." He paused and turned toward his mother, who stood by the stove, pouring herself a cup of coffee. "Both of you."

His parents exchanged glances as his mother took a sip of coffee, eyeing him over the lip of her cup. She nodded, put her coffee on the counter, and turned back to the stove. Lowering the flame on the burner, she flipped the frittata in the frying pan as its aroma filled the kitchen. Then, wiping her hands on her apron, she stepped to the kitchen table but remained standing.

Tony cleared his throat. This wouldn't be easy.

"We're all ears," she said, crossing her arms across her chest. Carla Miracolo was the key. In matters of the house, Anthony Miracolo deferred to his wife.

Tony inhaled, studying his mother as his nose twitched and his stomach growled at the aroma of peppers, eggs, and onions. "It smells great, Mom." His voice cracked. "Ahem, well, as you know, I've been asking if we could get a dog for some time now."

His father offered a slight chuckle, his calm presence helping the boy relax. "Yes, I seem to remember a full-press campaign a while back where every morning we'd wake up to find notes and drawings taped up all over the house, on the refrigerator, the bathroom mirror: *Can I have a dog?*"

Tony groaned, recalling the failed childish crusade. His father was trying to help pave the way, but Tony wanted to focus on the future. He needed to sell his indomitable mother.

"Yes, well, I put together a contract detailing my commitment to a family dog."

He took his hand from behind his back, offering his mother the rolled-up document tied neatly with the red ribbon, but with a tip of her head, she directed him to give it to his father.

His father untied the ribbon and studied the paper momentarily. A smile flickered across his face as he said, "Carla, I don't have my eyeglasses. You'll have to read this." He signaled for his wife to sit next to him as he surreptitiously slipped his hand over his reading glasses resting on the table next to his cigarettes and snuck them into his pants pocket.

Carla Miracolo stared at her husband, but he averted his eyes as he gazed intently out the kitchen window, seemingly fixated on the travails of a lone paper bag blowing down the rain-swept street. With her husband unwilling to meet her stare, Tony's mother lowered herself into the chair beside him.

"Why don't you read it out loud, Hon? For both of us." Tony's father leaned back, struggling to suppress a grin as he laced his fingers behind his head.

His mother tried again unsuccessfully to make eye contact with her husband. But finally resigned, she turned her gaze to the paper and began to read aloud.

THE
DOGMA CARTA

FIRST, THAT WE GRANTED TO GOD, AND BY THIS OUR
PRESENT CHARTER CONFIRM, THAT ALL BOYS SHOULD
GROW UP KNOWING THE LOVE OF A DOG.

AS SUCH, ANTHONY MIRACOLO WILL BE ALLOWED TO
EXPERIENCE THIS GOD-GIVEN RIGHT TO POSSESS
JUST SUCH A LOVING DOG IN PERPETUITY.

NOW APPROACHING HIS FOURTEENTH YEAR
AND HAVING REACHED THE AGE OF ACCOUNTABILITY,
CITIZEN MIRACOLO UNDERSTANDS THE
RESPONSIBILITIES OF DOG OWNERSHIP AND HEREBY
COMMITS TO THE FOLLOWING:

HE WILL PAY TO FEED THE DOG THROUGH MONEY
EARNED FROM CUTTING LAWNS AND SNOW
SHOVELING
HE WILL TRAIN THE DOG TO ENSURE APPROPRIATE
BEHAVIOR AT ALL TIMES
HE WILL RISE EARLY EACH DAY TO OVERSEE THE
DOG'S MORNING ABLATIONS

AND WILL ACCEPT ALL OTHER RESPONSIBILITIES
FOR SAID FRIENDSHIP

ALL THIS WE SO SWEAR, IN THE YEAR OF OUR LORD,
1969.

Tony's mother let the paper drop to the table as her smiling husband lit a cigarette. Previously fixated on the happenings outside their window, he now turned to silently blowing smoke rings as he waited for his wife to speak.

"I'm guessing you've had your nose buried in another of those history books you love so much, and you've been reading about the Magna Carta," she said, stalling for time.

Tony nodded.

"Perpetuity and ablations?" His father reached out to wrap an arm around his son's shoulder as he beamed with pride.

"I kinda took the opening bit and perpetuity from the Magna Carta and looked up ablations in the dictionary," Tony said, studying his mother for any crack in her armor. "I thought it made it all sound more official."

His mother nodded. "Well, you know the doctor said he thought your sister might be allergic."

"Pop says only Americans have allergies." Tony jumped in to shoot down this red herring.

"You're American," his mother said, her eyes throwing darts at her husband, exasperated with the man's recycled theories.

"Yeah, but Pop says, first, I'm Italian, and Pop says we're from hardy Sicilian stock. Working in the fields all day or on fishing boats, all that hard work has made us, like, immune to allergies an'stuff."

His mother continued to stare at Tony's father, who once again seemed fascinated with the happenings outside their kitchen window and remained unwilling to meet her gaze. "And what about when I got my bad case of poison oak last summer?"

"Yeah, Pop explained that, too," Tony said. "He says it's cuz your father came from north of Naples. He said you'd be half-German if Italy lost just one more war."

His mother bit her lower lip. "Uh-huh, well, you've obviously picked up some fascinating scientific and historical data from your father. Why don't you leave this, um, *document* with us."

Tony's eyes shot from his mother to his father, but both looked away. His mother returned to biting her lower lip as she slowly rocked back and forth in her chair while Tony's father linked his fingers on the table in front of him, as if in prayer, bringing his hands to rest under his chin.

"Tony, why don't you get dressed for school and let your mother and me talk."

Tony rose from the table, thinking, *It will be okay if Pop musses my hair.* But his father sat motionless, waiting for the inevitable showdown with the indomitable mistress of the house.

III

"Mister Mi-ra-co-lo, you seem even more distracted than usual. Would you care to come back to the land of the living?"

Tony rose from his chair, anchoring his hands by his side as students were instructed to do when called upon. He squared his shoulders and turned away from the window. "Sorry, Sister Agnes Helen."

"Come now, Mister Mi-ra-co-lo. We have you in this classroom each day from eight thirty to two forty-five. Is it too much to ask you to join us in our quest to produce future soldiers for Christ and productive citizens?" The nun hollowed her cheeks, making soft sucking noises through her pursed lips. "To fail to do so insults your classmates . . . and me."

Tony stood, silent. He'd been down this road

before, and nothing he could say would change the resolute ministrations to come. Best to remain quiet and let the ancient nun rail away.

"Has a cat got your tongue, boy? You owe the people in this classroom, working hard to better themselves, an explanation for your rudeness." Sister Agnes Helen paced, her floor-length black frock ominously rustling as the sucking sounds grew louder. "Do you think your time is somehow more valuable than the others in this classroom?"

The other kids giggled, fidgeting at their desks in anticipation of the continuing attack. They understood every moment of abuse focused on Tony prevented the nun's withering scrutiny from turning on them.

Tony stared at a spot on the wall above the nun's head, willing the interrogation to end. "I apologized for my lack of attentiveness. Can't that be *enough*?" Tony cursed himself as his heartbeat quickened. He couldn't let her see she was getting to him.

"Are you sassing me, boy? Don't you dare sass me." The nun's alabaster skin flushed pink as she continued to hollow her cheeks and make her odd sucking sounds. "Now tell us, what fascinating thoughts pulled you away from our lesson plan?"

Tony exhaled, long and slow. "I was thinking about the dog I'm gonna get," he finally said. "I pictured him running and playing in the parking lot between the school and the church where we have recess." Tony's voice grew louder as he spoke, the idea of a dog taking on a palpable life of its own with the words finally said out loud.

"A dog?" The nun stared at him bug-eyed as the

hollowed cheeks and noises continued. "Mister Mi-ra-co-lo, you are wasting valuable class time thinking about some stupid dog?"

Tony clenched his fists. He hated how the nun said his name, drawing out each syllable, as if calling attention to its foreignness—so different from names like Tompson, Walsh, or Collins. And he hated how she made his wanting a dog seem childish and frivolous.

"Dogs aren't stupid. They're one of God's great creatures," he said.

The class struggled to hide their giggles as Tony put himself in the crosshairs of their vitriolic teacher.

"You dare lecture *me* on God's creatures?" The nun fired back. "You are a silly boy who lacks the maturity to care for a goldfish. Report cards come out in a few weeks, and I will be certain to disavow any perception your parents may have about you being ready for additional responsibilities outside the classroom. I'll assure them anything that detracts from your studies would be most inadvisable." The nun stood in front of her desk, staring at Tony as her constantly hollowed cheeks morphed into a smug smile.

Tony's fingers dug into his palms, his dreams of a dog slipping away. He clenched his jaw, fighting back tears. Mindlessly, he grabbed a thick textbook from his desk and hurled it at the blackboard behind the nun, where it hit with a thunderous bang.

"Go suck a bushel of lemons, you miserable old coot!" Tony shouted, his voice filled with rage. Then he leaned forward, insolently staring into the older women's eyes as he perfectly mimed the nun's hollowed cheeks and her incessant sucking sound.

Initially stunned by the audacity of the thrown book, the classroom exploded in laughter at Tony calling out "Sister Lemon Sucker" to her face with his perfect imitation.

"Up the hill, boy." A bright-blue vein popped in the middle of Sister Agnes Helen's forehead as she pointed her gnarled index finger toward the parish rectory. "Do not disturb Monsignor Hanrahan or I will box your ears in, boy. Tell Mrs. O'Donnell I will be up when class lets out to discuss your future at this school with the Monsignor." Catching herself from hollowing her cheeks, the nun cleared her throat as her chilling stare shot across the room, silencing the snickers from the class before turning back to Tony. "Leave now, you uncouth child. I will deal with you later."

Tony shoulders dropped as the magnitude of what he's just done settled over him like a thick fog. He wanted to hold his head high but couldn't. He'd let his temper get the better of him again, potentially blowing his chances of getting a dog. Tony trembled with anger and frustration as the eyes of the entire class followed him, their whispers and titters growing with each quickening step.

Don't let them see you cry.

He left the room and headed up the hill. Halfway to the rectory, Tony lost his battle, and tears freely flowed when his unsteady hand reached out to ring the rectory bell. His mother would be angry, his father disappointed, and Tony didn't know which he dreaded more. Tony feared the cold wrath of his mother, but often, the *You're better than that* look in his father's eyes cut the deepest.

Why couldn't he be more like his father? But if he were, would he ever meet his mother's all-but-unattainable expectations?

Tony leaned on the rake as the smoldering pile of wet leaves at his feet turned slowly to gray ash and drifted into the late-afternoon sky. The last forty-eight hours had passed in a blur. An evening sit-down at school with his parents followed the afternoon session with Monsignor Hanrahan and Sister Agnes Helen. It ended with the four adults agreeing Tony wouldn't be expelled, but his actions warranted severe punishment at home and in the classroom. Disciplinary action at school was left in the "capable hands" of Sister Agnes Helen, while Tony's mother assured everyone she'd see to punitive measures at home. All while sister Agnes Helen continued to insist any future infraction would most certainly appear on his "permanent record."

Tony had remained silent throughout both sessions, except for several weak acknowledgments of guilt and a passionless apology. He struggled to enthuse any genuine remorse and felt almost certain he saw a flicker of a smile on both his father's and the Monsignor's faces. Did they exchange sympathetic looks at one point when Sister Agnes Helen slipped into one of her more dramatic moments in her description of Tony's insolence? Tony looked away, studying his hands, afraid to be caught joining the two adults in their brief exchange. But his chest swelled with a sense of comradeship. Surely, he wasn't the only one who could see how unbearable Sister Lemon Sucker could be?

His parents had been surprisingly quiet that evening. His mother told Tony his behavior was totally unacceptable and there'd be no TV or playing after school for the next two weeks, but the hellfire scolding he'd expected never came. The subject of a dog didn't come up, either, and Tony decided it best to quietly accept the punishment and bide his time.

A strong gust of wind whipped more sodden leaves from the heavily wooded area behind the house into Tony's backyard. He lowered his head and added them to the sputtering fire with several quick rake strokes, creating a brief glowing flash of orange. Nothing generated more goodwill with both of his parents than seeing a job well done. So, he'd spent his weekend completing one task after another. But he had a long way to go to return to his mother's good graces. He cursed the nun as he battled against the endless supply of leaves. Losing his temper had derailed his latest efforts at convincing his parents the family needed a dog, but the boy was resolute. He'd find a way.

Tony turned from the fire at the sound of a car approaching the house next door. He walked toward the front yard, picking up the basketball he'd left in the driveway, pounding hard to dribble the cold ball as he went. A man in khaki pants and a weather-beaten leather bomber jacket stepped out of a station wagon, opened the back of the attached U-Haul trailer, grabbed a box, and headed toward the front door. A girl about Tony's age—wearing blue-jean bib overalls, a Chicago Bears Sweatshirt, and an opened heavy-knit sweater—grabbed a second box and followed the man into the house. The girl nodded at Tony as she passed, like one of the guys on the corner would when someone new arrived on the stoop.

Odd, Tony thought, *girls don't nod. Girls giggle and whisper with mouths covered by fast-moving hands.* Tony hesitated before returning the nod, but the girl had already passed, carrying the large box.

The sound of tapping from his house caught Tony's attention, and his mother now stood at the window, her flashing hands signaling for him to help.

"Can I give you a hand?" Tony said as the man walked back toward the station wagon.

"That would be great. Thanks, champ."

Tony smiled. His father called him champ.

Tony tossed the basketball into his backyard, accepted a box marked "Pots and Pans" from the man's outstretched arms, and headed up the stairs toward the house, receiving another nod from the girl as he passed and the instructions, "Those go in the kitchen."

Duh. Does she think I'm an idiot?

He made several trips, his eyes searching everywhere, before finally lowering himself to address the girl. "Where's your brother?"

31

"He's in the back seat, taking a nap. My mother's watching him." The girl's arms trembled under the weight of a box marked "Good China."

Tony's eyebrows arched. "Why does your mother have to watch him take a nap, and why isn't he helping?"

"Helping?" She lowered the box to the ground and brushed a shock of golden-brown hair off her face with the back of her hand as her ponytail slowly unraveled. "He's a baby," the girl said with a dismissive shake of her head.

Tony's mouth flew open. He turned to find his mother standing by the station wagon, bundled in a thick handmade sweater and wearing a pair of his father's too big work boots. In her arms, she held a chubby baby with a shock of blond hair while she made those faces women always seem to make when there's a baby nearby. The other woman stood next to her, talking and wrapping a small blanket around the baby as she joined Tony's mother in *oohing* and *aahing* at each drooling gurgle the kid made.

The girl looked back at Tony. "Something wrong?"

Tony exhaled. With a flick of his head, he gestured toward the car. "Is that your *only* brother?"

His mother caught his gaze, but her typically intense eyes softened as she smiled like the cat with a canary and said, "Tony, I see you've met Jo."

IV

"**J**o Jo seems very nice."

"Huh?" Tony sat at the kitchen table, his algebra book open in front of him.

He had a test on Wednesday, and one sure way to dig himself out of this hole was to get his grades up.

"I said, Jo seems very nice."

Tony rolled his eyes.

"Don't give me that look," his mother said, turning away from the stove to stand over him with her arms crossed. "What's the problem?"

Tony groaned, his pleading eyes shifting from his mother to his silent father, who gave his son a *Don't get me in the middle of this* shrug and turned his open palms skyward, offering the classic Italian *Hey, what can I say?* pose.

Tony looked away. The old man would be no

help. "The problem is . . ." Tony paused, searching for the right words, and started again. "The problem is, she's a girl. Or hadn't you noticed?" He threw up his hands with all the built-up sarcasm only a fourteen-year-old could muster.

"Well, she is a very nice girl. And awfully pretty." His mother smiled as Tony winced at the word pretty. "So, whether or not it pleases you, the fact is, Jo Jo Trocki is a girl, that pretty young girl has moved next door to us, and she and her family are coming over for dinner tonight."

"Nooo!"

"Carla, this was such a lovely gesture." Donna Trocki leaned back from the Miracolo's red Formica-topped kitchen table and sighed, patting her waist. "Everything tasted delicious. I swear, I couldn't eat another bite. And inviting almost total strangers over for dinner was so thoughtful of you."

"Don't be silly. You and Frank were on the road for two days and haven't had time to open half your boxes. What kind of neighbor would I be if I let your family eat one of those terrible new frozen dinners on your first night in your new home?"

Donna Trocki smiled, showing small, perfect white teeth. "Well, anyway, thank you, and next time at our house."

Tony's father and Frank Trocki, who'd seemed to hit it off, immediately clicked the necks of their beer bottles at Donna's announcement of future family get-togethers while Tony's sister, Rosa, who'd taken to Jo immediately, perhaps seeing her as a potential exotic older sister, smiled. She'd been in heaven, feeding Frank Junior, but lowered the spoon to take the baby's hands in hers, delivering a series of quick claps. "Yes! Did you hear, Frankie? We're all gonna be spendin' lots of time together."

Tony slouched lower in his chair, burying his tongue in the side of his cheek, wondering if this would ever end.

"Tony, I understand Jo Jo's quite the basketball player. Why don't you two go out and play a couple of games of twenty-one?" Tony's father stood and handed him his coat. "Jo, go easy on him. Your dad told me you can shoot the eyes out of the basket. Tony's more of a KC Jones-type player."

"She doesn't know who KC Jones is," Tony said, shaking his head as he reached out to take the coat from his father.

"KC Jones was a starting guard for the Celtics and always covered the other team's best scoring guard." Jo paused as the two male Miracolos stared at her in open-mouthed surprise. Then she shrugged. "You know, guys like Jerry West or Oscar Robertson."

"That's my girl," Frank Trocki said, slapping Tony's father on the back. "I told you she's something special."

"Nothing but straight-*A*s since her first day of school."

"Mom, please," Jo interrupted. "Not that again."

"C'mon," Tony said, heading toward the back door. He refused to look back to see if Jo followed him as his father turned on the lights in the backyard. "Let's get this over with."

The girl could shoot. She broke her ice on her first shot, one point, and made the following three shots. 7-0. Surprised, Tony tightened his usual fluid form and short-armed his first shot, before dropping his head and sticking his hand on his hips as the ball clanged off the front of the rim.

Jo rebounded the ball and made an easy shot off the backboard. 8-0. She stepped forward, toed the white line Tony's father had painted on the driveway, bent her knees, and released the ball. Perfect swish. Jo would win by a shut-out if she made the next one, with Tony only having shot once.

Tony held his breath as Jo toed the line again, bent her knees, and rose slightly to release the ball in textbook form. It floated toward the hoop in perfect rotation, nicked the back rim, spun around the inside of the cylinder several times, and froze on the lip of the basket before dropping to the ground.

Tony breathed a massive sigh of relief as he retrieved the ball and walked to the free-throw line. He shrugged his way out of his coat and threw it to the ground behind him. Tony tried to bounce the ball several times, but the cold night air had taken all the spring out of the ball. He paused as he took two deep breaths. Then, keeping his eyes locked on the back of the rim, he dipped his knees, rose slowly, and released the ball with seamless follow-through. Nothing but net. Tony made his next three shots to close the score to 10-7.

But, just like her father said, Jo Jo Trocki could shoot the eyes out of the basket, and she had too big of a lead. Jo made her next three shots before missing again, ultimately winning 21-14.

"Rematch?"

"Sure," Tony said, his jaw tight. The girl's performance had to be a fluke.

Jo won the next two games before Tony got hot, making five shots in a row to narrowly win the last match 21-19.

"Getting colder." Jo brought her hands to her face and blew into them. "Your mother said you'd show me the neighborhood. Why don't we go for a walk, and you can show me around.

Jo wore a half smile, and Tony studied her perfect white teeth, like her mother's. Did she think she was letting him off the hook, allowing him to quit while he was ahead?

"Okay, but we better tell our folks," he said as he pulled his jacket back on.

Tony stood in the doorway while Jo spoke to the grown-ups, saying they planned to take a walk. He bit his tongue when she succinctly answered her father's question about who had won: "Pretty evenly matched."

Tony turned away. *Evenly matched. I'd love to hear what she tells her old man later.* He stuffed his hands in his pockets, blowing puffs of white smoke into the cold night air with throaty huffs.

As they walked along the sidewalk, Tony explained the nearby homes and the surrounding streets were known as the Heights. The church and the several dozen adjacent houses were the oldest buildings in that part of the city and sat at the base of a rocky, wooded hillside in the highest point in the neighborhood. His grandfather—a skilled carpenter—had bought their big old house that had fallen into disrepair and spent years fixing it up.

Tony pointed down the hill past rows of smaller single-family houses toward a steeper decline, leading to a cluster of awninged storefronts on the left.

"A couple of neighborhood shops are this way. A small variety store, butcher, and drug store, but most of the shops are at the bottom of the hill by the river. If your mother sends you to the store, you'll end up here or down on River Road. There's a movie theatre, diner, supermarket, library, a couple of autobody shops, cobbler, bakery, and hardware store. There's also a big playground and baseball diamond. That's most of what you can walk to. People take the bus to Forest Hills and grab the train for downtown for bigger stuff, like if your mom wants to shop at Filene's Basement or Jordan Marsh." Tony turned to study Jo, who looked past him down the hill. "Am I boring you?"

"No, just thinking about something." Jo quickened her pace, getting ahead of him.

Well, excuse me. This one-on-one time wasn't my idea. "Yeah. Let's pick up the pace and get this over with."

Tony lifted his head at the sound of a dog's lonely howl. He balled his hands into white-knuckled fists. *Is that him? What's wrong with that guy, leaving a dog outside on a cold night like this?*

If he was my dog . . .

They walked silently as the lonely dog's howl mixed with Tony's damaged boyhood ego. Losing three of four games to a girl gnawed at him. His jaw clenched, remembering Jo's solicitous *Pretty evenly matched.*

Bull. She'd won fair and square. Tony froze as a frightening thought left him colder than the winter's night air. It couldn't be. He'd won the fourth game fairly. Didn't he?

They passed a row of three-family homes at the bottom of the hill, walked past the supermarket, and turned onto the main street. Then they passed a bridge that crossed a slow-flowing river marking the border of the small, tight-knit neighborhood. Tony caught Jo staring up at the marquee of the neighborhood theater—*True Grit* and *Easy Rider*—the light illuminating the face his mother insisted was so pretty. Wide-set green eyes, golden complexion, even at the end of a long winter, and a slightly oversized aquiline nose that seemed to fit perfectly with the rest of her features. Tony wanted to ask her if she liked movies, but the dog's howl, now more of a plaintive weep, drove him deeper into silence. They passed a diner and stood in front of the town library, where Tony stopped.

"Something wrong?"

"No," Tony said. "That's about it. The rest of the shops run all along the river here, then a big park, playground, and the factory. Second shift." Tony pointed in the distance to a brick smoke-billowing, factory next to the playground. He turned away, wanting to get off the main boulevard and back up the hill, gone from the dog's plaintive howls.

"You play a lot of baseball?" Jo's words faded, unanswered, in the night air, like the dissipating white puffs of her breath.

"Huh?" Tony turned to stare in the direction of the persistent howls.

"Your father told us you love baseball." Jo pointed past the shops to the distant baseball diamond.

"Yeah," Tony said absentmindedly, his brain continuing to ping-pong between worries about the dog and the sting to his boyish pride at his defeat in shooting baskets.

"I saw the greatest hitter who ever lived," Jo said.

"What?"

"I said, I saw the greatest hitter who ever lived. My father took me to see the Cubs play the Cardinals, and I saw Stan Musial in his final game in Chicago."

Tony ignored the excitement in Jo's voice when describing this precious memory and sullenly struck back. "*Ted Williams* is the greatest hitter who ever lived."

"Stan Musial is the greatest hitter who ever lived," Jo said, her voice firm, all the joy gone.

"Williams."

"Musial."

"Williams."

"Musial!" Jo's voice echoed down the deserted streets.

Tony turned to face the girl who'd done nothing but disappoint him since appearing in his life. With disgust oozing from every pore of his body, he said, "And why do you believe Stan Musial was the best?"

"My *father* saw him play over a dozen times, and he told me Musial was the greatest hitter who ever lived."

"Your father knows Jack," Tony said, smiling, the hook set.

"Jack? Jack who?" Jo's eyebrows furrowed in confusion.

"Your father knows *Jackshit*."

Jo's eyes glowed with balls of fire as her nostrils flared like a bull in front of the matador's cape. And Tony, much too busy smirking with delight at his seamless delivery of the line he'd heard his father use many times, failed to notice Jo's clenched fist hurtling toward his left eye.

Tony's father struggled to hold back a grin as he pressed an ice-cold bottle of Ballantine Ale against the boy's eye. He slowly pulled it away for a peek while Jo's parents, dripping in mortification, looked on. Tony had wanted to say he'd fallen, but Jo, with all the color drained from her face, shook her head. She wouldn't lie.

Anthony Miracolo pulled the bottle away and turned to look at Jo. "Well, Smokin' Joe. That's a terrific right cross you caught him with. It looks like he's gonna have a hel . . . a heck of a shiner."

"Smokin' Joe Frazier, nothing," Jo's father said.

Jo's mother paced back and forth in the crowded

kitchen. "You're in a world of trouble. We taught you better than this."

All the color from Jo's washed-out face seemed to have transferred to her mother's now candy-apple cheeks.

"Tony knows better than to say someone's father knows Jack . . . well, you know," Anthony Miracolo said, coming to Jo's rescue as he glanced at his daughter Rosa, who knelt on the floor, absorbed in playing with the baby, barely noticing the maelstrom of activity bubbling over in the family kitchen. "And even more, he knows he shouldn't talk that way around a lady."

"I'm not a *lady*." Jo stood up, her body trembling in renewed rage.

"Jo, enough!" Her father's voice took on an edge, and a vein popped in his temple. This was clearly a recurring theme in the Trocki house. "You are a lady. Or at least you will be someday. Please, dear God. Now, thankfully, Tony proved himself enough of a gentleman not to hall off and pop you back."

Jo's father paused and gave Tony an appreciative nod. "This behavior is simply unacceptable. And for the record, what I told you is, Stan Musial was the greatest hitter *I* ever saw. I grew up in the shadows of Wrigley Field, so as a kid, I only saw National League teams. I never saw Williams, but if you forced me to choose, as great as Musial was . . ." Frank Trocki stopped and turned from his daughter to lock eyes with Tony. "I'd probably have to choose Williams. Now, both of these guys are long retired and coaching or doing beer commercials, so

I suggest we move on. And you two, shake hands."

Tony nodded. At least her old man had some class. He offered his open hand across the table out of grudging respect for Jo's father. She accepted the gesture, and Jo, proving, at least at that point in their lives, she was the better man, looked Tony in the eye and articulated a clear, seemingly sincere, "I'm sorry."

Tony, trying not to be outdone, said, "Yeah, me, too. I'm sorry."

Their hands locked and Jo's cool, dry hand melded firmly with Tony's. His grip tightened, acknowledging the mutual peace-making efforts as the handshake lingered. Tony was the first to break slowly, pulling his hand away, their fingers the last to come free.

Tony had to admit, she had a pretty good handshake, for a girl.

Splat. Splat.

Tony rolled out of bed, flipped on the light, and stumbled to his window. He wiped frost from the glass and saw Jo in the driveway below, holding a snowball and signaling for him to open the window. Over a white knee-length nightgown, she wore the Chicago Bears sweatshirt she'd had on earlier in the day.

He forced the window open and stuck his head out.

"Tony." Jo stood in the glow of the soft light from his room. "I thought you mentioned your bedroom was next to the driveway." She giggled. "I'm glad I guessed right," she said, letting the clump of snow drop from her hand.

"What?" He shivered and hugged himself as a blast of cold air rushed in. *She must be freezing out there.*

"I really am sorry about your eye." Jo hopped from one foot to the other in oversized boots as she flapped her arms. "Does it hurt?"

"Nah. . . . I kind of like the way it looks," Tony said, surprised by his honesty.

"Yeah, my father said it makes you look like even more of a rascal than you already do." Jo paused, nervously cleared her throat, and quickly started in again. "He meant it as a compliment."

"I know," Tony said, smiling. "Your father . . . He's a good guy."

"He's the best."

Tony fell silent. It looked like they might finally be getting along. He wouldn't contradict her, but Tony knew who had the best dad. "Yeah, he's pretty special," Tony said with all the diplomacy he could summon.

"Listen," Jo said, continuing to hop back and forth in the cold air. "I overreacted, but I was already in a bad mood. I hated having to move in the middle of the school year, and I could tell you didn't want to be showing me around. Then, as we left for our walk, my father whispered I had to ask you to walk me to school the first few days."

"I get it." Tony nodded. Nobody wants their parents treating them like a helpless kid. "Listen, I leave at eight fifteen each morning. If you just happen to go at the same time, we can walk together for a couple of days."

Jo stopped jumping and blew into her hands. "That would work. And if anyone asks about your shiner, I *guess* we could tell kids your father was hitting you grounders in the backyard, and the baseball hit a chunk of ice."

"Thanks for that." *Smart kid*, Tony thought, grinning, *and she is willing to stretch the truth, if needed.* "I'll see you in the morning."

"Well, good night." Jo turned, and as her footfalls softened, she faded from the light of his window into the shadows of the night.

V

Jo stood in front of Tony's house, leaning against a beat-up old Volkswagen Beetle, when he stepped out his front door. She acknowledged his arrival with an upward tilt of her head and fell comfortably in step beside him. They didn't speak for the first few minutes but took turns kicking chunks of ice that skittered and crumbled along the sidewalk. Every few hundred feet, one of the kids would stop at a shrunken, black-encrusted snowbank and break off another chunk of ice with the heel of their shoe before sending a new target skimming across the sidewalk.

Halfway there, Jo asked him about school and the teachers. Upon discovering they'd be in the same class, Tony opened up about Sister Agnes Helen, sharing all the gory details of his near expulsion.

Jo snorted with laughter. "'Go suck a bushel of lemons, you miserable old coot.' Wow, that's beautiful." She gave Tony a two-hand push in the back that hurried him down the street. "I'd love to have seen that."

She caught up with a grinning Tony, who rewarded her with an NHL-quality hip check, sending her bouncing off a chain-link fence.

"Good one," she said, smiling. "Number four, Bobby Orr."

Tony smiled back, temporarily forgetting the question still bugging him from last night. Had he really won that last game?

Jo's arrival made Tony's first day back after his blowout with Sister Agnes Helen much easier. The class's interest moved on quickly, excited by the rare occurrence of a new student in the middle of the year. At least for now, Tony's actions seemed consigned to the historic dusty shelf of other students' hilarious malfeasances.

Sister Agnes Helen—discovering, after a series of prodding questions, that Jo's father was the new general manager of the neighborhood Westinghouse factory—couldn't stop fawning over the girl. Delores DePalma and Kathleen Collins, the most popular girls in the class, asked Jo to sit with them for lunch, and Danny Walsh, "the cutest boy ever," offered to share his book when the class took turns reading *Anne of Green Gables*.

At first, Tony was pleased with the redirection of attention from his bad behavior. But his mood soured as the day wore on and the classroom's fascination with the new girl grew. With his teeth doing a slow grind, Tony drummed his fingers on his desk in petulant displeasure as his dark eyes took in the school's love affair with Jo Jo Trocki.

When the end-of-school bell rang, Tony approached Jo, who stood surrounded by half a dozen classmates, and he brusquely suggested she accept Delores and Kathleen's offer to walk home.

Jo smiled, thanking the girls but said she'd already made a commitment. She and Tony had agreed they'd walk home together so Tony could show her the rest of the compact neighborhood. But Jo bit her lower lip, a quizzical look on her face, as Tony flew past her.

He walked out the school's front door, with a wordless flick of the head indicating his planned direction and hurried down the concrete stairs two at a time.

Jo lowered her head and pumped her arms to catch up as Tony headed, not back toward their homes, but down the hill in the direction of last night's uncompleted walk. The homes grew smaller as they descended the Heights, and then a series of multi-family houses appeared as they got closer to the small downtown and the adjacent river.

Jo matched Tony stride for stride as her breathing grew heavy. "Something bothering you?"

"What?" Tony said, moving faster.

"I asked if something's bothering you?" Jo said through clenched teeth. "I know we got off to a lousy start, but after our talk last night and the morning walk to school, I thought you might be a pretty nice guy. But you're back acting like the jerk I first met."

"Okay, I'm a jerk. Well, what about you?" They crossed the street, dodging a big rig truck, and Tony stopped to stare at the sprawling brick factory that ran along the banks of the river. "Do you have any more secrets?"

"Secrets?" Jo turned to face him. "What're you talking about?"

"Okay, little Miss Priss, why didn't you tell me your father's the new manager of this place?" Tony pointed at the factory. "Kids' parents are talking about big changes coming that could cost even more jobs than when they stopped running the graveyard shift last year. And last night, your old man tried acting like some regular Joe Blow." Tony put his hands on his hips, shaking his head. "I thought he was just some kinda foreman or something. Not this college big shot."

"Wow, I was right the first time. You are a jerk. Yeah, my dad's a real big shot. He dropped out of high school, lied about his age, and enlisted the day after Pearl Harbor, ended up a waist gunner on a B-17. After the war, he went to college on the GI Bill while working full-time in a Chicago meatpacking house. Some big shot."

Tony paused, clearing his throat. "How come he didn't say that?"

Jo stared at him. "He told your father he was the new manager when he showed us his workshop."

"Oh." Tony's face flushed. Anthony Miracolo loved showing off his woodshop, and Tony, who knew every inch of it, had bowed out when his father led Jo and her dad downstairs to the basement.

"That's right." Jo flicked her tongue in the side of her mouth, making half-moons appear and disappear in her cheeks. "Any other *secrets* troubling you?"

"Why'd you let me win at twenty-one?" Tony fired back. He had her now.

"What?"

"You heard me," he said, his voice rife with indignation.

"Wow, you really are a dope if you believe that. I wouldn't let my baby brother win at a game of marbles. My father says that's how it should be," Jo said, her arms clutched tightly across her chest. "And he says screw anybody, girl or boy, who can't handle it."

Tony exhaled in one long breath, his silly boyish pride battling against his father's voice in his head: *If you screw up, admit it and move on.* He took a deep breath and exhaled again—a long, slow purge. *Pop's right, as usual.*

"I'm sorry," he said, his hooded eyes staring at the ground.

"I thought you might be different." Jo wiped a tear as she turned away. "But nope, my choices here are the same as at my last school. Hang around with boy-crazy gigglers like Delores DePalma and Kathleen Collins or self-absorbed pretty-boys like Danny Walsh."

Tony kicked a crumpled beer can into the gutter and shrugged. "Well, I guess there is one thing we can agree on. . . . I am a jerk."

A generous smile slowly curled the corners of Jo's lip, and Tony, with all the linguistic skills of a teenage boy, smiled back and gave Jo a good-natured two-handed push. "But I really am sorry."

Jo fell back two steps and caught her balance. "Hey!" She grinned, then sprang toward Tony, pushing him against a mailbox.

"Hey, yourself," Tony said, laughing. "So, you didn't let me win?"

"Never would."

"Good." Tony offered his outstretched hand. "Promise?"

Like the day before, Jo's grip was firm, her hands dry. The warmth of her touch lingered as their hands slipped apart.

"You hungry?"

"Starving," Jo said and shivered as she glanced up the hill at the afternoon sun slipping behind trees at the top of the Heights.

"Follow me." Tony nudged her with his shoulder. "I'm supposed to be grounded, but Mom said I didn't have to come straight home after school if I was gonna show you around town."

He reached out to take Jo's hand but pulled back, turning the movement into a half wave, signaling for her to hurry past the factory toward the playground and the long row of neighborhood businesses. He tucked his chin against his chest, hands stuck in his pockets, trying to make himself smaller as he leaned into the biting wind whipping his pant legs like a flag rippling high on a pole.

Tony stopped as they stood alongside the baseball diamond, and his nose twitched. "Smell that?"

Jo lifted her head and inhaled. "Umm, yeah,

smells great. What is it?"

"Best bakery in town."

Tony smiled as he hurried away from the park and past a hardware store to stand in front of a small bakery with a sign on its awning that read De Santo's. Met by a tingling bell, Tony shouted a greeting as the door opened to a warm, aromatic room.

"Hey Tony, how's ya'mom?" A dark, broad-shouldered, middle-aged man dressed in white pants, baker's cap, and t-shirt stood behind the counter, adjusting his apron.

"Doing good, thanks." Tony reached into his pocket, pulled out a solitary dime, and pushed it across the counter. "Two rolls, please, Zio Rico."

"Two today. Big spenda. But you know your money's no good here." The baker pushed the dime back across the counter as he tipped his head toward Jo. "And who's your friend?"

Tony smiled proudly, jerking his thumb at his companion. "This is Jo Jo Trocki. Her family bought the Prescott house. Jo, this is my Uncle Rico."

"Uncle?" Jo said, raising her eyebrows.

Rico chuckled. "It's kinda an honorary position. I've known this guy's folks since we were little. Most of the kids in the neighborhood call me Rico. But Tony here, his parents are what you'd call old-school, so he calls me zio. You know, uncle."

"Yeah, well, like I told you my, Zio Rico's got the best bakery in Boston, and he knows more about this part of town than anyone around."

"Oof, best in all Boston. There's a couple in the

North End that ain't bad." The baker wiped his hands on his apron and reached out to shake Jo's.

"Very nice to meet you, Mister De Santo," Jo said, shaking the baker's hand. "My parents are old-school, too. Maybe once I get to know you, I can call you zio."

The baker smiled at Tony and said, "You did good with this one. Hold on. I got some rolls just come outta the oven, nice'n warm." He walked away and returned, handing a golden, fist-sized roll to each of them. "Taste."

Jo took a bite and swallowed. "Delicious," she said before quickly taking a bigger bite.

Tony nodded, smiling widely, before taking his own bite, enjoying the crunchy crust and warm, chewy center that made his mouth water.

"So, the Prescott house." The baker raised his eyebrows. "Lotta history in that old place."

Jo swallowed another mouthful of food and turned to the baker. "My father was excited when he told us about the old Victorian house, and now I see why. The high ceilings and huge stone fireplace. It's so different from the ranch house we lived in outside Chicago. It feels like there's a story in every room."

"Come on, Uncle Rico, tell us about the old place."

The baker pointed at two wooden stools and grabbed one from behind the counter as his face grew somber. "Okay, but this ain't a happy story, and some people would say it's only for grown-ups. But not havin' kids of my own, I've seen lotsa young people are often smarter'n some of the grown-ups who make up those rules."

Tony laughed. He'd often talk to De Santo about his problems at school, and several months ago, the boy had listened, mesmerized, as his uncle told him the sad story of Sacco and Vanzetti, the tragically doomed Italian immigrants electrocuted for a crime many insisted they'd never committed. Since that day, Tony suspected his kind-hearted uncle, like the long-dead factory worker and fish peddler, was a bit of a radical at heart. Tony popped the last corner of the roll into his mouth and leaned forward on the stool. No one could tell a tale like Rico De Santo.

"The Prescotts owned the house for three generations. Old Alistair was as big as a bear, mean, and smart. The Prescotts were old Yankees, and some say they had old family money, while others say the Bear made his money bootleggin' with Joe Kennedy. Either way, he was rich and gettin' richer. He opened the foundry in the twenties, and half the men in the neighborhood ended up workin' there. The Prescotts made a bundle with Navy contracts, but the depression hit them hard. Alistair dropped dead on the factory floor, and when his son couldn't drink himself to death, he blew his brains out, but not before sellin' the factory to Westinghouse."

Jo bit her lower lip. "I think that's someone different. I heard my father say he bought the house from the estate of two sisters who never married."

"That's old Alistair's daughters. Yep, sad story, the whole family. After their brother lost the business, the sisters locked themselves behind their yellowin' lace curtains and slowly faded away."

Tony smiled, loving how Rico never treated him

like a kid. The lonely widower touched corners of Tony's soul the boy's ever-joyful father never could. His father's sunny disposition failed to recognize any of the unseemly sides of life, while his mother appeared to see it all but refused to discuss so many things with the boy.

"No one knows the history of this neighborhood like my Zio Rico," Tony said, filled with pride. Then his face twisted, all the joy gone. "Any changes?" He flicked his thumb toward the shops farther up the street.

"Nothin'," the baker said with a slow shake of his head. "Dominic, the cobbler, called the cops the other day, but same old story. There ain't nothin' they can do. But I hear the poor bastard howlin' in the night." The baker caught himself, raised his hand to his mouth, and offered an apologetic shrug. "Sorry, it gets me mad—the poor thing."

"Gotta go." Tony stood up, slapping his hands together as he brushed away the last of the breadcrumbs, and headed for the exit, his heart pounding. He'd heard enough. "C'mon, Jo. I've got to check on something."

"Hey, don't do nothin' stupid. You got the same look your mother used to get as a kid when someone was pickin' on your Auntie Flavia. I swear your mom hadda beat up half the kids in the neighborhood before they learned their lesson."

Tony stopped at the door and turned. "Yeah, but they did learn."

He pushed through the doorway, trusting Jo to follow, and tucked his head against the wind. They passed a tailor's shop and stopped in front of a shop with dozens of boots and shoes in the display window. Tony waved to a white-haired man with a walrus mustache behind a counter, then grabbed Jo's sleeve, pulling her to join him in leaning against the storefront out of the wind.

He turned away from the window, scanning the street, eyes open wide. "Listen, you can't tell my parents about this."

VI

Tony and Jo stood along the far wall of Dominic Caputo's cobbler shop. Tony signaled her to follow and walked into the alley formed by the shop on one side and a tarp-shrouded, eight-foot-high chain-link fence on the other. Attached to it hung a hand-painted sign on an oversized piece of plywood that read:

BIG A 's CARS

WE BUY, SEL & REPAIR

Tony's breathing came shallow, and he chewed his lower lip as he walked. Like his mother, there was nothing he hated more than a bully. And knowing an animal was suffering set him on edge.

He reached the back of the alley, placed an index finger in front of his lips, signaling quiet, before carefully pushing two aluminum trashcans against the fence and climbing on top of one. He removed his jacket and placed it over the barbed wire crisscrossing the top of the barrier so he could lean forward and see into the yard below. Then, grabbing hold of the chain links with one hand, he reached out to help Jo. Once up, she steadied herself and rested her chin on Tony's coat as they looked down into a crowded lot filled with old, rusting cars.

Jo lost her footing on the trash can, and Tony wrapped his arm around her waist, pulling her onto his can as the one Jo stood on flipped on its side with a clang. Tony winced at the sound but relaxed when no one working in the garage reacted to the clatter. Then he pointed to a dark back corner of the lot, where a large, scrawny dog was chained to the bumper of an old car set on cinder blocks. The mangy, malnourished animal lay panting. An empty pan sat flipped upside down in front of him as the dog huddled against the wind in the shadows of the brick wall that ran along the back of the property.

The dog's nose twitched, recognizing the boy's approach long before his appearance. The boy had been coming often, just as the sun dropped lower in the sky. His head would appear, popping up over the fence, and if the giant or the others weren't nearby, the boy would call out to the dog. The boy's words held no meaning to the dog, but he could tell by the lilting, gentle tone, the boy meant him no harm.

Each day, the boy brought some bits of food, and when no one was watching, he'd hurl it across the yard to where the dog could reach. The dog never wagged his tail or barked a greeting. His contact with humans had brought him nothing but pain, but he needed food, constant hunger a way of life. The dog never looked directly at the boy but would move forward—his body tense, shoulders low, still keeping his head high, watching for the giant and his thick, hard stick—before gobbling up the food.

Tony, frustrated with his inability to do more, clenched his jaw as he threw the hot dog he'd snuck into his book bag that morning. Every night, he'd wrap scraps in tin foil to stuff in his book bag to bring to the dog after school. But with last night's distraction of company and his argument with Jo, he'd forgotten and could find only the lone hot dog that morning.

What's the matter with these people? With his hands clutching the fence, Tony watched the dog limp toward the food—moving cautiously, as he always did, before quickly dropping his head to swallow the prize in one giant gulp.

A large man exited the garage's side door, leaned against the building, and lit a cigarette. Despite the near-freezing weather, the man's work overalls were rolled down to his waist, exposing tree-truck arms nearly as grease-stained as his sleeveless, once-white t-shirt. Tony pointed to the mountain of a man with a bald head the size of a watermelon, a florid complexion, and a nose much too small for his broad face.

"That's Big Al Ridgeway," Tony whispered. "He owns this place. Calls it a used car and repair shop, but it's nothing much more than a junkyard."

The dog bristled at the sight of the man. Fur rose high on his back, and his legs spread wide, as if anticipating an attack.

Ridgeway sneered at the dog's reaction before taking another long haul on the cigarette. "Don't have time for you today," he said, spitting a bit of tobacco leaf onto the ground. "But we'll have some fun later."

The big man took another drag on the cigarette, flipped the butt at the dog, and walked back into the garage. The dog tensed, his eyes following the burning ember flying toward him, prepared to jump away, but he dropped weakly to the ground as the cigarette flew over his head.

"C'mon," Tony said, cursing himself for not bringing more food.

"What? We can't leave him like that," Jo said. "Look at him. He's starving."

Tony grabbed his coat from the fence, jumped from the trash can, and hurried out of the alley as he struggled back into his jacket.

"Tony, wait!" Jo shouted, running after him and catching up with the boy in front of the cobbler shop. She grabbed him roughly by the arm and pulled him around to face her. "You're crying."

"No, I'm not." Tony wiped his coat sleeve across

his eyes as he tried to stare past her.

"Come on," Jo said, placing her hand on Tony's shoulder, gently leading him away from the junkyard as the boy struggled, blinking back his tears.

The two walked around the neighborhood for the next half hour, and Tony told Jo about the sad situation. How he'd spotted the dog a few months earlier, chained up outside, and been sneaking food to him ever since. He said neighbors, including his Uncle Rico, had called the ASPCA and the cops, but it seemed there wasn't anything they could do. The animal was legally purchased, licensed, and working as a "watchdog." So being chained and forced to sleep outside didn't break any laws or warrant taking the dog away from Al Ridgeway.

"It's not right." Jo sat on the top step of her front porch with Tony beside her. "Life isn't fair."

"My pop says, 'Life is what we make it.'" Tony set his jaw. "And I don't know how, but I'm going to do something to make that dog's life right."

Jo's eyes grew distant. "'Some men see things as they are and ask why—'"

"'I dream things that never were and ask, why not?'" Tony said, finishing the quote, then shrugged, embarrassed by the surprised expression on Jo's face. "George Bernard Shaw's one of Uncle Rico's favorites."

Jo laughed, shaking her head. "Anthony Miracolo, you are different."

Tony beamed. He'd often felt like he didn't quite fit in, forced to sit back and watch as others confidently navigated their place in the world. Tony wished he could be like the other kids, seemingly so comfortable as they slipped into the roles they played. But now being described as "different" by this curious new neighbor of his felt like about the greatest compliment a guy could get.

"Tony, suppertime."

His mother stood at their front door with an odd smile as she waved hello to Jo. Tony walked toward his mother, wondering what she was so happy about.

He looked back and called to Jo, "See you tomorrow."

The two stopped by the junkyard every day after school for the next two weeks, their pockets filled with scraps of food they'd taken from home. Watchful for Al Ridgeway or any others working at the junkyard, they'd throw treats to the dog, who offered no response beyond the swift gobbling of the food. Tony would call softly, but if the animal heard, his reactions never showed. With the food gone, the dog would turn away, searching for a spot out of the cutting wind.

Tony's previous solitary, selfless act of compassion had become a shared experience. Each day on the walk to school, the two young people delighted in showing the bits of food they'd snuck from the previous night's dinner table. And with each passing day, the passion of the friendly competition grew as both tried to outdo the other with the food quality they pilfered. But oddly, neither seemed disappointed on the days their table offering had been bested. Instead, they'd celebrate together in the shared knowledge of the badly needed nourishment they could bring the dog.

Then, with the assessment of the food they'd brought to the dog that day addressed, the conversations moved on. The topics were as limitless as the dreams of youth. They might discuss books, movies, school, music, or sports, along with topics as profound as: Does God really see everything? What did they think their parents were like when they were their age? Would they have wanted to hang out with them? So, the two grew closer, coming to appreciate the strange way they seemed to anticipate the other's thoughts.

Despite this unique bond, or perhaps because of it, hardly a day passed when the two didn't find something to argue about. Possibly because they'd grown to secretly value the other's opinion, a differing view cut more profoundly, or maybe it was hard-wired in both their natures. But as sure as night followed day, after hours of pleasure in each other's company, Jo and Tony would slip into a teeth-gnashing argument. Each regarding the other's failure to agree with a point of view they found utterly irrefutable as a personable affront.

"*El Dorado* was okay," Jo said, "but it was just a rehash of *Rio Bravo,* with Robert Mitchum playing the drunken deputy instead of Dean Martin."

After stopping to see the dog, the two stood in the foyer of the movie theater to get out of the cold as they looked at some of the older playbills posted on the wall. With Tony's punishment over, the kids could now linger on their walks rather than having to hurry home each day after visiting the dog.

Tony nodded in agreement, pleased but not surprised Jo spotted the artistic ploy. Director Howard Hawks changed the town's name and the supporting cast but essentially rolled out the same story of a courageous sheriff and a small band of misfits taking on a corrupt cattle baron. "My father thought it should have won the Academy Award for Best Picture."

Jo giggled. "Your dad's a great guy, but I don't think I'd depend on him for the latest film reviews."

Tony smiled. If those words came from anyone else, the boy would have bristled and rushed to his father's defense, but he knew how much Jo liked his easygoing father. And she wasn't wrong.

"Yeah, Pop's the best, but there're so many things I can't talk to him about. I swear, there isn't a book my Uncle Rico hasn't read where, Pop doesn't make it past the box scores in the *Herald's* sports page." Tony shrugged, walking on to the next billboard, *The Trouble with Angels*.

"Still, I think he's got it figured out."

"Got what figured out?" Tony turned to look at Jo.

"You know. Life. Your father's one the happiest people I know. He seems to accept life for what it is and finds pleasure in the simple moments."

"I wish I could be more like him." Tony sighed. "I don't know. It's just, sometimes I look at my mom and think she wants so much more from life, from my father, and then she blames Pop for something he can't be. I see them fight, and I can't figure out why. I don't think he can, either. I feel the same way around her. I'm always coming up short. Pop bites his tongue and walks away. I'm not so good at biting my tongue, but it doesn't matter. Mom ends up mad, whether I try to do what my father would or if I'm just myself." Tony turned and headed toward the exit, leaving Jo to hurry after him. "Let's get out of here."

Once outside, he dipped his shoulders against the wind and buried his hands in his pockets, walking swiftly up the hill toward home.

"I think Westerns are overrated," Jo said.

"What did you say?"

Jo gave him a sideways glance. "Westerns. They're a thing of the past."

Tony pulled his hands out of his pockets, his face lit and ready for battle. Whenever he got excited, Tony needed his hands to talk.

"*Red River, The Searchers, Shane, High Noon, Stagecoach.*" The boy rattled the films off with the fingers and thumb of his right hand. "I could go on, but I've run out of fingers," he said, waving his hand. "Goodbye, debate over."

"Those movies are all ten, fifteen, even thirty years old. Look at the way they portray women."

Tony exhaled deeply. "Please, not this again."

"Yes, this again. The women all stand around waiting for the men to do their heroic deed and then run into their arms at the end of the movie."

"That's not true. Look at Joanne Dru in *Red River*. She stops the gunfight. Or Grace Kelly in *High Noon*. Jeez, the woman's a Quaker, and she kills a guy."

"Small potatoes," Jo said. "I bet women buy more than half the movie tickets in America, and Hollywood acts like they're an afterthought. It gets me so mad sometimes I want to . . ." Jo stopped and stared at Tony, facing her with his hands hanging loose by his side, laughing. "What's so funny?"

"You," Tony said, trying to control his laughter. "Telling me Westerns are overrated. You just wanted to get me going, but you're worse. You need to argue like other people need air."

Jo stamped her foot. Then she blushed as a smile crept across her face. "That's not true," Jo said slyly. "I just have lots of opinions others would benefit from hearing, so I often feel the need to share my thoughts."

"That's what you call it, *sharing thoughts*?" Tony said, miming Jo's delivery. "Admit it." Tony's posture and voice took on the persona of a TV show courtroom attorney. "And I remind you, you're under oath, Miss Trocki. Admit it. You'd argue with a rock."

"Maybe, but I'd rather argue with you," Jo said, laughing.

"The defense rests." Tony theatrically waved his arms to an imaginary jury as his laughter mixed with Jo's to brighten the gray, cloud-wrung March sky.

When they arrived back at Jo's house, Tony stared at the ground, kicking a blackened snowbank. "Thanks. I know you were trying to get my mind off thinking about my parents. I appreciate it."

"It's nothing."

Tony watched as Jo fidgeted with the zipper on

her coat. He wanted to thank her for being there for him and ask if she, too, had fears she could barely admit to herself. But the words stuck in his throat.

"My mom's making a pot roast tonight," he finally said. "Our friend will eat well tomorrow." Then he spun away and ran toward his house.

VII

"**M**iniskirts are a mortal sin."

Sister Agnes Helen stood at the front of the class in rare form, her cheeks hollowing in and out as she sucked away at her bottom lip. With a long pointer rapping against her open palm, she paced back and forth, staring out at the class, defying any student not to join her in the glorious quest of growing closer to God. Somehow, in the middle of English class, she'd taken a hundred-and-eighty-degree turn from the lesson plan and spent the last twenty minutes detailing a litany of sins these young soldiers for Christ needed to be on guard against. Most of the class sat straight in their chairs, hands clasped and resting on their desks. The wise knew only someone with a death wish would call attention to themselves when Sister Agnes Helen had the saving of young souls on her mind.

The nun finished with the latest proclamation, challenging anyone to question the veracity of her logic, causing Jo to anxiously look over her shoulder for Tony. She groaned. Just as she feared, his hand pointed high in the air. Her new friend wished to contribute to the conversation. The rest of the class shifted at their desks, leaning forward in gleeful anticipation as Jo locked eyes with Tony. She shook her head, mouthing the words *Don't go there*. But Tony only smiled his crooked smile, and Jo surrendered, lowering her face into her hands. When Tony got that look, nothing she could do would stop him from going down the rabbit hole.

"Sister, excuse me."

The room grew still in anticipation. The show was about to begin. Tony Miracolo had something to say.

The nun, who had judiciously tried to ignore the raised hand, finally relented, turning her icy stare toward the irredeemable boy in the back of the room. Her lips pursed, and the rapping of the pointer against her open palm sped into overdrive as she collected herself.

"Mister Mi-ra-co-lo, you have a question?" The nun's voice tightened, preparing to battle, but Jo thought she heard a hint of anxiety in the older women's voice at the prospect of yet again having to match wits with the *incorrigible child.*

"Yes, Sister." Tony stood beside his desk, arms by his side, his face glowing radiantly. "Yes, I do."

Despite her dread, a low chuckle escaped when Jo saw the joy on Tony's face. He waited silently, baiting the nun, as the old woman's expression grew more dour with each passing moment. Helpless to intervene, Jo sighed. This wouldn't end well for Tony, but she suspected it would be a day they'd not soon forget.

"Well, go on, Mister Mi-ra-co-lo. Cat got your tongue?"

"It's about miniskirts being a mortal sin, Sister." Tony's relaxed delivery had the nun bristling, only the slightest nudge needed to push her over the edge.

"You question the accuracy?" the nun said, the pointer now rapping on the desk of a frightened girl in the first row.

"Oh no, Sister, not at all." The defrocked altar boy wore his most earnest funeral-mass face. "It's just, I'm only looking for some clarification."

"Clarification? What sort of clarification?"

"Well, Sister, I just wanna be sure I don't commit a mortal sin, so I'd like to better understand what exactly about miniskirts is the mortal sin. Girls wearing them? Boys looking at girls in them?"

"Look out!"

Tony, too busy enjoying the reaction of those around him to notice the nun storming down the aisle toward him, fell deaf to Jo's warning and grinning, continued with his list. "The people who manufacture them? The stores that sell—"

Thwack. The pointer cracked across Tony's shoulder, splitting the staff in two as the class gasped in voyeuristic delight.

"Get out! Get out! Get out, you godless child." The nun stood frozen, hovering over Tony, her bug eyes blinking as she stared at the broken stick left in her hand. Then she turned to point the shattered stub at Jo. "And you, Miss Trocki, since you feel the need to contribute to this young man's foolish display with your outburst, you can join him."

Jo's face turned crimson as the class shifted their giggling attention to the new girl in school, who'd acted so cool and distant to their advances since her arrival. Jo grabbed her coat from the back of her chair and collected her books. Then she rose, clutching the books tightly to her chest, and left the room, staring at Tony's back while the boy strutted out of class like a proud rooster.

"What's wrong with you?" Jo said, her nostrils flaring.

"What?" Tony, leaning against the flagpole in front of the school, stopped smiling, his smug face now looking like an incredulous victim.

"Don't give me that look! You know what you did. You deliberately baited Sister Agnes Helen, knowing the reaction you'd get and knowing it had to end badly. For you, Tony, it had to end badly for you."

Tony lost his pleased expression, and his tone grew defensive. "She just got on my nerves. I couldn't stand listening to her know-it-all babbling." Tony turned and slapped his open hand against the flagpole. "I bet the old witch has never even been kissed. What does she know about life? And we're supposed to sit there and listen to her."

Jo looked away. Tony wasn't wrong. Each day,

they were forced to listen to the self-righteous woman prattle on about life. But Sister Agnes Helen didn't have a clue about their fears and dreams.

"Miniskirts a mortal sin. What a fool."

"That's not the issue," Jo said, still unwilling to acknowledge Tony's point. "Exactly what do you think you accomplished with your silly stunt?"

"It wasn't silly. I just got tired of listening to her stupid voice."

"Oh, you got tired, like your hero in *Cool Hand Luke*? He got tired of looking at all those parking meters, so he got drunk and cut their heads off." Tony had shared how he'd related to the tragic character in the film, and Jo put her hands on her hips, pleased her comments hit a raw nerve. But she wasn't ready to let up.

"So, tell me, Tony, how'd that end for him?" Jo could tell her words hit home. She should quit but couldn't. Jo needed to twist the knife and knew just the words. "Honestly, you can be so childish sometimes."

"Oh, screw you. School's letting out in ten minutes anyway." Tony spun away. "I'm going to see the dog. You don't have to come if you're afraid to be seen with someone so childish."

"I brought cold cuts. I won't deny the dog just because you're a jerk," Jo said, following Tony down the hill, neither looking at the other.

"The Trockis are coming over for a piece of cake."

"What?" Tony lifted his head from busily

rubbing linseed oil into his new baseball glove to look up at his mother. His parents, perhaps feeling guilty over once again freezing any conversation about his getting a dog, had bought him a new glove for his birthday. Tony tried to act disinterested through the whole Happy Birthday charade, but the sight of the Brooks Robinson model glove momentarily broke through the cold demeanor he'd been working so hard to maintain. With the announcement that Jo and her family would be coming by for a piece of birthday cake, his cold visage was back in full force. "What'd you invite them over for?"

"Well, I happened to mention it was your birthday, and Mrs. Trocki said Jo had bought you a present." Tony's mother was wearing that Chesire smile she always seemed to have whenever Jo's name came up. "So, I said they should stop by after supper and have a piece of cake."

"It's my birthday. You should've asked me!" Tony hadn't spoken to Jo in two days. And the thought of having to talk to her in front of his parents after their latest argument, their biggest one yet, left him with that funny feeling in his stomach he'd been getting anytime he thought about the unbelievably annoying Jo Jo Trocki.

Anthony Miracolo placed his hand on his wife's, temporally silencing her with a shake of his head.

Tony saw the interplay and, recovering his senses, jumped at the opportunity his father's actions afforded. "Sorry, I thought it would just be the family," he said, searching for an excuse for his behavior.

"I hope you and Jo didn't get into—" A knock at the back door interrupted Tony's mother. "They're here." She gave Tony a look before turning away to answer the door.

"Come in, come in. Where's Jo?"

"She's not feeling well, and Frank's working late." Donna Trocki stood in the doorway with Frank Junior in one arm and a wrapped package in the other. "Happy Birthday, Tony. Jo . . . um, I mean, *we, the family,* got you a little something."

Tony squirmed, trying to hide his discomfort as he rose to accept the present.

"Thank you, Mrs. Trocki," Tony said. "You really didn't need to." Embarrassed by the gesture, he dropped back into the chair, uncomfortable with the attention the unexpected gift brought.

"Nonsense. Jo insisted we get you something." She sat down at the kitchen table and exchanged a knowing smile with Tony's mother as a thick slice of Italian rum cake was placed in front of her. "Jo's just sorry she doesn't feel well enough to have given it to you herself."

"I hope she's okay," Tony said.

"Oh, she'll be fine." The mothers exchanged that look again. "We found the gift at an old bookstore on Milk Street when we went downtown to Filene's Basement to look for a dress for Jo to wear to the CYO spring dance." Donna Trocki smiled, pointing at the wrapped package. "When Jo saw it, she lit up like a Christmas tree. She said it was the perfect gift for Tony."

"Go ahead, open it." His sister Rosa, now holding Frank Junior, hovered over Tony as she bounced the baby in her arms. "You love books. I wonder what it is," she said, her voice filled with adolescent excitement.

Tony tore the seam on the neatly wrapped package and looked down at a weathered hard-covered copy of a book entitled *A Shropshire Lad: The Collected Poems of A.E. Housman.*

Tony swallowed hard. Several weeks ago, he'd told Jo how much he'd liked a poem by Housman, "To an Athlete Dying Young," and stopped at a streetlight on the way back from the junkyard to recite the poem from memory. Jo hadn't said much at the time, while Tony grew withdrawn, and the two soon found themselves arguing about one of the many silly things they seemed to battle over.

"She remembered."

"What, dear?"

"Oh, nothing, Mom," Tony said, his smile shining brighter than the birthday cake lit with its fourteen candles half an hour earlier. "It's just a very nice gift. Thank you, Mrs. Trocki, and please thank Jo for me."

"Why don't you thank her yourself?" Tony's mother said. "I noticed you two haven't been walking to school together the last few days."

"Oh, I'm sure Jo Jo will be feeling better tomorrow," Mrs. Trocki said, raising a forkful of rum cake to her mouth before pausing. "And I'll be sure to tell her how much you liked the gift."

VIII

Tony knocked on the Trockis' front door, a box with a corsage for Jo in his free hand.

He'd insisted to his parents it wasn't a date, saying he and Jo had merely agreed to walk together to the Catholic Youth Organization's spring dance held in the church basement. But his mother asserted that since he and Jo agreed to attend together, it was the gentlemanly thing to do, and Tony felt rather pleased with himself that he could pay for the small white corsage with some of the money he'd earned from shoveling driveways that winter.

A solemn Mr. Trocki met Tony at the front door, and Tony gulped when he saw Jo in a thigh-high, Twiggy-styled summer-blue dress. Her hair, usually tied in a ponytail, was down, curled, and glowed like honey. Jo's cheeks were pink, and she looked like she had a touch of mascara and lipstick on. What had happened to the Jo Jo Trocki he knew?

Mrs. Trocki spotted the small flower box in Tony's hand and helped him pin the corsage on Jo's dress. He squared his shoulders in his hand-me-down blue blazer and nervously adjusted the knot in his father's too-long tie. *She even smells different.* He wasn't sure if he'd ever smelled jasmine, but in Tony's mind, that's precisely what standing so close to Jo made him think of.

Mrs. Trocki then yelled for her husband to "Get the Brownie," and the two kids posed, smiling painfully for a series of photographs in front of the large stone fireplace. For the last photo, Mrs. Trocki told Tony to put his arm around Jo, and Tony's smile grew even more strained as he placed his trembling hand on the lovely young girl's slim waist.

As the two walked toward the church, Jo unbuttoned her spring jacket. "It's warmer than I thought it would be," Jo said as she slowed momentarily to brush a long curl off her face with the back of her hand.

"Yeah," was the best Tony could manage, cursing himself for his silence. But the sight of Jo dressed fancy and made-up left him tongue-tied in a way he'd never felt before.

The day after his birthday, Tony had risen early and stood outside his front door, waiting for Jo to walk by. He'd thanked her for the book, and the two fell into step, walking toward school and slipping into comfortable conversation, as they had so often since Jo moved next door. Tony wasn't quite sure how it happened, but before they reached school, they'd agreed to go to the CYO dance together.

They visited the junkyard each day that week, bringing food for the dog, and soon it seemed like the argument never happened. Through it all, the spirited conversations never lagged as they talked endlessly about books, movies, whether Bill Russell had one more championship run in him, and how the Red Sox looked at spring training in Winter Haven. Although, much to Tony's chagrin, Jo insisted she still planned to remain a long-distance Chicago Cubs fan.

But now, walking toward the dance, Tony breathed deeply, taking in the scent of the pretty young girl beside him. He couldn't think of a thing to say.

They entered the steamy church basement and, after hanging up their coats, were immediately separated. Several giggling girls surrounded Jo while Delores DePalma grabbed Tony's hand, dragging him out to the dance floor, squealing, "My favorite song" as a portable record player set up next to a microphone blared out "Cherish" by The Association.

"I think this song is *so* romantic." Her upper lip beaded with sweat, the busty fourteen-year-old girl rested her head on Tony's shoulder and hummed to the music.

After the song, Tony slipped away from Delores, brought Jo a soda, and they danced to Creedence Clearwater's "Proud Mary." Tony watched Jo move seemingly without thought in rhythm to the music as he proudly wondered if there was anything his pretty neighbor wasn't good at. But as Jo's head bobbed to the music, Tony prayed the next song would be a slow one. Because, suddenly, the thought of having Jo rest her head on his shoulder, like Delores DePalma had only moments earlier, seemed like the only thing in the world he could possibly want.

They were soon separated again, and blond-haired, blue-eyed Danny Walsh appeared, hovering around Jo, asking her to dance multiple times as half the other girls looked on with green-eyed envy. The room grew hotter and noisier. Tony and Jo danced to another fast song, and he tried to talk to her above the din of the crowded room but was again separated from Jo at the end of the song.

The night passed quickly until a heightened energy filled the hall—only one more song. Everyone knew the last record would be one the kids could dance to slowly. After a long night of being cautioned by the nuns and priests chaperoning the dance to "Leave room for the Holy Spirit" if they held each other too closely, the kids hoped these earnest watchdogs may have lost some of their zeal.

"Ba da da da da da da," the opening notes of Orpheus's "I Can't Find the Time" crackled over the microphone as Tony pushed his way through the crowded basement. At last, standing behind Jo, he reached out to tap her on the shoulder but found his hand pulled away. He spun around to face a starry-eyed Delores DePalma.

"My favorite song." The girl cooed. Tony's shoulders dropped as she locked her fingers behind his neck, and whispered in his ear, "I think this song is *so* romantic."

Delores pressed up against Tony in the crowded church basement as the lyrics to the song spoke of looking at a pretty girl's face and falling in love. But Tony, immune to Delores's attention, couldn't take his eyes off Jo, who danced nearby in the arms of Danny Walsh.

The song ended, and Delores pulled Tony's face toward her, kissing him hard as other kids pushed past them, heading toward the cloakroom to grab their jackets. The two had kissed once before, last summer, when they'd been stuck at the top of the Ferris wheel at the church carnival. And now a surprised Tony found himself momentarily kissing back and thinking—Delores must have been practicing.

A strong hand fell on Tony's shoulder, and he broke from the embrace. "Don't forget your coat." Monsignor Hanrahan seemed to suppress a smile as a surprised Tony spun away and headed toward the cloakroom, searching for Jo.

But Delores grabbed his hand, pulling him back. A crowd now stood by the door, and Tony froze when he saw Danny Walsh, a full head taller than Jo, smiling his toothy *Pepsodent white* smile. Danny helped Jo put on her coat and confidently put his arm around her waist as he led her out into the cool night.

Tony stepped toward the door but was stopped by another aggressive tug on his hand. "Your coat, silly."

"Oh yeah," Tony said mindlessly looking back at

the rapidly dispersing crowd as Jo disappeared.

Delores, still holding tightly to Tony's hand, led him back to the cloakroom. She handed Tony her coat, let him help her into it, and turned, beaming, as she slowly buttoned her short, red leather jacket.

"It was such a wonderful night. Thanks so much for asking me to dance and offering to walk me home."

IX

Tony stood on a trash can next to Jo as she reared back and threw the last slice of meat at the dog's feet. The animal lowered his head to gobble it up.

They hadn't spoken all weekend after the dance. Still, Jo surprised him during recess when she broke free from a serious-looking conversation with Danny Walsh to tell him her mother had made prime rib for Sunday dinner, and she planned to join him when he visited the dog after school. Tony was still mad at Jo for leaving the dance with Danny, but seeing the dog devour the meat felt good.

"You stupid son-of-a-bitch! I told ya to drain the radiator first. Shit for brains, that's what ya got, Charley. Shit for brains. Get outta my sight."

The shouting came from the garage, where the gravelly voice of a yelling man mixed with the sounds of banging pipes. Then the crash of metal skittering across concrete and a second voice, younger and scared. "You're freakin' crazy, Al? Ya coulda killed me with that damn lug wrench."

"I got a thirty-eight in my desk, top draw. If I wanted'ya dead, I wouldn't use no wrench. Now get outta here. Before I split your head with this pipe. You cost me enough money."

"Rot in hell, ya miserable bastard."

Then the sound of more metal clanging as a young man in mechanic's overalls ran out of the bay doors toward the street, hands held protectively over his head.

"You're crazy, an' all the booze is makin' ya meaner by the day."

The kids ducked low behind the canvas-covered fence as Ridgeway stumbled out of the shadows of the garage, reached back with his right arm, and threw a pipe the size of a kid's baseball bat at the fleeing man. It somersaulted through the air, barely missing its intended target before smashing a car's windshield, where it quivered and settled, impaled in the windscreen next to a sign that read:

1963 CADLLAC

LIKE NEW

$1,50 0

"Son-of-a-bitch!" Ridgeway bellowed, reaching into his back pocket to pull out a clear, flat bottle half filled with a dark-brown liquid. He removed the cap, brought the bottle to his lips, tossed his head back, and emptied it with an uninterrupted series of throat-gurgling swallows. With a feral howl, the mechanic stared at the empty bottle and sent it spiraling across the lot, where it smashed against the back wall.

The dog, panting heavily during the argument, yelped at the sound of the crash and jumped up, taking several quick bounds to escape. But the dog's short leash spelled danger. Tony grimaced, averting his eyes moments before the chain cinched and snapped the poor animal back like he'd run into a wall. The dog fell to the ground with a painful thud.

"Stupid mutt." Ridgeway staggered to the back of the lot, where the dog lay on his side, stunned and panting. "Waste of friggin' money. Can't fight no more with that bum leg. Ya good for nothin'. Some friggin' watchdog you are. Not even smart 'nuff to know how long your chain is."

Ridgeway snapped off the antenna from a crumpled car, reached back, cracking the stunned dog across his bony ribcage with a merciless swipe, and then caught the dog's shoulder with a returning backhanded swing of the antennae. Breathless, the man sucked in air with quick gasps as he repositioned himself, hovering over the dog, intent on inflicting more pain.

"Stop that, you Goddamn son-of-a-bitch."

Heart pounding, Tony threw himself over the fence, leaving his jacket draped across the barbed wire and tearing his pant leg, opening a gash in his thigh. He landed hard and stumbled, falling with a grunt, scraping his knees and palms and drawing more blood. He quickly righted himself, oblivious to the pain, and stood tall, his bloody hands clenched in rage.

"Get outta here, you pissant." Ridgeway stepped toward him, lips curled, exposing large, yellow, misshapen teeth. The big man snapped the car antenna against his pant leg as each step brought him closer.

Tony's jumping over the fence and calling out this giant of a man might not have been the best idea, but what else could he do? He couldn't let the man beat a defenseless dog. His heart racing, Tony's eyes darted across the ground, looking for something he could use to defend himself—nothing.

Ridgeway lumbered forward, the only sound the vicious snapping of the antennae.

Tony took a deep breath and slowly exhaled, hands trembling. *If I'm gonna take a beating, I'm gonna make sure Ridgeway knows he was in a fight.* His father always told him: Never start a fight, but if you know one's coming, be sure you throw the first punch and, win or lose, don't quit throwing them till it's over.

Tony tucked his head, taking several long strides before hurling himself in the air and catching Ridgeway with a solid right to the face that would have ended a battle against any kid in the neighborhood.

But Big Al Ridgeway wasn't a kid. He was a 275-pound man.

Caught by surprise, Ridgeway spit a mouthful of blood onto the ground, wiped the back of his hand across his lips, and sneered, his yellow teeth now masked in a pink hue. He closed on Tony and grabbed him by his shirtfront, pinning the boy several feet in the air against the chain-link fence, with Tony trying desperately to claw at Ridgeway's face.

"Kid, I'm gonna make you wish you wuz never born."

Tony's heart pounded, and he struggled for breath as the man's massive left hand wrapped around his throat.

Ridgeway's bloodshot eyes narrowed, and he cocked a menacing right hand. "I'm gonna enjoy messin' you up."

Wide-eyed, Tony continued to flail and kick, pressing his head against the fence, hoping to dodge the crushing blow.

A blur whipped toward Ridgeway from the shadows, and a *thwap* echoed off the back wall. The man's eyes rolled back in his head, and he fell to the ground with a thud as Tony, gasping for air, dropped to his knees beside him.

"Is he . . . ?" Jo stood over the two of them, shaking, holding a two-by-four. Her face turned crimson as she tossed the board away, burying her face in her hands. "Did I *kill* him?"

Tony crawled to Ridgeway and anxiously brought his face close to the big man's. Tony's nose flared. His throat contracted at the smell of whiskey and stale sweat as his lips slowly spread into a wide smile.

"You didn't kill him, but he's going to have a beauty of a headache when he wakes up." Tony stood, wincing, grabbed a handkerchief from his back pocket, wiped the blood from his palms, then tried to stanch the blood darkening his thigh.

"You okay?" Jo asked, studying the battered boy. "You look like you fell off the back of a truck."

"I feel like it, too." Tony jumped back as Ridgeway began to stir. "Come on. We don't have much time."

Tony ran toward the dog, who stood snarling, guarding against the next human who might try to hurt him. Tony called, but the dog growled once and turned away, crawling under the car.

"I'm not gonna hurt you, buddy. I'm gonna get you out of here." He tried to coax the dog, who backed farther under the car, its teeth gleaming in a protective snarl. Tony grabbed the dog's chain and tried to free it from the bumper. "We can't leave him here."

Ridgeway got to his knees, shaking his head, trying to clear the fog as Jo joined Tony. With their feet braced against the car's chassis, the two struggled to break the dog's chain free from the bumper. Tony's hands grew bloodier. His arms quivered, and the bumper popped, slipping free on one side. But the chain welded tightly around the bumper didn't shift.

"Whata'ya bastards doin'?" Ridgeway struggled to his feet, unsteady, and stumbled toward the kids.

Time was running out.

"The pipe. Get the pipe." Tony pushed Jo toward the pipe Ridgeway had embedded in the Cadillac's windshield.

With the big man almost on top of him, Tony dropped the chain and sprinted to grab the two-by-four, where a shocked Jo had sent it skittering away. He fell to his knees, scrambling to grab it as the snarling dog backed deeper under the car. Tony stood between Ridgeway and the dog, locking eyes with the much bigger man while holding the two-by-four extended, making small circles in the air, like a batter finishing up in the on-deck circle.

"Don't think I won't use this."

Ridgeway smirked as he closed on the boy. Tony recognized the look of total confidence. Most people probably turned and ran or were so rapt with fear they fought ineptly when facing a foe as threatening as Big Al Ridgeway.

But Tony Miracolo wasn't like most people. Ridgeway took a quick step but stopped, his eyes opening wide, and snapped his head back as the flashing two-by-four missed his chin by inches.

"Told you I'd use it."

Tony's heart pounded, and his arms ached as he swallowed hard. He hadn't meant to get quite so close. He took a calming breath and repositioned the two-by-four menacingly, flashing the weapon as he listened for the pounding of metal on metal behind him. "Jo, hurry."

Clang, clang, clang. Jo swung the pipe like an ax, pounding away at the dog's chain, trying to free it from the bumper. "Almost."

The clanging continued as the board grew heavier in Tony's hands.

"Got it." Jo stood triumphantly, holding the chain high in the air, its stub still tightly wrapped around the bumper. "Let's go!"

Tony took another swing, forcing Ridgeway to jump back, then dropped the two-by-four and sprinted toward Jo, who pulled on the chain, trying to drag the growling dog out from under the car. "Run, Jo! Run!"

"The dog." Jo leaned back, tugging on the chain with two hands but having no more success than when they'd tried to pull it free from the bumper.

The dog snarled and backed away, his claws digging into the ground, refusing to move as he dragged himself farther under the car.

"Go, go! I got him!" Tony shouted as he reached for the chain.

But Ridgeway got to him first, pinning the boy against a car as he buried a massive fist in Tony's gut. Tony fell to his knees and doubled over, struggling to breathe. Ridgeway lifted a booted foot, aiming at Tony's ribcage, and swung it forward as a gasping Tony tried to spin away.

But the blow never arrived. A blur flew at the man, fur meeting flesh, knocking the massive man to the ground and leaving him staring up into the crazed eyes of imminent death.

The dog had crawled out from under the car. Surprised by his ability to move beyond the usual confines, he spotted the open gate: Freedom.

He hurried toward it but stopped, gripped by the sound of the young girl's cries, and turned to find the giant towering over the boy. Escape beckoned, only moments away. But the dog froze at the sight of the man who'd caused him so much pain. An emotion more intense than his desire to escape blinded him. Rage.

The dog lowered his head and closed on the man. Then, airborne, hurtling forward like the great gray wolf he descended from, he crashed into the big man, knocking him to the ground. The dog scrambled back onto all fours to stand over the giant, the animal's fist-sized paws spread wide on the man's chest. The primal synapsis fired in his canine brain, telling the dog to strike again and end it now. His foe's vulnerable throat lay exposed, inches from the animal's vice-like jaw.

Forced to fight other dogs as men stood around a caged pen screaming, the dog had killed before. It all came rushing back. The noisy, smoke-filled rooms, the stench of their adrenaline, and the men's sweat heightening the animal's survival instinct and bloodlust.

With his fur high on his back, his body trembled in anticipation. He closed, ready to strike, but the boy shouted something.

"Stop!"

The dog hesitated. The word meant nothing, but the animal responded to the boy's voice. He raised his head, smelling the cool air, fresh and clean. The bloodlust slipped away. The dog just wanted to be free. He glared down at the cowering giant, but the desire to avenge the brutality faded. His entire life, these cruel, strange-smelling creatures had only hurt him. His lone-wolf brain told him to run—not from fear, but from a burning desire to be alone, away from the evil, and free.

The dog looked down. His stare locked on the giant whimpering underneath him. The animal's sensitive canine nose twitched as the smell of the man's cowardly release of bodily fluids added to the stench of the giant. The man who'd beat him again and again, always acting brave around others while the dog struggled to escape his chains, now trembled like a frightened pup. This man had nothing he needed.

The dog jumped off and ran toward the gate, past the girl, and into the street, dragging the chain behind him.

Tony watched from his knees, in awe of the animal's raw power. The dog could have ended Ridgeway's life with one savage attack. But instead, he turned away.

"We have to go." Jo now stood behind Tony, her hands under his armpits, helping to pull him up. "He's coming."

Back on his feet, Ridgeway staggered toward the kids, the two-by-four now in his hand.

"The dog." Tony pointed to the fast-moving animal.

The kids chased after him, their feet barely touching the ground, followed by Big Al Ridgeway, gasping for air, struggling to keep up. The dog moved at a manic pace, the chain clattering along the sidewalk. Oblivious to the danger, he narrowly missed being hit by several screeching cars, leaving scarred pavement and an acrid stench of scorched rubber to fill the late-afternoon air. He ran down the street, dodging cars, past the shops, through the stone archway onto the playground, then down toward the wetlands and the riverbank. The kids lost sight of him when they had to stop for a delivery truck blocking the sidewalk as it backed up next to the hardware store while Ridgeway—doubled over, gasping for air—quit the chase.

They ran into the street, mindful of the oncoming traffic, but could find no sign of the dog. Tony froze at the faint, far-off sound of a distinctive whistle.

He lowered his head, kicking at a can lying in the gutter. "That's my pop. It's suppertime." He turned away. So close, and he'd let the dog, his dog, slip from his grasp.

They snuck back into the alley, grabbed their book bags, and headed up the hill. Tony, brooding, walked on in silence as Jo tried to get him to focus on their success of freeing the dog from his terrible existence.

But Tony couldn't stop worrying. "The dog's spent his life tied to the bumper of a junkyard car. I can't leave him running around these busy streets, dragging a length of chain behind him. What if Ridgeway catches him?" Tony said, his mind filled with imagined horrors. "My parents are in bed by ten. I'm sneaking out after they're asleep. I gotta find him."

"I'll come, too," Jo said.

"No. I don't need anyone's help. I can do this alone."

"Well, you sure needed my help today. I'm

coming."

But Tony wasn't listening. He was already planning how to slip out of the house without being seen.

At home, his mother reacted to Tony's tattered appearance with shocked displeasure, going on about the cost of replacing his ruined school clothes while his father offered nothing more than a mere *boys will be boys* shrug. But Tony's explanation that he forgot his coat at the ballpark and his ragged appearance came from an overly intense tackle football game didn't pass the sniff test with either parent. His mother, on high alert, studied his every movement as she probed for the truth while his father's usual trusting countenance carried a sad look of disappointment.

Tony sunk low in his chair as he thought of how angry his mother would be if she heard the language he'd used in the junkyard. The swearing would get him at least five Our Fathers at confession, but Tony had never known a sin to feel so right.

Lying to his parents only added to the list of sins, but he had to stick to his story. So, as Rosa deliberately kept the conversation of his tattered appearance alive, Tony, drawing on all his story-telling skills, offered elaborate game details. His face lit with faux excitement as he described catching the fleet-footed Danny Walsh from behind in the open field and the long touchdown pass he grabbed from little Billy DePalma. Fortunately, the mention of Billy DePalma brought Rosa back to the May Procession conversation, and Tony slipped into silence. Head down, he played with the food on his plate, worrying about the dog out there, alone and frightened.

After supper, Tony went into the bathroom to inspect his wounds. His mother knocked on the bathroom door, handing him Band-Aids and a bottle of Mercurochrome. She offered to help, but Tony's embarrassed face signaled that the days of Mom nursing her cut or bruised son had passed, and the wall between Tony and his indomitable mother grew taller. She walked away in a huff, yelling at his sister. The girl better have her homework done before turning on that TV.

Tony took a long bath, wincing as the hot water settled over his open wounds, thankful for the distraction the stinging pain brought. His parents doubted his story, and he feared the repercussions if his mother caught him outright in his lie. But Tony dreaded the conversation he'd have with his father even more. The *You're better than that* look in his eyes would be agonizing. Yes, he had much to confess this week to Monsignor Hanrahan, but what truly was the greater sin: a bit of foul language or looking at someone you love with all your heart and lying to their face? Tony flushed as the significance of swearing at Al Ridgeway dropped precipitously.

But all that would have to wait. The dog was out there—his dog—alone, cold, and frightened.

"He needs me," Tony said in a whisper as he pulled clean blue jeans over tender knees. He didn't say the rest, but it hung over him like a full moon in the night sky.

I need him.

X

The house rested in darkness, and Tony lay in bed as the headlights of cars flashed across his bedroom wall before passing on. He listened to his father's heavy breathing and then his mother's lighter murmurs coming from down the hall—asleep at last. He rose, quietly pulled on a pair of winter boots, and grabbed his heaviest sweatshirt from the radiator, where he'd placed it to warm. As he drew the sweatshirt over a long-sleeve, thermal shirt a beam of light flashed on and off into his room. He walked to the window, wiped away the frost, and looked out at Jo, waving for him to follow.

Tony shook his head as he stared down at the girl. He'd told Jo he didn't need her help. Tony signaled her to stay and crept down the hall, the old wooden floor creaking under his feet with each step as he snuck toward the fire escape. Once outside, he nodded to an annoyingly determined Jo, and they walked in silence down the hill, slipping into the shadows anytime they saw car lights heading toward them.

First stop was back to the junkyard to grab his coat from the top of the fence, where he'd left it that afternoon. Tony grabbed Jo's hand to pull her back as she started to cross the street toward the alley.

"Mister Caputo's still up," he said, eyeing a small well-lit room above the cobbler shop that overlooked the junkyard.

Tony's Uncle Rico had told them Dominic Caputo complained about how Ridgeway treated the dog, but Tony still couldn't afford to let the old cobbler see them wandering the streets late at night searching for the animal.

"I shoulda grabbed the coat when we got our book bags, but I was afraid Ridgeway might spot us," Tony said, flapping his arms to stay warm. "C'mon, I'll come back for it later."

"You'll freeze," Jo said, pointing toward a broken streetlight in front of the junkyard. She crossed into the shadows and snuck down the alley with an angry Tony behind her as she climbed the chain-link fence to free his coat. The barbed wire had severely torn the jacket, and Tony simmered, angry at Jo for risking their being spotted and imagining the earful to come from his mother. *What were you thinking? Your cousin's coat was almost brand-new. Money doesn't grow on trees.*

"You didn't have to do this," he said, buttoning his coat as they hurried out of the alley, staying in the shadows, and headed toward the park where they'd last seen the dog.

"I'm not-one for quitting." Jo tucked her shoulders, making herself small against the biting wind.

"Sure," Tony said between clenched teeth before quick-stepping around Jo on the sidewalk to be closest to the street, just like his father had taught him a gentleman must do when walking with a lady. *You sure quit on me the night of the dance.*

They crossed under the WPA-built stone archway to the park. Filled with thoughts of his beloved grandfather, who'd died the previous summer, Tony ran his hand along the cold stone wall and sighed. His grandfather had worked on the government project during the Depression, and he'd often told Tony stories of those hard-scrabble times. Tony looked up at the dark, cloud-shrouded, sky remembering the gentle old man, and said a silent prayer, asking for help.

Jo pulled the flashlight out of her coat pocket and zigzagged a beam of light past the playground and basketball courts down to the baseball diamond. Nothing. Tony stopped, placed his right thumb and middle finger in his mouth, and produced a sharp whistle in a reasonable facsimile of his father's call to supper.

"Pretty good," Jo said.

Tony shrugged. He'd been practicing for months, and that was his best yet. But he found little pleasure in this newly developed talent. "Who knows if he'll even respond to a whistle?"

The two walked across the baseball diamond, through the outfield, and down toward the riverbank, to the sound of the last remnants of frozen snow crunching under their feet. As they walked, they mixed calls of "Here, boy" with Tony's whistles while their eyes darted everywhere, sometimes following the flashlight's trail or off into the darkness. They reached the end of the park and stood at the lip of a wooded wetland that ran close to a hundred feet wide along the banks of the river on the backside of the shops.

Tony frowned. "It's a swampy mess in there. Just give me the flashlight, and you can head back. You've already done enough." He reached out to take it but had his hand pushed back.

"No way. I told you, I'm not one for leaving a job half done."

Tony exhaled, long and slow. What was she trying to prove? Sure, bringing the flashlight had proved smart, but walking through these wetlands in the dark could be dangerous, and she'd already risked everything by going after his coat. But the tone in Jo's voice made it clear she wouldn't go home.

"Okay, but don't say I didn't warn you." He paused. "Listen, this marsh is a tricky, wet mess. Let me have the flashlight. I know the trails. Stay close behind, and only step where I do."

The flashlight slapped across Tony's open hand, and he turned his back to hide the look of pain on his face. Directing the flashlight across a trail of matted grass flanked by shoulder-high brush, he switched it to his other hand as he flexed his right hand open and shut, wincing with each stretch. She did that on purpose, but he wouldn't give Jo the satisfaction of letting her know it hurt. He probably deserved it. He'd barely spoken a word to her since they'd snuck out, and despite everything else, she only wanted to help. But Tony didn't have time for bruised feelings—Jo's or his own. *Who cares if she likes Danny Walsh.* His dog was wandering out there alone, maybe hurt, and he had to find him.

Snow started to fall, flakes the size of quarters, signaling the arrival of the predicted "last major storm of the year." The graying sky had hinted at the looming threat since early afternoon, and now the stars were whited out by swiftly swirling snow. Tony's father's meteorologically gifted knee had been correct, and the kids were soon coated in the huge flakes.

Tony stepped carefully along the trail, but even at the high points, the ooze of the crystalized muck sucked at his boots. Jo gasped, and Tony looked back to find she'd lost her footing on the snow-covered trail and was down on one knee with her other leg calf-deep in the freezing-cold marsh.

Tony slapped the flashlight against his thigh as he let out sigh. He'd feared the dog might end up in the marsh and had put on his thick-ridged, rubber-soled boots before leaving the house. Jo wore knee-high, leather-soled boots—warm enough, but not the best on ice and slush, leaving her slipping every third step. Tony mumbled under his breath, blaming the girl for the delay. He turned the flashlight on her and grudgingly asked, "Do you need help?"

"I'm fine." Jo pulled her boot out of the muck and stood, directing her eyes past Tony and deeper into the marsh. "Let's go."

"You're wet. You really should head back."

"My feet are still dry. I said, let's go."

"Whatever you say, tough guy," Tony said with a frustrated wave of his free hand.

"I'm not a *guy*, but yeah, I am tough," Jo said through clenched teeth. "Now let's get going. We're not going to find the dog standing here."

"Just watch your step," Tony said, shaking his head as he turned back to the trail.

They walked on, the conversation over, their intermittent whistles and calls the only sound. Tony peeked back as Jo nimbly jumped over a fallen log and landed on the high, dry point on the path, perfectly following his trail. *She didn't lie. Pretty tough.*

He stopped in front of a narrow trail running through an expanse of muddy water. They needed to be careful crossing. Jo removed her wet gloves and blew into her hands, an aching shiver escaping her small frame. Tony groaned, watching her tremble. She needed to go back before she got pneumonia.

"Listen, I know you want to help, and I appre—"

"Quiet." Jo held her hand out like a traffic cop and froze with her head cocked to one side. "I hear something."

Tony froze, mirroring her pose with his ear tilted toward the sky. "I think I hear it, too." He stepped off the trail and wove through a thicket of trees down toward the riverbank, where the ground grew even muddier, the muck sucking on his boots with every step.

"Here! Over here." Tony moved so fast he slipped, falling hard to his knees, but bounced up quickly.

Pushing through thickets, he found the dog lying on his side in six inches of mud along the riverbank. The chain had caught and wrapped around the exposed root of a rotted, half-submerged tree trunk, leaving the dog stuck and panicked. Unable to lift his head from the muddy water, the exhausted dog struggled to keep his mouth and nose from slipping into the ooze.

Tony dropped to his knees and reached to touch the dog's flank.

The animal snarled and tried to pull away, only managing to push his snout deeper into the muck.

"He can't breathe!" Ignoring the dog's feeble, frightened snarl, Tony lifted the animal's head and slid his legs under it. The dog's snout now rested in the boy's lap as the lower half of Tony's body sat caked in icy mud. "See if you can free the chain."

The freezing water sent bone-chilling shudders through Tony's body as Jo, unable to unravel the chain, tried beating it with a rock, attempting to free the dog.

She stood up, breathless, steam rising off her head and her coat covered with snow. She exhaled a long, torturous groan as she dropped the chain from her raw, red hands. "I'll be back."

She bent down to pick up the flashlight, which Tony had dropped on a rotted tree stump, and turned away, disappearing into the misty white of the swirling snow.

"Nooo!"

Tony's cry got lost in the hushed darkness of the tree-shrouded swamp.

Panicked, he reached out with frozen hands, pulling on the chain, trying to free it. But his efforts only sunk him deeper into the muck, his thighs now covered and leaving the dog struggling to lift his snout above the rising muddy water.

Tony lifted his head and, in carnal fear, howled into the soulless night.

He'd failed.

"I'm sorry. I'm sorry. I should have left you alone. Should have left you in the junkyard. It wasn't much of a life, but it was something."

Finding a last bit of strength, the dog thrashed against the chain, his eyes wide with terror as he struggled to hold his snout above the icy water of the swollen river. Tony placed a hand under the dog's chin, trying to help, while the boy's cries turned to sobs and tears froze on his cheeks.

Shivering uncontrollably, it became impossible to concentrate. Tony's head fell forward his thoughts disjointed and angry screams of betrayal.

Not one for quitting or leaving a job half done. What a joke. She disappears the moment things get tough.

The boy stopped shuddering, his body growing still and his mind blank, enveloped by the falling snow and the stillness of the night. Even the sound of the dog wrapped in the throes of final panicked thrashings fell muted under the covering blanket of swiftly falling snow.

Tony pitched forward, his head resting on the thick fur of the dog's heaving chest.

And everything went black.

XI

MIRIAM

My phone vibrated on the arm of the chair, where I'd placed it when I first sat down to talk to AJ. I grabbed it before it slipped off the slick metal arm, glad for the distraction from the depressing, frozen demise of the boy and the poor dog. I spotted the caller ID and let out a long sigh.

"Something critical?" AJ looked at me like I was the most important person in his world, reminding me of how my father would close his laptop, look up at me anytime I walked into his home office, and with a smile on his face say, 'What's up, kiddo?'

"My mother thinks it is."

"That's kind of a mother's job," AJ said, trying to suppress a grin.

"It can wait."

"Are you sure?"

"She made an appointment for me to see that magician plastic surgeon." I shrugged, feeling my face flush.

AJ's weathered face lost its glow. "That's the silliest thing I've ever heard."

"Tell my mother that."

AJ reached out, motioning for me to give him the phone. "Love to."

I pulled back my hand, not sure if he was serious, and said, "I don't know. She says I lack confidence, and that why I can't do anything right."

AJ frowned. "Hard to believe that's true."

"Oh yeah? Well, you heard my tale about how ancient Popeye the Sailor Man died on me while I was feeding him. I didn't tell you the promising start to my day was delivering a giant balloon shaped like a stork with a message 'It's a girl' to the room of a sixty-four-year-old man who'd just had his prostate removed."

AJ snorted and said, "Hey, I bet you brought a smile to his face." Then he gave me that look again. "Find something you love, and you'll be great at it."

"That's what my father always says."

"Smart man, your father."

I smiled. Something about this gentle soul seemed to loosen my tongue, and before I knew it, I found myself telling AJ more of my sad story. How my father had worked for the ACLU until they went "bat-crap crazy." His words, not mine. And how, after that, he hung out his shingle doing more and more pro bono work. How my mother nagged him about becoming an even worse provider, and he finally moved out, getting an apartment in Brooklyn, to the undying mortification of my mother.

I described how I spent every weekend with him visiting museums, going to off-Broadway plays, or just sitting in Central Park people-watching and making up stories about their lives. But within a year, Mom got a call to do voice-over work in LA, and I'd been here ever since.

"Another sad story," I said at last. "Just like your unhappy tale about the kid and the dog."

AJ smiled. "Hey, the story isn't over yet." He stopped and looked out the window as the sun slipped lower in the sky. "I should just be able to finish before I have to go. Now sit back and remember I told you this is a love story, but it's no neatly packaged Debbie Macomber paperback. I'll leave it to you to decide if the story's dark or full of light."

XII

Tony opened his eyes to find himself propped against a log with a dry blanket wrapped around his shoulders. Jo stood with her back to him, ankle-deep in mud, trying to pull the dog away from the riverbank. She'd managed to turn the animal around, addressing the immediate danger of drowning, with the dog's head and shoulders now out of the muck. But she struggled to move him any farther. Tony's lips trembled as he tried to speak, his brain and tongue disconnected. The boy fought to rise, but the primordial ooze of the riverbank and freezing water had beaten him, body and mind. And he couldn't stop shivering, his body shaking like the pistons of a racing car.

"Jo?" he finally managed.

It was nothing more than a croak, but she turned, her wide eyes a mixture of pleasure and relief.

"Welcome back."

She stepped toward him, fixing the blanket more tightly over his shoulders. Then she looked back at the dog, who lay still, with its eyes closed, the only movement a shallow rising and falling of the animal's malnourished chest.

"He won't last long if I can't get him out of there," Jo said, her face beaded with frozen bits of sweat. "Here, eat this." She pulled off her gloves, reached into her pocket, and tore open the wrapper of a candy bar with her teeth before handing it to him. "Chocolate will help." Then she turned back to continue the efforts to pull the dog free from the icy goo of the riverbank.

Tony bit off a chunk of the chocolate and slowly chewed. He tried again to stand, but the effort proved more than his shuddering body could handle. He shoved the rest of the chocolate bar in his mouth, wiped his hands on his pants to bring some life back to his fingers, then pushed himself into a kneeling position before standing unsteadily.

"Let me help," Tony said, his voice splintered, as if speaking for the first time.

"If you're up for it." Jo bit her lower lip as she studied him, her narrowed gaze filled with doubt. "I could use the help. The dog's awfully weak, and I'm afraid he's going to die if we can't dry him off and get him someplace warm. I cut the chain with a bolt cutter I brought from my dad's toolbox and turned him so his head's away from the riverbank, but I can't get a good hold to pull him the rest of the way."

Tony eyed the length of the cut chain lying in the

mud and said, "I got an idea."

He grabbed the chain and knelt beside the dog. Wrapping the chain around the dog's chest, he positioned it snugly under the pits of the animal's front legs and handed Jo one end while he held the other.

She nodded her approval and handed him gloves. "Here, I grabbed us both a dry pair."

"Thanks. All right, on three."

The two tightened the hold on their ends of the chain and bent their knees in grunting unison, quivering arms aching, as they slowly dragged the dog onto the dryer footpath. Jo wrapped the blanket over the dog, rubbing its fur vigorously to warm the trembling, frozen animal.

"Okay, how do we get him out of here? He's not much more than fur and bones, but big. He must weigh eighty pounds."

"Here, slip this under him," Tony said, grabbing a corner of the blanket. "We can each take an end to carry him out of the marsh, but the snow's getting heavy." Tony dropped his head in despair. "We won't get far."

"We don't have to," Jo said with a knowing smile. "Just be sure we take the chain with us."

The two struggled, retracing their steps out of the marsh, each holding two corners of the improvised stretcher. As they slipped and stumbled forward, Jo described how she ran home to get the supplies from the large carriage house in the Trockis' backyard that her father had turned into his work area. As she'd turned to leave, Jo, realizing she could sled down to the riverbank quicker than trying to run, grabbed a sled she spotted in the corner of the massive old barn. She detailed how she tried to stay on the sidewalk, but fortunately, only a handful of cars appeared on the snowy streets.

Tony staggered through the marsh, his mind slowly recovering as his body warmed with the exertion. Jo had taken a foolish risk, coasting down some of the neighborhood's most traveled roads. But he shuddered, imagining what condition he and the near frozen dog would be in if she hadn't been so resourceful. He tried to speak, to say thank you, but the words wouldn't form, his mind locked on the trail ahead. The boy lowered his head, moving forward one step after another along the icy, muddy track.

Lights flickered high up on the street above them as the path opened onto the park. Their arms aching, the two lowered the dog onto the sled where Jo had left it at the entrance to the marshland, and a still-weak Tony slumped to the ground, his back resting against the sled.

Jo handed him another candy bar. "Eat."

"Snickers, my favorite," he said weakly before biting hungrily into the chocolate bar.

"Good thing my father's got such a sweet tooth. The drawer in his workbench is always packed with candy." She tied the chain around both runners at the front of the sled, improvising a harness, and looked up at Tony. "Ready?"

Tony rose slowly, slipping into the harness, and with a grunt, started out of the park. The two took turns pulling while the other pushed from behind. As they dragged their precious cargo up the hill,

Tony called out, directing which streets to take to avoid the steepest inclines as the snow continued to fall. It proved a longer route but more manageable. In just over thirty minutes, the two, sweating and panting, staggered into the Miracolo's backyard before dropping to their knees in front of Tony's basement door.

They rested a few minutes before Tony struggled to his feet. "C'mon, let's get him inside. Here, slide him back onto the blanket, and we'll carry him down."

Careful not to make any noise, they navigated the steep cellar stairs, placing the dog close to the warmth of the furnace. Then Tony, almost as if talking to himself, outlined his sketchy plan to keep his parents from discovering what they'd done.

"Are you sure this will work?" Jo said, her voice filled with doubt.

"No, but it's the only thing I can think of. Pop's just started a new job, remodeling a kitchen for some rich doctor in Newton. I heard him say the wife's a real . . . well, she'll keep him busy."

Tony stepped out from behind the oil tank, wearing dry blue jeans as he put on a clean t-shirt he'd taken off the improvised clothesline his father hung in the basement during winter months. Jo, already changed out of her wet clothes, wore one of Anthony Miracolo's thick flannel work shirts that hung down to her knees and a pair of Tony's coarse woolen knee-high socks that he wore ice skating.

"But won't anyone be coming down here?"

"Pop's got all his tools in the truck or already on the job site. He shouldn't be coming down here for a couple of days, and Mom hates the steep stairs. She'll hang the clothes outside when the weather's good, but it's my job to take them down here when it's too cold or wet to hang them outside. Besides, it's only till morning."

Jo nodded and pulled a blanket tighter over the dog, who lay on a pile of burlap bags.

"He looks better, don't you think?" Tony said, stepping away from the oil burner to join her, kneeling beside the dog, his anxious voice pleading for any sign the animal would be okay.

"Don't know," Jo said with a sad shrug. "He's still trembling like crazy. I guess dogs can get hypothermia, just like people. At least we got him in a warm, dry place. That should help." Her eyelids drooped as she fought off exhaustion and worry. "I just don't know if we got him out in time."

Tony cleared his throat, swallowing his pride. "What's hypothermia?"

He sat silently while Jo told him stories about her father's experiences flying in an unpressurized B-17 during World War II. When the heating unit in the plane's flight gear failed, crewmembers were at risk of hypothermia, frostbite, or death if they didn't quickly address extended exposure to the numbing cold. The crews learned how to deal with all sorts of exposure issues. That's how Jo knew to give Tony the chocolate bar to help him.

Tony nodded as he listened. *Smart kid.*

The dog lay on his side, his breathing shallow and unsteady. Tony found a metal pan on a shelf near the paint-stained sink, filled it with water, and placed it in front of the dog. But the animal remained lost in another world, the bone-thin ribcage's slow rise and fall the only sign of life.

"So, I guess all we can do now is try and keep him warm." Tony said, fighting to hold back tears while slipping behind the dog and wrapping his arms around the dog's chest, pulling his body snugly to the trembling animal.

Jo offered a weak smile. She shifted, lying down on her side to face the dog, and placed her head on his dry, mud-caked neck. She yawned and threw her arm over the dog's shoulder, where it brushed against Tony's face.

The dog's breathing seemed to steady, perhaps some instinctive memory of being back with siblings as a pup, drawing warmth from the surrounding bodies, calming the frozen, battered animal.

Tony's tears dried as the aching need to sleep fell on him like a thick morning fog. He shook his head. He had some things to say first.

"Jo."

"Yeah?" Her voice sounded lost in the same fog.

"Thanks." Tony cleared his throat. Apologies didn't come easily. "I couldn't a done this without you. I owe you."

"Maybe I'll collect someday, but for now, how about we just agree to be friends?"

"Deal," Tony said as he nuzzled closer to the dog.

There it was. She'd said it. She just wanted to be friends. But Jo had proven to be a great one, and he needed that now more than ever.

Tony yawned, long and deep, his eyes fluttering

shut, his breathing syncing to the rhythm of the dog's.

Tony woke several hours later with the early morning light filtering through the basement's narrow window. The dog, breathing steadier, slept with Jo's arms wrapped around his neck. Tony jumped up, heart pounding as he checked the clock on the wall above his father's workbench. Five thirty. The house would be coming to life soon.

"Jo. Wake up," Tony whispered, shaking her gently. "You need to get back to your house before anyone gets up."

Jo stirred, smacking her lips as she mumbled sleep-filled nonsensical words.

"Sssh," Tony said, placing his hand over her mouth. "You need to *get home.*"

Jo's eyes flew open, her morning grogginess gone, the memory of last night's rescue a better wake-up call than any screeching alarm clock.

"He's still with us," Jo whispered, removing her arms from around the dog as she wobbled to a stand.

The dog eyes blinked open, and stirring he tried unsuccessfully to lift his head, like a prize fighter struggling to rise from the canvas. The two fell silent as Jo's comment about the dog's condition heightened the somber mood.

Tony stretched, feeling every cut and ache of the previous twenty-four hours. He replaced the pan with fresh water, and the kids held their breath while the dog's nose twitched and slowly lifted higher to drink.

Tony and Jo talked in hushed tones as they watched the dog empty the pan. After leaving him more water, Tony shook off the worst of the clumps from last night's muddy clothes before loading them into the washing machine. He bit his lower lip as he worked, thinking of all the things that could go wrong with his plan. He hadn't intended on kidnapping—no, not kidnapping, rescuing—a giant, skeletally malnourished dog from the meanest guy in the neighborhood. But it had happened. So, Tony had to keep the dog out of sight until he could figure out his next step.

"Look, I know I already said it, but we could get in a mountain of trouble for this," Tony said. "If you want out, I'll say I did it myself. If I get caught, you were never there."

Jo flashed Tony a look, and he held up his hands in surrender.

"Okay, Trocki, I get it. *Not one for leaving a job half done.*" He mimicked Jo's I'm ready to fight voice, bringing a broad smile to the girl's face. "Anyway," he said, growing serious again, "I meant what I said last night. Thanks, but none of this works unless—"

"I know. But all we can do is wait." Jo turned away. She ran her hand along the dog's flank, and between shallow breaths, his lips curled in a weak protest at being touched. The dog tried to lift his head and pull away, but the effort of drinking seemed to have sapped all the energy he could muster. He closed his eyes and slept again.

"We'll know soon enough," Tony said, unable to look away from the exhausted and beaten dog. "I'll wash your clothes and get them to you later. And be sure to get your father's bolt cutter and gloves back before he sees anything's missing."

The clock showed five forty-five. They had to hurry and sneak back to their bedrooms to make their regular morning appearances at their family breakfast tables. Jo soundlessly slipped out of the cellar, a blast of cold air hitting the room as she pushed the door closed behind her.

Tony dropped to his knees beside the dog, who continued sleeping. He trailed his hand along the dog's side, but the animal's only response was the rising and falling of its gaunt rib cage. The boy sighed, heartbroken by how thin the dog looked, and ran his sleeve across his runny nose. He turned away to fill a laundry basket with dry clothes and headed upstairs. If anyone saw him coming up from the cellar, he could tell his parents he'd started his chores early.

At the top of the stairs, he stopped, listening for voices. Nothing. But he heard the scraping of a shovel outside in the driveway. Tony glanced back at the dog and said a silent prayer as he slipped into the kitchen.

Please, God, let him be okay.

XIII

Tony sat next to Rosa, both kids hunched at the kitchen table, listening intently to the radio on the counter. Their mother, standing at the sink finishing the breakfast dishes, sighed, unable to join the kids in the excitement—their heartfelt morning wish appearing to only complicate her already busy day. Tony raised the radio's volume as the announcer started again at the top of the alphabet.

"Abington, Amesbury, Andover, Arlington, Ashfield, Ashland, Athol, Avon, Bedford, Belmont, Beverly, Billerica, Boston, all schools, no school—"

The kids flew from their chairs in celebration, whooping and hollering, their hands pumping in the air.

"Boston, no school, all schools," the two chanted in a sing-song delight as they danced around the room.

Their mother turned away from the sink to face

them. "You know I have to work at the rectory this morning, and your father was up early digging the truck out. He's already at the job site in Newton. You're on your own for the day. I won't be home till after three."

"I'm going coasting all day with my friends," Rosa said, barely listening to her mother.

"Honey, I'm not sure—"

"Don't worry, Mom. I'll take care of things here. I'll get Rosa's sled out of the cellar for her and make her a sandwich she can take for lunch." Tony paused. He needed to be careful. He couldn't overdo the good son act. She'd already commented on the laundry basket being brought up unsolicited. It didn't take much to set his mother's radar on high alert. But he'd run this through in his head all morning and knew how to play it. "I wanna go skating at the MDC rink and don't need Rosa and her goofy friends tagging along."

"The rink may not even be open with all the snow."

"Please, Mom, the plows have been out for hours, and I'll look after everything here before I go."

Tony almost offered to put the dishes away but held back. His mother's eyes had already narrowed, locking on his, sensing something. Tony fought to hold her gaze, but far better men than he had surrendered under the indomitable scrutiny of Carla Miracolo. Tony shifted uncomfortably, his facade of casual innocence crumbling. His right eye twitched as he struggled not to turn away. The no-school announcement happened more than five minutes ago. *Come on, Jo. What's keeping you?*

His mother cleared her throat, potentially preparing to ruin all his plans, only to be stopped by the ringing telephone. She wiped her hands on her apron and walked across the room to grab the phone off the wall.

"Oh, hi, Jo. Yes, school cancellation is great news." Tony's mother smiled, nodding her head.

Tony had seen his mother take an immediate liking to Jo and he'd noticed how her typically suspicious nature seemed to melt if any of Tony's activities involved their new neighbor. His mother continued smiling and nodding as she toyed with the long extension cord. Tony held his breath, listening to one side of the conversation. It all rested in Jo's hands, but she appeared to be playing it flawlessly.

"Oh, so *you and Tony* planned to go ice skating." His mother's smile grew wider as she continued to wrap and unwrap the phone cord around her finger. "That would be lovely, but . . . Oh, you haven't been yet? Yes, Tony's right. When they built the rink a few years ago, the Metropolitan District found extra funding to add a canopy over the rink so it could stay open if it rained or snowed." Tony's mother hesitated. "Well, I was about to suggest Tony take Rosa, but perhaps she'll have more fun with her friends. . . . Uh-huh. . . . Uh-huh. . . . You, too, dear. . . . Okay, here's Tony."

Tony took the phone from her and turned away. It wouldn't do to have his discerning mother catch the look of relief on his face.

"Yes, we are lucky. . . . Yes, the plows did get

out early this morning. . . . Okay, I'll meet you out front in half an hour."

He hung up the phone with his mother watching him intently, but her earlier grim expression had disappeared. Her face now radiated a schoolgirl flush, perhaps remembering some distant childhood pleasure.

"Wow, look at him go. That's his third can of tuna fish." Jo elbowed Tony in the ribs as the two watched the dog lick the final morsels from his nose with his long, probing tongue. "And your plan worked great."

"You called just in time," Tony said, bobbing his head. "My mother planned to stick me with Rosa for the day, but her face lit up when she heard your voice. She had me worried for a minute, but you played it perfectly."

"She's nice, your mother."

"Yeah, I guess." Tony shrugged. "But she was at it again last night. She tore into me about ruining my school clothes, and then she got back on me about the Sister Lemon Sucker blowout. It's been almost a month. I've been on my best behavior, but no matter how good I do at something, I feel like she thinks I could have tried a bit harder. . . . You know, been a bit better." He looked away. "I think that's why I got in the miniskirt battle with Sister Agnes Helen last week. I figure if I can't be a good kid in anybody's eyes, I can at least be the best bad kid possible."

"That's about the dumbest thing I ever heard," Jo said. "Well, I see how it makes sense in a perverse Tony Miracolo sort of logic. But ultimately, it only comes back to hurt you. And anyways, I always figured it's sort of a parent's job to push us to be as good as we possibly can be. I know my parents can be pretty hard on me." Jo gave him a sideways glance. "And you know, that pushing thing and always wanting more from everyone around them kind of reminds me of *someone else* I know."

Tony sat, studying the dog, Jo's advice and teasing wasted on the boy, whose attention remained fixed on the animal. "Listen, my mom's working till three, but Rosa could get cold or wet and be back anytime. We've got to get him out of here and to the bakery this morning."

"What if your uncle won't—?"

"He has to," Tony interrupted. "All I need is a couple of days. Look, I know it's not perfect. The bakery's close to the junkyard, but Zio Rico knows how Al Ridgeway treated that dog. You saw how much it upset him. There's a storage room in the back of the bakery. Zio Rico's got to help. Plus, he's one of the few people my mother might listen to."

Tony refilled the dog's pan, careful not to scare him with any sudden movement as the still-weak dog raised his snout. His nostrils flared at the presence of the water, and Tony reached out to run a hand along the dog's flank. The animal snarled as his body tensed. But slaking his thirst won out as he slowly calmed and sat up, lifting his head to bury a long pink tongue in the water.

Tony frowned as his hands gently explored the dog's thick fur. "He's all bone," he said, frowning as his eyes drifted to an open wound on the dog's leg, where a discolored scab refused to fully heal.

The dog quickly emptied the pan, and Jo filled it again, sitting by the dog's side. She reached out to join Tony in petting the dog, but he pulled her sleeve and mouthed the words *not yet*.

The animal flinched at the sudden closeness of another person but hesitated, sensing no immediate danger. Still dehydrated from last night's ordeal, he continued drinking, his snout buried in the bowl. With his tongue slopping away, the dog's tension ebbed as he slowly grew more comfortable.

Tony recognized the change and signaled Jo, who reached out with trembling hands to bury her fingers in the thick fur.

The dog froze at the new presence and tried to pull away, but the kids continued with their tender pets. Too tired to fight or even growl, he dropped his head onto his forepaws. Perhaps confused by the nearness of the two strangers, the dog struggled to keep his eyes open—trying to deal with the unsettling closeness of the boy and girl—before falling back into an exhausted sleep.

"Okay," Tony said a few minutes later as he looked at the clock above his father's workbench. "Can't wait any longer. Gotta find out how strong he is." Tony stepped back and clapped his hands. "C'mere, boy."

The dog looked up, eyes blinking, nose twitching him awake in anticipation of more food. Jo stood beside Tony, waving a treat. Despite eating well, the prospect of still more food had its effect. The dog shifted his hind legs underneath him, pushing off with his front and back paws to bring himself into an unsteady standing position.

"Oh, good boy," Jo called out, showing the treat again, willing the dog to keep his tottering balance. Then, glowing with excitement, she grabbed Tony's hand. "He's standing," she said as she tossed the treat a few steps in front of the animal.

The dog moved slowly toward the food and gobbled it whole before dropping back to the ground, his energy spent. But the dog bristled as the kids shouted and danced in a celebration dwarfing the morning's no-school announcement.

Tony noticed the change and grabbed Jo's wrist. "We're scaring him," he said, his heart pounding. "What was I thinking?"

"It's not your fault. You were just excited."

"I shoulda known better," Tony said, shaking his head. "C'mon, we need to get going."

It took close to ten minutes and half a dozen slices of Italian cold cuts, but with the kids' help, the dog, on wobbly legs, navigated the cellar stairs to the backyard. Head hanging low, he briefly sniffed the snow before lifting his hind leg to relieve himself. Exhausted by the small effort, the dog allowed the kids to lead him onto the sled, where he plopped down unsteadily, and they covered him with a few burlap sacks Tony had taken from the cellar.

"Let's go," Tony said, slipping into last night's improvised harness. He winced as he freed the sled runners from the snow, his cuts and bruises a painful reminder of the previous day's battle. "Going downhill will be easier than coming up, and where the snow isn't too high with drifts, we can cut through some backyards to avoid traffic and people. If anybody sees us, pull the sacks over his head. If no one gets too close, it'll look like we've got groceries."

The sky shone crystal-blue without a cloud—one of those glorious, sun-filled, arctic-blue-sky days that follow a winter storm. With faces raised to the warming sun, the kids zigzagged down the hill from Tony's house. Cutting through backyards to avoid heavily traveled streets, they waved and turned the other way if Tony spotted kids he knew coasting or having snowball fights. The sled picked up speed several times on steep hills, and Jo had to dig in her heels from behind with her rubber-soled hiking boots buried in the snow to prevent the sled from knocking Tony over. But, at last, the bakery stood in sight.

To avoid being seen, they approached from the direction of the playground, away from Big Al's Garage and the longer row of shops. They hurried across the street, past the park, and slipped behind the hardware store, where the small, unplowed backlot lay covered with drifts running up to their thighs.

Now Jo took the lead, lifting her knees high through the deep snow. She cleared the path for Tony, who followed, shoulders bent, pulling the sled. He pointed to a gate separating the hardware store from the bakery. Jo nodded, striding on as she cut a trail in the snow for the gate to swing open and walked the final fifty feet to the bakery's back door.

She stopped, placing her hands on her hips, sucking in air. "Made it," she said, catching her breath.

Tony dropped the harness from around his waist and took off his gloves, finding his hands had started bleeding again. He ran a coat sleeve across his sweaty brow and wiped his bloody hands on his pants. Exhausted, the two exchanged triumphant smiles as wisps of white smoke rose from the bakery's chimney and the aroma of freshly baked bread filled the air.

"Now comes the hard part," Tony said with a nervous laugh. If they couldn't convince Rico De Santo to help, freeing the dog from the junkyard and getting it safely unseen down the hill would be meaningless. "C'mon, boy." He pulled the burlap sacks aside and looked down at the animal.

The dog, who'd kept covered during the trip, with only his snout popping out occasionally from under the burlap to enjoy the sun, now gathered himself. He stepped cautiously into the deep snow. Still unsteady, he shuffled toward a tree and sniffed before raising his leg and marking it.

Tony nodded in approval. "Making himself at home." Then he turned to face Jo. "Wait here. I'll be right back." He steeled his nerve and walked toward the bakery's back door.

A few minutes later, the door opened, and Rico De Santo, mindless of the cold, stood in the doorway dressed in his ubiquitous short-sleeve white t-shirt and apron.

"You two actually did it," he said, shaking his

head and looking at Tony, who'd walked past him to stand over the dog, now lying on the sled again. "Stole that dog from under the nose of the meanest, craziest guy in town. And now you wanna get me in the middle of—"

"Only for a couple of days," Jo said before the baker could finish.

"Until I can talk to my parents," Tony said, his voice rife with desperation.

"Your parents." Rico took a deep breath, his lips making a motorboat sound as he exhaled. "You forget, I grew up with 'em. And your mom's one single-minded lady."

Tony lowered his head, the emotions of the last twenty-four hours leaving him beaten and weak. It couldn't end this way. He dropped to his knees, wrapped his arms around the dog's neck, and buried his face in the fur.

The dog tried to pull away, but something stopped him from instinctively snapping. Instead, he allowed the boy to continue kneeling by his side, holding him as some of his anxiousness seemed to slip away.

Rico stepped toward them and placed a hand on Tony's shoulder. He reached out to touch the dog but stopped as a flash of teeth warned to stay away.

"He's just a little skittish around strangers," Jo said defensively as the baker nervously pulled his hand back.

"I can tell," Rico said, staring at his hand as if counting fingers. "Come on. I'm probably gonna regret this, but we can put him in the storage room while we figure out what to do."

XIV

With the dog watching them from the far corner of a small room in the back of the bakery, the three sat on sacks of flour as the kids detailed to Rico how they'd helped the dog escape from the junkyard.

"So you see, we had no choice."

Tony's head bobbed in approval as Jo spoke. "Yeah, we couldn't just leave him there after all we saw."

The tinkling bell at the bakery's front door interrupted her. Rico placed his hands on his knees and pushed himself up from where he sat.

"Got another customer. Hold that thought, but I don't know if the police would agree with the word *rescue*."

Rico left the room, and Jo looked at Tony. Her face red, she mouthed the word *police*. Tony shook his head, hoping he showed more confidence than he felt. Then, anxiously flicking his tongue to wet his lips, he said, "We didn't do anything wrong or, you know, break any laws."

"I'm not so sure. I hadn't thought of it till now, but he's right. We took a dog that didn't belong to us, but not before you punched a grown-up in the mouth, and I hit him across the back of the head with a two-by-four."

"Well, yeah, I guess there is that," Tony said with a mischievous grin.

The two fell into a fit of laughter as the exhausted dog, beginning to relax, merely raised his eyebrows in curiosity before blinking a few times and rolling onto his side to continue sleeping.

"What's so funny?" Rico returned with a bowl of water and a brown paper bag. "Lunchtime," he said as he handed the bowl to Tony, who placed the water in front of the dog.

The movement woke the animal, who raised his head, taking in the activity around him.

Rico pulled a crate next to the kids, handed them each a submarine sandwich on thick-crusted rolls, and peeled back the tin foil from a third. "Meatball subs. Not as good as my Isabella used to make, God bless her soul. But not bad for an old widower."

Tony swallowed hard and stared at a water-stained spot on the wall, anything to keep from seeing the heartache so evident on his uncle's face.

Rico De Santo had lost his wife two years earlier. The entire neighborhood stood by helplessly and watched the heartbreaking withering away of Bella De Santo from a robust, joyful surrogate mother to every kid on the block to a pallid skeleton who was gone within six months.

For weeks, Tony was sent down the hill carrying trays of lasagna, eggplant parmigiana, or manicotti. Until one summer afternoon, when Rico came to visit. Tony's mother stood in the doorway, her eyes sweeping the street. Rico fidgeted, shifting from one foot to another and shaking his head before taking Carla Miracolo's trembling hand. He kissed her open palm, whispered something in her ear, and turned to hurry down the hill. Tony, fixing the chain on his bike, watched from across the street where he knelt, hidden from view, behind a parked car.

Tony had ducked lower as Rico passed on the other side of the street, and his mother dropped her head in numbed silence. Burying her face in her hands, she began to weep, and Tony no longer brought food to the baker.

Tony blinked, forcing the memory away as Rico took a large bite. The baker rolled back some more of the tin foil as his eyes turned to rest on the dog. He tore off a piece of meatball and waved it in the air, trying to capture the dog's attention, before leaning forward with the food in his hand. "Want some? Hey, *come si chiama,* want some?"

But the exhausted dog remained unmoved.

"What's come si . . . ?" Jo asked between bites of her sandwich.

Rico laughed, raising his shoulders in mild apology as he popped the piece of meatball in his mouth and swallowed, giving up on his attempt to feed the dog. "Sorry. *Come si chiama.* It's Italian. It means, like, whatta'ya call it? Or what's ya name?"

"Wow, Tony, I hadn't thought of that," Jo said

excitedly. "You haven't named him."

Tony sat on the stack of flour, chewing on his lower lip, his knees pinging up and down with nervous energy. He'd been thinking a lot about this, and the question touched a nerve. "I've been afraid to name him cuz there'd be no going back." Tony shrugged, turning to look at the baker. "You know, like about the fall of the Roman Republic, in the book you loaned me."

"You mean how when Julius Caesar crossed the Rubicon? The die had been cast?" Rico said with avuncular warmth. He'd winced the moment Jo raised the point, perhaps fearing the naming of the dog could be the boy's own personal Rubicon. But he couldn't keep the pride from showing in his voice. "I thought Plutarch might be too much for a fourteen-year-old, but I shoulda known better. You're no regular kid."

"Thanks," Tony said, his chest swelling with pride. No one's opinions meant more to him than his Uncle Rico's. "It's pretty slow reading, but I think I got most of it."

"I'm glad someone does. Because I don't know what you two are talking about," Jo said, her eyebrows raised in mild amusement. "And what's this about loaning books?"

"What? You think the library up the street is the only place my young friend goes when lookin' for interestin' books to read. Besides, whatta'ya figure we do here when business is slow?" Rico placed a powerful arm on Tony's shoulder and pulled the boy toward him. "We have deep conversations about great books, films, and the meanin' of life."

"Yeah, I thought I told you," Tony said. "You should see his books upstairs. There must be more than a thousand of them, stacked everywhere. He's got everything from Milton and Chaucer to Louis L'Amour, Zane Grey, and Harold Robbins."

"Wow, I wouldn't have guessed."

"So, you figured Rico the Baker's some kinda dummy?" Rico smiled. "I read. Even quote some Shakespeare, from time to time." He stood up and cleared his throat. "Okay, here goes, and this line may be appropriate for what you two started last night. 'Cry, Havoc! and let slip the dogs of war.'" Rico swept his hand with a theatrical flair and took a short bow. "That, my young friends, is from *Julius Caesar*. There's more, but maybe another time. Right now," he said, pointing a thick finger at the dog, "I wanna know what'ya gonna call this guy."

Tony smiled, never prouder of his working-class corner of the city that could create men like his Zio Rico. Then Tony's face grew bright. As they often did, Rico De Santo's words had helped him find his way.

"That's it. *Release the dogs of war. Crossing the Rubicon.* They're all signs. I'm gonna call him Caesar." Tony grabbed a slice of meatball from his sub and, moved closer, calling out to the dog. "C'mere, Caesar."

The dog stirred now and sniffed, his eyes following the movement of Tony's hand.

"C'mon. Caesar, c'mon."

The dog stood and moved tenuously forward with his snout extended and nostrils flaring. Eyes wide, he stopped and inhaled.

"It's okay, Caesar. No one's gonna hurt you ever again. I promise."

Tony leaned forward, tossing the food onto the ground near the dog. The animal reached out, turning his snout sideways and flicking his tongue to cautiously take it. Tony tore off another piece of the sub and lobbed it to the dog, who snapped it out of the air.

"All hail Caesar," Rico said with delight. "Our boy has picked a winner."

For the next five minutes, Tony fed portions of his meatball sandwich to the dog, who cautiously allowed the boy to move closer. With the food gone, Caesar emptied the bowl of water with sloppy relish and circled slowly several times before dropping to the floor in front of Tony with an exhausted huff. With his stomach full and the room warm, he closed his eyes and sighed. For the moment, the dog was safe.

But the dreams still came. The pup huddled in a cold place, where the only chance of warmth came from lying by his mother's side. But his mother had changed. When the pup was smaller, barely able to walk or see, his mother let him and the others lie and suckle all day while she nuzzled against their bodies, licking them clean with her warm, wet tongue. But she'd lost her milk, and with her milk gone, she lost her patience toward the now energetic little ones. She'd nip at them, pushing them away with her long snout, forcing them to explore the confines of the dark, dirty warehouse.

Instead of the warm, reassuring suckling, the pup learned to sit back, controlling his anxiousness and watch the others foolishly waste their energy. He pulled away from his potential pack as he waited for the morning light to rise higher in the sky until it finally snuck in weakly from the hole in the roof above. The room shifted from black to gray as the hungry, cold pup watched. Sometimes, if the morning grew late and gnawing hunger overrode his youthful resolve, he'd try to suckle, but a quick flash of his mother's teeth and a painful nip would send him scurrying away.

So, the young pup would sit alone as the sun climbed. He knew the man always arrived before it stood high in the sky.

The small man walked with a limp, smelling of a strange, unfamiliar scent, something powerful and foul. The pup didn't recognize this new odor but learned that the later the man arrived, the more overpowering this foul smell would be. Less steady on his feet, the man would stagger toward them, sometimes spilling food from the bag he carried on his shoulder to the delight of the puppies scurrying to greet him. Some in the litter ignored the food, their need for a loving touch overriding their hunger. But the pup, bigger than the others, pushed his way through, ensuring he got his share of the fallen prize.

The man always looked right past the puppies, ignoring the mass of wagging tails surrounding him. He'd shake them off his foot with angry kicks, sending them skittering across the hard floor. But the young dogs greeted each visit with the same delight, hoping perhaps for a moment's affection to replace the nurturing love of their mother, which no longer came.

The visits of the brooding little man meant only one thing to the pup. Something far more essential than a meaningless pat on the head. He'd pour fresh water and dry food into large bowls, grumbling while he worked as the puppies raced to feed, careful not to anger their mother, who always ate first. While the dogs nipped and fought over the food and water, the man, continuing to grumble, swept up the previous day's waste before throwing a new layer of wood shaving onto the floor.

But this day was special. The other man—older, with large, active hands—reappeared and walked toward them. The puppies went wild. This man's alert, darting eyes seemed to take in their every move. He'd picked each one up, as if studying them, checking their eyes, teeth, and limbs while nodding or shaking his head with pleasure or disapproval.

Today, the man stopped in front of the pup and paused, standing over him for the longest time. Unlike the others, whose tails whipped across the floor as they peed excitedly, the pup held back, observing the man who towered over him. The man placed his hands on his hips, eyes narrowed, locking on the pup, and nodded as his lips twisted into a calculating smile. Ignoring the other puppies buzzing around his feet, the man picked up the pup, slowly evaluating, as he did with each visit.

"Yep, you're different all right. The pick of the

litter. Bigger'n stronger than any two. Someone wantin' a fightin' dog's gonna pay top dollar for you."

The man tossed the young pup on the ground next to the others and walked away. The pup took several steps to trail the man before stopping, confused by his instinct to follow. His tail dropped. He was searching for something, but like with the foul-smelling man, the pup didn't see it in the cooly efficient older man.

The pup turned away from the others, who continued to race after the quickly disappearing man, their whipping tails calling out for attention. But the pup didn't look back. He'd go it alone.

He'd eaten his fill, but a hunger remained, an unknown emptiness he didn't understand. The pup found a stick and holding it between his paws, ground at it with his powerful young teeth, gnawing at the emptiness in his spirit. He'd once looked to his mother and followed her every move, but no more. And these men could never replace her. They were not ones to follow. He redoubled his efforts on the stick, grinding away and accepting how it must be.

Caesar yelped, his head jerked, and his paws twitched, as if escaping some imagined foe.

Tony dropped to the floor and curled up next to the dog, who tried to pull away. Still tired and weak, Caesar lowered his head, allowing the strange boy to lie beside him, and his twitching stopped.

But it took a long time before the dog fell back to sleep.

"This poor guy has been through a lot in his life," Rico said, his usually happy face sad and distant. "He ain't like most dogs."

"What do you mean?" Tony sat up, his face flushed.

"Look, Tony, I'm not tryin' to get you mad, but you gotta know the truth. Just look at him. He's got scars on his snout and shoulders." Rico pointed at the sleeping dog. "He was a fightin' dog. Lookin' at the scars, I'm guessin' fightin' to the death."

"No," Tony said, unwilling to consider the unimaginable. "Nobody would do that to a dog."

"Sorry, kid, it's true. The world's made up of all kinds of people, and some are just downright evil," Rico said. "Look at his leg. The scar around his knee. It's infected and looks to me like some messed up tendons." Rico knelt beside Caesar and cautiously traced his hand along the sleeping dog's haunch, careful not to wake him. "See how this leg is thinner? My guess is he's got some permanent damage. I figure he'll walk with a limp. It's a shame, but the bum leg just might've saved his life. Ultimately, I'm bettin' the injury forced Ridgeway to stop fightin' him. His life as a watchdog wasn't much, but it was better than dog fightin'."

"He did seem to walk kind of funny this morning when we got him out of your cellar," Jo said as she reached out to place a comforting hand on Tony's shoulder.

"Shut up," Tony said roughly, slipping out from under Jo's hand. "You saw him flying like the wind when he ran yesterday."

But even as the words formed on Tony's lips, the picture of the dog racing away from the garage, with his long gait slightly off, locked in his mind. He refused to look at Rico or Jo, instead fixing his gaze on the dog. Caesar's left hind quarter did appear smaller and less muscled than the other.

"Just shut up, the both of you. He's perfect." Tony turned away. *Please, God, let him be okay. He has to be.*

Tony lay back down and wrapped an arm around the dog, who stirred again from all the noise. Caesar surrendered to the boy's nearness and closed his eyes as he fell back into a deep sleep.

XV

Rico stood, signaling Jo to follow, leaving Tony alone with the dog in the storage room.

"The kid's exhausted. You both are," he said, sitting on a stool behind the counter. "Tony didn't mean it when he told you to shut up. He knows better. His parents raised him better. I'll talk to him. Set him straight."

"You don't have to."

"Yes, I do. But with Tony, time's gotta be right."

"I'm learning that," Jo said, sitting across from the baker, "but I'll tell you, sometimes it's hard to keep up with his mood swings."

"I know, but you gotta understand." Rico sighed. "He's a good kid, with a heart big as the ocean. He's just so hard on people. You know, lettin' 'em get close. But I'll tell you a secret. The poor kid's twice as hard on himself as he is on anyone else."

Rico leaned in, resting his hands on the countertop as he snuck a peek at the storage room. "Tell you somethin' else. He's lonely."

"Lonely? That's crazy. I've watched him at school, always joking with other kids, or when he's playing street hockey at recess. He fits right in."

"He's fakin' it," Rico said, shaking his head. "You heard him today, talkin' 'bout Shakespeare and Plutarch. He's an old soul in a kid's body. Why do you think he spends so much free time with a beat-up old baker like me? He's lonely, and he needs a friend."

"So why me?"

"He likes you."

"He's sure got a funny way of showing it," Jo said.

"Are you any better at showin' your true feelings?" Rico smiled. "You wanna tell me how Tony really got that black eye the first time I met you?"

"He told you?" Jo said, her cheeks flushing.

"Wo-ah, no one told me nothin'." Rico raised his hands jokingly in front of his face, like a boxer ready to block a blow. "Now, don't get mad." The baker smiled. "But I see how you two are 'round each other, and knowin' Tony like I do, I figure it wouldn't take long for him to say somethin' to make you wanna haul off and hit'm."

"I guess you're right." Jo looked away. "I'm not much good at making friends, either."

"Don't feel bad," Rico said. "I think you're an old soul, too. I bet hangin' 'round kids your age every hour of the day drives you crazy. You're always needin' to get away, you know, to be alone with your thoughts so you can dream your dreams."

Jo's sad expression shifted to a challenging glare. "You don't know anything about my dreams," she said, jumping off the stool and heading for the front door.

"I'm sorry, kid. I didn't mean to upset you. You're right. I don't know nothin' 'bout your dreams, but I know you got 'em, and whether you leave or stay here talkin', the dreams will follow. You can't run away from your dreams."

Jo turned back to face the baker but averted her gaze when the older man's knowing eyes settled on her.

"I'm sorry. Maybe I've been living alone too long." Rico showed his palms in the ubiquitous Italian apology. "When my Bella was alive, she'd tell me I didn't know when to shut up." He shrugged. "Smart woman, but it's not my only curse. I have many. First, I see things, things other people don't always see. And then I complicate things by being unable to keep my yap shut."

"Like now?" Jo said, her hands clenched tightly.

"Yeah, like now." Rico smiled. "Tony and you are good for each other. There's a connection between you two that doesn't happen often."

Jo shook her head. "I'm sorry, Mister De Santo. Tony's a good kid, but I think you're seeing things that just aren't there."

"Possibly," Rico said. "But indulge an old man. My boy's gonna need a good friend. Can you be that for him? I know you'll never find a better friend in return. Can you promise to be there for him? You know, be a friend?"

Be a friend? Jo took a deep breath. She'd seen Tony kissing Delores at the dance. It hurt, but she'd vowed not to let it show. She was too proud for that. That's why she agreed to let the mind-numbingly boring Danny Walsh walk her home. Yes, Tony was frustratingly argumentative and stubborn, with terrible taste in girls. But he could also be kind and brave. The way Tony cared about Caesar and stood up to Al Ridgway to free the dog said it all. Who cared if Tony was attracted to the busty, dimwitted Delores DePalma? He was still someone Jo wanted as a friend.

Jo smiled, truly at peace for the first time since the night of the dance. "I promise."

"Excellent," Rico said, slapping his hands on the counter in celebration.

"What's excellent?" Tony stood at the back of the store, rubbing his eyes.

"Jo just said she's ready for a slice of pizza." Rico reached into the display case and slipped a spatula under a thick slice of Sicilian pizza before sliding it onto a piece of wax paper. "I can heat it up, but my pizza's great hot or cold. Whadda'ya say?"

"Cold's fine, thanks," Jo said, surprised by Tony's appearance and wondering how much the boy overheard.

Rico handed the pizza to Jo, gently smiling when their eyes met.

"And what about you? Wanna slice?" Rico asked, pointing the spatula at Tony.

"Please, Caesar ate nearly my whole sub," Tony

said, sighing. "Maybe a full stomach will help me come up with an idea on how to convince my parents to let me keep him."

The three sat on stools at the front counter, eating pizza, while the battered dog slept locked safely in the back room, away from the prying eyes of random customers. Their efforts to drag the dog to the bakery had produced ravenous hunger in the kids. So, Rico sat smiling, watching the two devour several slices of the thick pizza as they detailed their adventure of getting the dog down the hill to the bakery unseen.

They'd accomplished a lot: freeing the dog from a terrible existence in the junkyard, saving him from drowning in the marsh, and then getting him half-way across the neighborhood unseen. But Rico feared the kids' daring act had set wheels in motion no one could stop. His gut told him things were only going to get tougher.

Rico cleared his throat. "You did a good thing, gettin' him away from Ridgeway, but don't you think the dog might be better off if we called the ASPCA?"

Tony swallowed a bite of pizza. "Why would you say that? You know I can't give him up. I'm going to keep Caesar."

The baker nodded, silently listening, biding his time as Tony described presenting his Dogma Carta document and detailed his speech about how a dog was a great responsibility for a boy and how a watchdog would be a great value, with his father having so many expensive tools in the house.

Despite his uneasiness, Rico roared with laughter, almost falling off his stool at Tony's story of how he'd torpedoed his well-planned efforts with the Sister Lemon Sucker episode at school. "How come I'm just hearin' 'bout this now? *Sister Lemon Sucker*, that's priceless, kid. But I bet it didn't win ya any points with your parents." Rico wiped away tears with the back of his hand.

"No. But I think I caught Pop grinning out of the corner of my eye, but my mom . . . well, you know my mom. I can't talk to her. Sometimes, I just want to—"

"Don't go there, kid. I love ya, but I won't let anyone talk bad about your mother. Even you." Rico took his baker's cap off and ran his fingers through his thinning hair before pushing stray curls back under his baker's cap. "Your mother would walk across white-hot coals for the people she loves, no one more so than you and your sister. Sure, she's a tough nut." Rico closed his eyes, picturing the hard-shelled women he'd known his entire life. "No one's more demandin', but she's got a heart a gold. You just gotta know her story."

Rico brought his hands together and steepled his fingers, staring at them for the longest time.

"I've known your mom all her life. Little Carla Pagano, the prettiest and sweetest girl in the neighborhood. Everyone liked her, and she was the happiest kid, always wearin' a freshly ironed dress and always singin'."

"Singing?" Tony raised his eyebrows, his

expression showing the thought of his intractably demanding mother as a little girl, happily singing, as inconceivable as the Moon landing the guys down in Cape Canaveral kept promising.

"Yeah, Tony, your mother had the most beautiful voice and always so full of joy. But when she was eleven years old, her mother, your Nonna Graziella, died. Your mother had to grow up overnight. She had to cook and clean for your grandfather and the younger kids." Rico bit his lower lip. "I never heard her singin' again. But when she laughs, I can still hear the music—sweet, clear, and joyful." Rico stopped and pointed a finger at Tony. "So don't let me hear you say a bad word about your mother."

"I'm sorry, it's just—"

"I know, kid." Rico's voice grew soft, his intensity replaced by a gentle, nurturing tone. "Life's complicated. Growin' up's complicated, and all the sh . . . all the stuff that happens along the way changes us. Our job is to try to make it change us for the better. Your mom couldn't always do that, but God knows, she tried. And you gotta, too. I see a lot of your mother in you. You've got her spirit, her passion for life. Hell, you even got her quick mind and bitin' tongue. *Go suck a bushel of lemons, you miserable old coot.*" Rico smiled. "Fourteen-year-old Carla Pagano couldn't a done better."

Rico's smile slowly faded as he reached across the counter, placing his hands on Tony's shoulders, and turned the boy to face him. "But your mom, she passed some of her pain and anger on to you. You gotta fight that. Look to your father to see the beauty in life. Your mother will give you the strength to take on the world, but when you put your head down to sleep at night, to count your blessings, think of your father. He's a very special kinda man, your father." Rico placed his index finger under Tony's chin, so the boy's raised eyes stared directly into the older man's. "Understand?"

"I . . . I think so."

The baker looked away. "Good. Now, 'bout the dog." Rico stood and stretched, collecting his thoughts for the conversation he'd been dreading. "You kids did a good thing, gettin' that poor guy outta that junkyard. A real good thing. But that dog scares the—"

"I know."

Rico raised his hand like a traffic cop. "Tony, please, listen. The dog's scars, they ain't just physical. And if you're honest with yourself, I think you'd see it—"

"He's fine," Tony said, clearly unwilling to listen.

Rico turned and looked at Jo. He hoped she'd meant it when she promised to be there for the boy. "I'm sorry, he's *not* fine, and you gotta face it. That animal's damaged emotionally, and he may never be quite right.

"Look, kid, we don't know what kinda life he had before you two freed him, but there's somethin' off with the dog. I can see it in his eyes and how he tenses anytime anyone comes near. Tony, he barely let's ya touch him, and you saved his life." Rico paused. "You know me, I never met a dog I didn't like. Had one my whole life growin' up. But this dog, this one scares me. Anytime I get near him, I swear his eyes are locked on my throat like he's tryin' to decide if he should tear it open. A hard shell surrounds him, and I don't know if anyone can break through it.

"I know you want to argue, but you see it, too. He's different. Whatever pain the dog's experienced in his life, those unknown horrors have marked him, perhaps leavin' him unfit for a normal life."

"I have to try," Tony said. "I owe him that."

"I dunno. I don't think it'll ever be safe for the dog to be 'round people, families, your sister. I hate to say it, but the poor guy might have been better off if . . ." Rico turned away, staring out the window at the snow-covered street, unable to look at Tony to share his darkest thoughts and break the young boy's heart.

"Give us a week," Jo said.

Rico turned back as the girl reached out to take Tony's hand, her eyes locked on the baker's.

Tony squeezed Jo's hand. "Yes, give us a week. If we can't prove to you it's safe for Caesar to be around people then . . ."

"Okay, a week. You can keep the dog here for seven days. But if I don't see a real change in that time, I mean *real* change . . . well, I've got a friend." Rico stopped, fighting the urge to turn away from the boy's intense gaze. "This friend, he's got a farm up in New Hampshire."

Tony nodded. "Okay, a week. Let me say goodbye to Caesar, and then I have to go. My mother will be back from work soon."

Rico feigned, busying himself, wiping down the

nearby pastry racks as Tony walked to the storage room to see the dog. Jo followed him and stood in the doorway, blocking Rico's view as Tony entered to be met by a low growl. The growling continued as Tony spoke gently to the dog.

"It's okay, buddy. It's okay. I promise you, I won't let anyone hurt you ever again."

Rico watched Jo for any sign of danger, but the girl stood frozen in place except for the anxious biting of a knuckle. The baker moved closer, a rolling pin in his hand, ready to pounce. But Tony's tender voice held Rico at bay.

"Here's the plan, Caesar. I'm going to come over there and sit next to you. I won't try to pet you if you don't want me to. We'll just sit together for a few minutes before I leave."

Rico couldn't see Tony, so he watched Jo, still standing in the doorway, as she lowered her hand from her mouth, her body relaxing, while Tony continued, "That's right. We're just going to sit here. Two old friends hanging out."

The growling stopped, and Jo smiled, her fingers locked in a seemingly silent prayer of thanks.

"That's right, Caesar. I won't try to pet you. I won't do anything until you want me to. We'll just hang out, you know, getting comfortable in each other's company. You'll tell me when you're ready for something more."

The baker exhaled and loosened his grip on the rolling pin, the color returning to his knuckles. He'd been half hoping the animal would show his true nature and snap at Tony, frightening the boy into admitting that cruel treatment had irreparably scarred the dog. But the kid's instincts were remarkable as the dog passed the first text. Rico moved closer. The growling stopped, and Jo no longer appeared primed to spring to the defense of her friend.

Rico waited for the snarl that never came. As promised, Tony never touched the dog, but as the boy left the room, the baker thought he heard a single soft swoosh of a tail across the floor.

Perhaps the boy, with his loving patience, accomplished something far more critical than momentary physical contact. Had Tony touched some long-hidden part of the battered dog's fractured psyche, a part that still understood the special bond a dog could have with a boy? Rico looked to the sky, praying it wasn't only wishful thinking.

Tony stood in the doorway, holding the empty water bowl—Jo by his side, the strain of the last day showing on both their young faces. "I'll get Caesar some fresh water before I go, and I'll stop by the market after school tomorrow to buy some dog food and get a collar and some antiseptic for his leg. Can you . . . ?"

"Don't worry about food for tonight. The dogs I had as a kid never ate store-bought dog food. They ate what the family did." Rico smiled, remembering simpler times. "I swear, old Butch could eat a pound of pasta. I can scrounge up somethin' for tonight."

Rico stopped as his doubts about this not ending well soured the happy memory, and his premonition returned, darkening his mood. "You two are exhausted. Hurry home. Your mom'll be wondering where you are."

Tony hugged Rico, something he hadn't done in years, and left with Jo walking by his side.

With the kids gone, Rico grabbed another slice of pizza from the tray and sat behind the counter, taking small bites as he struggled to avoid letting his mind fixate on the precarious future he feared awaited the dog. A disquieting unease settled on him. He finished eating, took another slice from the tray, and returned to the storage room. He inhaled deeply, slowly exhaling as he pushed in the door to find Caesar standing on the far side of the room. With the fur high on his back, the dog looked ready to attack. Caesar stared with those unsettling hunter's eyes that had unnerved the baker from the moment he'd first seen the dog.

Rico stepped cautiously into the room, leaving the door half open so he could quickly escape if he had to.

"Hey, boy, how ya doin'?"

The dog slipped into a predatory crouch, the lean muscles of his shoulders and haunches quivering like a coiled spring, ready to pounce. Caesar flashed razor-sharp canines as a low growl rolled from his throat. Even in his malnourished and weakened state, the animal's raw power set the baker on edge.

Rico stopped and tried to steady his trembling hand, knowing the dog could sense his unease, smell his fear. How had Tony done it? The kid was a natural with the dog, calm and reassuring. Rico tried to remember the tone of the boy's voice—soft and relaxed, like talking to an old friend. The baker took another deep breath and tried again.

"That's okay, fella, I won't hurt you. I see you starin' at me, but I'm not here to fight." Rico pointed at the pizza he was holding. "I just brought you a little somethin' more to eat."

Careful not to lock eyes with the dog, Rico focused on the pizza, tearing off a corner of the crust and tossing it underhand toward the dog.

Caesar's gaze settled briefly on the nearby food. His nose twitched, and some tension ebbed from his powerful body. Taking a short step, the dog arched forward, turning his head sideways as he flicked out his tongue to curl around the pizza crust before quickly gobbling it up.

"That's right. It's good, ain't it," Rico said as he tore off another piece and tossed it to the dog.

Caesar ate three slices over the next twenty minutes before falling into a deep sleep.

The baker came back several hours later and softly called to the dog. Closed for the day, it was time to get him outside. Rico grabbed his coat, stepped cautiously into the storage room, and forced open the rarely used side door leading to the fenced back lot. He stepped outside, lit a cigarette, inhaled deeply, and exhaled, trying to steady his nerves. Then he called for the dog to follow. It took a few minutes, but eventually, Caesar appeared in the doorway, his nose pointed high in the air as he took in the smells of the clear, cold night. Careful not to get too close, Rico let the dog pass before stepping back to stand at the door.

Caesar pushed his way through the snow. Still weak but moving better than at any point in the last day, he quickly marked several spots in the lot. He raised his snout, taking in all the scents of the night. Caesar's primal stare locked on the full moon as he spread his legs wide, raised his powerful chest, and bellowed a deep howl into the night, sky telling the world he lived.

Al Ridgeway, his head aching from an ugly hangover and the crack across the back of the head from some punk kids, lowered the near-empty bottle of Four Roses from his lips. He cocked his head, and his lips curled into a joyless smile.

Ridgeway knew that sound.

XVI

On the walk home, Jo listened while Tony detailed his plan for the next week. Seeking no affirmation, he'd detailed his intended action and presumptively included Jo in those plans. Her eyebrows arched in bemused surprise as he talked excitedly about what *they* must do.

Tony said they'd each tell their parents they needed to go to the library after supper because they had an assignment to work on. He didn't mention Rico De Santo's troubling comments about Caesar's physical and emotional scars, but admitted the trip to the library was so he could find some books on training dogs.

They stood outside Jo's house as Tony continued talking until the lights of Jo's front porch, flashing off and on, caught their attention.

"My mother," Jo said with an apologetic shrug.

Tony nodded. "Okay, so we'll meet right here at seven thirty. The library closes at nine, giving us more than an hour to get what we need. And remember to tell your parents as soon as you get in. That way, if my mother calls yours to check, she'll know I'm not trying to sneak out for a nighttime snowball fight or something."

"Don't worry, I got it."

Tony stood before her, a lopsided grin lighting his young face. Jo stepped toward him and, without thinking, leaned in to gently kiss him. Then she pulled away, shocked, only to see a similar look of shock on Tony's face.

Cursing her foolishness, Jo spun away and ran into the house.

Jo ate dinner in a trance. Her parents met her mumbled announcement that she planned to go to the library with Tony after supper with wry smiles. *Do they think I'm stupid and don't know what they're smiling about?* She stared at her food, mindlessly playing with the golabki on her plate. Donna Trocki's stuffed cabbage, usually one of Jo's favorites, lay barely touched.

"So, you and Tony must have had fun ice skating. You were gone most of the day," Jo's mother said in her third attempt to get Jo to talk.

Jo caught her father putting his hand on her mother's. He slowly shook his head as his eyebrows pulled tightly together, indicating Jo would talk when she was ready.

She took a mouthful of golabki, barely tasting the savory pork and rice, but the hunger of her growing body drove her to eat, even as her young mind struggled with so many new and confusing emotions.

She looked out the frost-covered dining room window to the street, where she'd first met the boy just over a month ago. Tony had stood there that day holding a basketball, offering to help her father. Jo nodding to him as they passed—oddly feeling like they were old friends, languidly comfortable in his presence. Even when Tony acted strangely aloof, Jo dismissed it like she'd seen her mother do when her Aunt Dottie was having a bad day. "We know each other too well and are too much alike to ever stay mad at each other," her mother always said.

And that's the odd sense she got around Tony. At his most petulant, he could bring Jo to an explosive wave of volcanic anger, crackling like fat on a hot skillet. But within moments of each snapping-firecracker misunderstanding, she'd pause as if she could hear the workings of Tony's brain struggling to articulate an apology for his latest offense. Rico De Santo's prescient words pecked at the dark recesses of her brain: *Tony and you are good for each other. There's a connection between you two that doesn't happen often.* He was right, but it wasn't what her parents thought, what anyone thought. Tony didn't see her that way, and she'd accepted that.

Jo continued staring out at the street where they'd first met. *Then why did I kiss him?*

They hurried down the hill, Tony in the lead with his arms swinging by his sides. The library closed at nine, and every minute counted. The plowed roads sat bare, the streetlights glistening off the icy blacktop. They stayed on the shoveled sidewalks until they turned a corner and came to a vacant lot with a hip-high drift across its un-shoveled sidewalk. They stopped and turned away to climb a huge snowbank. Tony helped Jo over the obstacle. Then with a soft nudge of his shoulder, directed her to the inside of the street, away from the traffic, as they continued down the road, alert for oncoming cars.

Jo noticed both gestures. Her impulsive kiss hadn't put Tony off too much. Maybe it was time to share her secret. Her mother managed to work it into almost every conversation about Jo. It was amazing she hadn't already said something in front of Tony.

"Do you know what your IQ is?" Jo asked, trying to sound casual.

"That's a weird question." Tony said, his brow furrowing. "Why would you ask something like that?"

"I don't know. You seem kind of smart."

"Smart? That's a joke. I'll show you my report cards sometime."

"Grades aren't always the best indicator of intelligence," Jo said, sounding like a high school administrator. She'd grown quite familiar with this subject.

"Hum." Tony turned to look at her. They'd stopped at the traffic signal leading to the bridge. "Last year, the district did some city-wide testing, and they said I read at an eleventh-grade level. And I've always been able to do math in my head. But, like I said, I've never gotten very good grades. The nuns always tell my parents I *lack discipline*, whatever that means."

"Grades are often a popularity contest with teachers," Jo said, remembering the coolness she sensed whenever Sister Agnes Helen addressed Tony in class. "I've got a feeling you're a lot smarter than the teachers know. I'm betting smarter than *you* know."

Tony blushed. "Light's changed," he said before running across the street, past the movie theater, as he hurried toward the library.

Jo followed, cursing herself. She'd embarrassed him, perhaps hurt his feelings, or left him thinking she was being condescending. She winced, remembering her mother the first night at the Miracolo's house, going on over dinner about Jo being a straight-*A* student. *He probably thinks I just wanted to brag.* She stopped short, bumping into Tony, who stood at the bottom of the library stairs waiting for her. Instead of the insulted glare she'd expected, Tony wore his trademark grin.

"You know, I always thought I might be kinda smart. But nobody's ever told me." He shrugged. "Except, you know, my father and Uncle Rico, and that don't count. What else is family supposed to say?" Tony's boyish face looked older and suddenly quite wise. "But you didn't just bring this up to make small talk. Something you wanna to tell me?"

Jo flinched.

"What, are you a genius or something?" Tony's voice had a teasing lilt but carried something more. He sounded *proud*.

Jo exhaled. The way Tony said it, she didn't feel like some oddball. He made her feel not just different but . . . special. She'd lived with this label a long time, and it still sat uncomfortably on her young shoulders.

"Please don't tell anyone. Of course, my mom gave all my test results to the school, but no one else knows. And yes, in answer to your question, according to the testing my parents had done, I'm supposed to be some sort of genius. My folks say that's why I can't make friends. I can make friends." Jo stopped and looked directly into the boy's eyes. "When I want."

Tony nodded. "I get it. Except for sports, there isn't much I've got to talk about with the guys at school." He turned away. "I think that's why I acted like a jerk around you at first. I saw someone named Jo Jo Trocki moving next door and hoped, at last, a boy my age I could talk to." He laughed. "You can imagine my surprise when Jo Jo had a ponytail."

"Sorry I disappointed you."

"More surprised than disappointed." Tony's face grew thoughtful. "But now, knowing you a bit, I think you might be easier to talk to than any guy I know."

"Thanks. I like talking to you, too."

"Come on, Einstein. We've got work to do," Tony said, smiling as he raced past her up the stairs.

"Don't call me that," Jo said, trying to sound angry. "At least not in public."

"Deal." Tony looked back at Jo as he held the door open for her. Then, with a conspiratorial glance left and right, said, "And if you're nice, I'll tell you a secret and my annoying nickname."

"Oh, so Mister Tony Miracolo, too cool for school, has deep, dark secrets, too."

"More than one," he said, looking away as he hurried toward the front desk.

Mrs. Browning, the ancient librarian, with a beehive-shaped pile of white hair and rimless glasses, looked up from sorting a pile of returned books and smiled. She was older than the first wheel and had an odd way of puckering her mouth, reminiscent of the dour Sister Agnes Helen. But the similarities ended there.

The kindly librarian's face lit up when she saw Tony. "Anthony, I haven't seen you in over a week. I feared you might have taken ill. But I see, like the prodigal son, you've returned to us. And brought a companion."

"Hi, Mrs. Browning. No, I haven't been sick, just kinda busy." Tony stopped and looked proudly at Jo. "And this is my friend Jo Trocki. You'll be seeing her a lot. I think she reads even more than me."

"Wonderful! A pleasure to meet you, Jo. Have your mother stop by to set you up with a library card. So, Anthony, what is your area of interest today?"

"I'm looking for books on dog training."

"Still trying to convince your parents, I see.

That's why I like you so, Anthony. There's no quit in you." The librarian's smile grew wider as she pointed to the far corner of the library. "Top shelf, and good luck."

With a quick thank you, the kids headed toward the corner.

Tony grabbed a book, *Training You to Train Your Dog,* fell into a chair, and began to read. But his face soon wore a mask of disappointment.

Equally frustrated with her book, Jo looked up at a frowning Tony. "Something wrong?"

"I don't know." Tony closed the book and pushed it into the middle of the table. "This one has all these specifics on training a dog on a leash. Then, it details all these ideas about punishing dogs for bad behaviors and rewarding them for good. It just seems like there should be more than that." He shrugged. "You know, a better way to connect."

Jo nodded. "This book is even harsher. It's like they're saying you're supposed to break the dog to your will. You know, *force* him to behave."

"Exactly. I don't wanna do that. I need to connect with Caesar, not beat him into obeying me. Caesar's been treated badly enough. He doesn't even know what it feels like to . . ." Tony stopped, his face lit with excitement. "Follow me."

Tony raced to the library's fiction section and dropped to his knees to take a book from the bottom shelf. Sitting cross-legged, he studied the back cover then looked up, smiling, and said, "One of my favorites." Then he began to read aloud.

"The man moves cautiously toward White Fang. The wolf-dog has been treated cruelly by others, and Scott's careful not to provoke the animal. His attempts to touch White Fang are initially met with flashing teeth and snarls. But slowly the wolf-dog allows Scott to come close and finally gently run his hands across his thick fur. And so, the fierce mistrustful dog comes to discover the wonders of a human's touch."

"That's it," Jo said, kneeling next to Tony. "We have to teach Caesar to love."

Tony's mind filled with visions of White Fang allowing a stranger to get close to him as he felt Jo's shoulder brush against him. He swallowed, his throat tightening. The boy turned, closed his eyes, and leaned in to kiss the pretty girl who knelt beside him.

"Library closing in five minutes."

The PA announcement broke the spell, and Tony opened his eyes to see Jo red-faced and staring at the floor.

"We better go," he said in a self-conscious mumble, saved from making a fool of himself by Mrs. Browning's closing announcement.

Looking away, Tony rushed to the checkout counter with copies of Jack London's *White Fang* and *The Call of the Wild*. He'd read both before, and the emotional connection between man and dog described by London had resonated with him. He squeezed the books tightly, hoping London might have more to teach him about bonding with Caesar than any of the how-to books they'd looked at.

"Wait," Jo said as Tony placed the books before the librarian. "There's one more I think you should read."

While an excited Jo ran back to the fiction section, navigating the aisles like she'd been there a hundred times before, Tony waited, talking with Mrs. Browning and trying not to think about his foolish attempt to kiss his new neighbor. Jo quickly found a book and returned, slipping the slender volume on top of the other two books. "I think this might help," she said with an embarrassed shrug.

They rushed out of the library. Despite needing to get home before it got late and his mother had a fit, Tony turned left at the bottom of the library stairs, compelled to take the longer route past the bakery.

What was I thinking? Tony kicked a clump of snow, smashing it into a giant puff as they walked. *The look on her face said it all.*

Sure, Jo had kissed him on the cheek, but that was no different than when his sister came home from the hospital after getting her tonsils out last spring. She looked at her old bike—freshly painted, with fancy white-wall tires and ornate, pink-tasseled hand grips Tony had bought with his own money— and squealed with delight. Rosa wrapped her arms around his neck, giving him a big, wet kiss on the cheek, calling Tony "the best big brother ever."

That's how Jo thought of him, and he'd better

not ruin it by getting all goofy over her. Jo had already proven to be the best friend a guy could find, and he vowed not to mess things up by making her feel uncomfortable. Besides, why would she be interested in him when everyone in the class knew she was with Danny Walsh, *the smartest, best-looking guy in school* ?

"I think these books will help. Have you read them?" he asked, breaking the silence and hoping Jo was willing to forget his foolish moment back at the library.

"Yes, both." Jo's voice sounded distant.

"Oh yeah, that's right. I forgot you're a *genius*," Tony said, trying to make her smile.

"Don't start," Jo said, some of the punch back in her voice. "And you still have to tell me your big secret. I already know the nickname. It's Hitchcock, isn't it."

"Yeah, figures you'd have heard that by now."

"Hey, a girl's got ears. So, what's the big deal? Everybody knows you love the movies. It didn't take a *genius* to figure it out."

"Okay, they know I like movies. But what *no one* knows is my dream of *making* movies. The guys think I'm strange enough already, spending time in my uncle's bakery or with my nose buried in a book when they're all hanging out on the corner. They'd laugh their butts off if they knew I was saving up to buy a used eight-millimeter camera I saw listed for sale in the *Tribune*. And forget about what the nuns would do. I can just imagine the note Sister Agnes Helen would send home, telling my parents they need to rein in their *daydreamer* son."

"Screw Sister Agnes Helen and screw the guys on the corner." Jo covered her mouth, looking at Tony out of the corner of her eye, and giggled. "You want to make movies." Her excited voice traveled far along the deserted streets. "I think that's great."

"Sssh," Tony said, staring at his feet. "It's stupid."

"Stupid?" Jo grinned and bumped him with her shoulder as they walked. "I think it's freaking awesome. Who knows movies better than you? What works in a scene and doesn't, camera angles, lighting, all of it. And you're a fantastic storyteller."

"It's nice to think about, but I know, deep down, life's not like a movie." Tony buried a hand into a snowbank to grab a clump of snow and aggressively squeeze it into a tight ball. Stopping to take aim, he tossed it at a glimmering streetlight, where it hit with a splat as white powder filled the night sky, before slowly falling toward them.

"Who am I kidding? Guys in this neighborhood grow up and work in the factory or for the phone company. They become cops or firemen, or they buy a pickup truck and become plumbers or electricians. Nothing wrong with any of that. Look at my father and yours. But guys who grow up here don't go to Hollywood and make movies." Tony shrugged. "My mom keeps saying I should take the civil service exam, whatever that is. I dunno, maybe she's right."

"That's at the top of the stupidest things I've ever heard you say, and that list is growing daily," Jo said, her nose twitching.

"I'm just being realistic," Tony said defensively.

"You're being dumb," Jo said with a dismissive wave of her hand. "Now, how much more money do you need to buy that camera?"

"Twenty bucks." Tony kicked another clump of snow. "I could've made at least ten bucks shoveling driveways today, but obviously, Caesar had to come first."

"Hum. I've been saving up for a leather jacket, but I always wanted to be a patron of the arts. I think I might be able to help you out with a small loan."

"Are you serious?" Tony said. "You'd really do that."

"I don't just say stuff." Jo smiled. "You, my friend, will make great movies, and I want to help."

Tony squared his shoulders, a giant weight lifted from him. Jo Trocki, the smartest person he knew, believed in him.

"Thanks. What you think means a lot to me." Tony looked away, afraid of what Jo might see if he met her gaze. "But right now, I need your help breaking through to Caesar. Here." He handed her a copy of *The Call of the Wild*. "I'm guessin' you read even faster than I do, but I want to start with *White Fang*. We can swap after we finish."

"Good idea." Jo took the thinner of the two books. "Two heads and all that."

They discussed Caesar and his unwillingness to let anyone get close to him as they walked. Tony tensed when Jo mentioned Rico's comments about Caesar's hidden wounds, and he fell silent when she said they might never know what left him suspicious of all humans. Tony couldn't go there. The dog's mistreatment was too painful to contemplate. He clenched his fist, vowing he'd find a way to reach Caesar's fragile psyche. The consequences of failure were unacceptable. There must be a way, and he vowed to find it.

The two passed the bakery, and Caesar lifted his head, the smell of the boy familiar and strangely comforting. The dog's chest swelled, and a bark formed in his throat. But he hesitated, fighting the instinctive impulse to greet a pack member. With his ears perked, snout raised in the air, and nostrils flaring, the dog froze as the scent and the sound slowly faded. He'd quelled the urge to call out to the boy, but the dog remained confused by the compelling desire to feel his touch again.

Caesar rose, restless, and made several small circles before plopping back to the ground with a harrumph. For the first time in a long time, he knew warmth, and at last, the constant hunger that had seemed a fixed part of his life was gone. But an unfamiliar new need arose, one strangely tied to the boy. Caesar lay there a long time until his eyelids grew heavy, and he began to blink, eyes staying closed longer each time until he fell into a heavy, dream-filled sleep.

Caesar was back with his mother, safe and warm, licking his mother's face, tasting the crumbs of her recent meal. Then he curled up next to her and felt the loving, gentle embrace as her paw rested on his side, holding him close to her warm body.

The dog snorted contentedly, remembering the comfort of the touch, but as he stirred, the dream changed. His mother faded, replaced by the boy who'd helped to free him from the giant. The same boy Caesar found sleeping with his arm wrapped around him when he woke, exhausted and weak, after escaping from the flooded river.

Caesar lifted his head, taking in the darkness. He was alone, safe and warm, but something was missing. He yawned, tired and oddly anxious. The dog closed his eyes to sleep, resting his head on his paws. Maybe the boy would return to him in his dreams.

Ridgeway left the print shop and got into his truck, throwing the package on the seat beside him. He winced as the lights of a car flashed past. The big man had slept most of the afternoon, waking with a crippling hangover, and he knew only one cure. He pulled a pint of whiskey out of his back pocket and unscrewed the cap, the smell greeting him like an old friend. He threw back his head to take a long, gurgling tug. The alcohol warmed him, soothing his jagged nerves, but his hands still trembled. He took another long draw on the bottle while allowing the palm of his free hand to brush against his hip, his fingers tingling at the reassuring presence of his .38 caliber pistol. Satisfied, he started the truck and pulled into the street, his hand heavy on the gun.

The mechanic had bought the pistol a few years

ago after hearing about some store break-ins, but he'd never felt much of a need for the gun. The big man's foes never stood very long. Between his ham-sized fists and any weapon he could pick up—bottle, pipe, or barstool—his fights ended quickly, leaving his rival bloody and beaten. Ridgeway could bully most people into bending to his will, and he'd pound into submission any who couldn't be intimidated.

All that had changed when the dog attacked him. The humiliating defeat at the hands of a couple of kids and a gimpy, malnourished mutt haunted him. Ridgeway had never known the shame of being bested until getting outsmarted by those punks and jumped by the dog. It cut at the core of his being. The big man ran a red light in front of the bridge, pounding the dashboard as he sped past the library, his face red with embarrassment remembering it all. He'd pissed his pants. That damn dog with those teeth bared at his throat caused him to cower like a baby, and the kids were there to see it all.

That dog would pay. As would the brats who'd helped the worthless mutt. His body trembled with a festering hunger the man vowed to feed.

He didn't know the kids, but the smart-mouth boy looked familiar. He'd seen him around the neighborhood somewhere and heard the dog howl nearby in the night. He'd find them. Mindless of the icy road, Ridgeway drove on, rocking back and forth in the car as he clenched and unclenched his massive fist.

Oh yeah, he'd find them.

XVII

The dog lay curled up in over a foot of snow watching—his thick fur protecting him from the cold.

The boy had been outside with the dog a long time now, sitting calmly on a crate as he stared at something in his lap. Every few minutes, he'd rise to throw Caesar a tasty bit of food and move his crate. The boy never looked directly into the dog's eyes. But Caesar felt the boy watching him each time he came closer.

"Nothing to worry about, buddy. I'm just out here enjoying the sunshine and reading my book." The boy rose, tossing him another slice of meat, and moved closer.

Caesar tensed but didn't try to move away as he leaned forward to gobble up the food that lay in front of him.

When the boy had first arrived, he let Caesar out of the storage room. The dog had exhausted himself with the effort of marking the perimeter of the small lot, so now he rested and watched, snapping up food each time it was tossed near him. The dog lay his head on his front paws, never taking his eyes off the boy. Caesar needed to build his strength to defend himself from the attack he knew must eventually come. It might not come from the boy, but sooner or later, some human would strike out. So, he remained wary. And when he grew strong enough, it would be time to run.

The dog blinked as he studied the boy, whose scent he recognized as the one who'd come each day to throw food to him over the fence when he was chained up by the giant. Caesar didn't understand why this boy had always been so kind to him. But this one carried himself differently from other men the dog had known. Maybe the boy hadn't yet learned the cruel ways of men, but Caesar knew all men ultimately were the same. In time, the boy would show his true nature. So, the dog waited as the memories of the cruelty he'd endured set his fur on end.

Caesar's muscles twitched, remembering the first time he saw the giant. His mother's litter had grown smaller. People came and visited, speaking with the older man. The visitors would pick up one of the pups and study them, looking at their teeth, eyes, and limbs, as the man had done when they were younger. The visitors and the man would talk back and forth, with the visitors soon taking a pup away.

Many people picked Caesar up, interested, and

had long conversations with the man, but he'd shake his head, saying, "Not nearly enough. This one's the pick of the litter, stronger than any two combined and a natural-born fighter." So, Caesar remained behind as littermates slowly disappeared.

Then, one day, the giant arrived, towering over the pup, casting a dark shadow across the room.

The giant reached down to pick him up, and Caesar smelled the evil. The pup flashed his teeth, snapping a warning. The big man pulled his hand back, laughing—a mean, shallow sound—and cuffed the pup across the head. The giant ignored the protest from the other man, and he reached again for the puppy. But Caesar snapped with intent, this time locking his sharp teeth deep in the man's massive hand. The giant howled in pain and cuffed the pup again, harder, sending him spinning across the floor. Then, ignoring the heightened protest of the older man, the giant glared at his bleeding hand, smiled his evil smile, and said, "He'll do. A hundred bucks it is, and shuddup. The animal's mine now. I'll smack him any goddam time I please."

He grabbed the panicked puppy by the scruff of his neck and threw him into a canvas sack.

The giant spoke again, words that meant nothing to the pup but somehow filled him with more dread than he'd ever known. "Oh yeah, I've got big plans for you. But first, I gotta teach you to hate. And when there's enough hate in your heart, I'm gonna give you a present. . . something to fight."

The man walked out of the warehouse with the sack on his shoulder as the frantic puppy scrambled wildly in the enclosed darkness, trying to escape this ugly man and the terrible turn his life had taken.

Caesar's nose twitched as another bit of food landed in front of him. He looked up to find the boy moving nearer, but he sensed no danger. With his eyes still on the boy, the dog dropped his snout, taking in the meat with one gulp as the memory of that painful day slowly faded.

Tony closed the book and rose again, moving the crate closer to Caesar as he tossed the dog another bit of roast beef. He'd stayed up half the night rereading passages from Jack London's *White Fang* as his plan slowly took shape. The boy scuttled his original thought to try and bombard Caesar with affection, admitting his Uncle Rico was right about one thing regarding the dog. They'd never know the details of Caesar's life before they'd freed him. As much as he'd like to, Tony couldn't deny Caesar wasn't like other dogs. The animal's bristling discomfort around people, his aversion to any physical contact, and his refusal to even consider taking food directly from anyone's hand all indicated a life of isolation and mistreatment. His approach with Caesar had to be different.

Tony sighed, looking at the copy of *White Fang* he'd been reading the past hour, the suspicious look in the wolf-dog's eyes on the book cover so eerily similar to Caesar. Tony traced his index finger along the image, as if petting the wary animal whose crouching posture and half-turned, dipped, shoulder signaled he might attack or pivot and flee at any moment. Weedon Scott had found a way to touch White Fang's soul, and John Thornton had connected with Buck in *The Call of the Wild* when no one else could. Tony vowed he'd find a way with Caesar.

"That's right, buddy, you and I are going to be best friends." He leaned forward, showing his open palm to the dog, who sniffed suspiciously. "That's all right. I told you we got all day. I packed us some sandwiches and told my folks I was going to a double feature at the movies."

Tony smiled as he reached into his coat pocket and unwrapped his second sandwich, making a show of taking a huge bite. "Um, um, delicious." He opened the sandwich and tore away another piece of meat, which he held eye level with Caesar before flipping it underhand to be snapped out of the air by the watchful dog.

He tossed the next piece in front of the dog, forcing Caesar to lean forward to get the meat as the boy crept closer with each subsequent toss.

With one piece left, Tony squatted an arm's length away from Caesar and the dog's powerful jaws. The boy slowly waved the thick slice of meat in front of Caesar's twitching nose as drool rolled off the dog's lips. Caesar turned his head and reached to take the roast beef from Tony's outstretched hand, gobbling the slice up in a flash.

Tony's heart raced as Caesar pulled back. *I did it!*

He'd gotten the cautious, fear-filled dog to eat out of his hand.

"I brought you some water." Rico stood behind Tony, wary not to startle the dog. He handed him a bowl, then stepped away slowly to let the boy place the water in front of Caesar.

Tony, mindful to make no sudden gestures, spoke reassuringly. "It's okay, buddy. It's okay. And remember my promise. I won't let anyone hurt you ever again."

The dog, watching every move, let Tony leave the water before burying his snout to empty the bowl as Tony pulled his hand away.

Rico waited before grabbing another crate and sitting next to Tony as the dog emptied the bowl. Finished, Caesar rose unsteadily, struggled to a corner of the lot to relieve himself, before returning and dropping to the ground just out of reach. With a quick glance at the two, he lowered his head and curled up to rest.

"He's moving better today," Tony said.

"Still got a long way to go, and not just physically."

"I know," Tony said, cutting the baker off.

"Okay, I'll say no more." Rico smiled. "So, where's your friend?"

"Couldn't make it."

Tony wasn't ready to discuss his Jo problems. Besides, what was there to say? He was sure she would have seen the changes his Uncle Rico couldn't or wouldn't. But she didn't come, and her absence weighed heavy on his young mind.

They'd parted last night with Jo's promise to join him, but this morning, when he'd knocked, she met him at her front door, wrapped in a bathrobe. Jo told him she didn't feel good. But she sure didn't look sick to Tony.

He grimaced, thinking back to the night of the dance. He closed his eyes, trying to clear his mind of the painful image of Danny helping Jo put on her coat and then confidently wrapping his arm around her waist to walk her home. Who was he to think he could compete with Danny Walsh: tall and good-looking? Even Sister Agnes Helen loved Danny. And just like Jo, a straight-*A* student.

Jeez, the girl's a damn genius. No wonder she doesn't want to waste time with a mope like me.

"You alright? You seem a million miles away?" His uncle's voice pulled Tony back.

"Yeah, just thinking about Caesar." Tony stood. "It's getting late. I better go. You need help getting Caesar back in the storage room?"

"No. I leave the door open enough for him to get in and out," the baker said, tipping his head in the dog's direction. "He still doesn't trust me, but he's too weak to run and smart enough to come in from the cold. So that'll work for the next few days. Just make sure you lock the gate when you leave."

The baker didn't say more, but he didn't have to. Tony understood. His uncle had promised he'd let Caesar stay at the bakery for a week so Tony could devise a plan to convince his parents to let him keep the dog. But as difficult as that might be, getting the wild, mistrustful animal to stay once he grew strong enough to run again could prove even harder.

Jo sat on her front steps, anxiously tapping her foot, as she waited for Tony. She didn't want to be late to Mass. She hated it when all the eyes turned on her. And Sister Agnes Helen would be sure to make an example of them on Monday morning if she spotted them arriving late.

Jo lied, saying she was sick yesterday, but the time alone did nothing to help. The other night, they'd shared secrets, but just as it seemed to bring them closer, she felt Tony tense up and pull away.

She knew he'd asked Delores to go steady. The dark-eyed girl had told all her friends about it at school the Monday after the dance. Then why did Jo imagine Tony wanted to kiss her last night at the library when he looked so intensely into her eyes, excited about the books they'd found?

Jo never made friends easily. She wasn't interested in what the girls her age were doing, while boys were looking for things she wasn't ready to give. But it felt so different with Tony. She bit her lip, struggling to understand where she stood with her young neighbor and afraid her phone call earlier that morning suggesting they walk to mass together had been a mistake

Jo's parents always told her she was a miracle. They'd tried to get pregnant unsuccessfully for years. Then, for years after she was born, they tried again until they accepted Jo would be an only child. So, they channeled all their love and attention into their brilliant and sensitive daughter.

Then, a second miracle, Frank Junior arrived,

premature and colicky. While her mother, older and recovering from a tough pregnancy, struggled with depression and exhaustion. Her father no longer came home from work shouting, "Let's play catch or shoot some baskets." His wife needed help, and he now had a son with whom he'd soon do those things. Jo needed to grow more independent, make some friends her age, and start acting like a lady.

She struggled to navigate the changes in her life. The baby's arrival altered her world, and the shy, lonely girl grew more distant as she buried herself in competing and being the best at everything she did. Her parents—wrapped up in a big promotion, a new baby boy, and the move to a new city—pushed on, oblivious to the stone-cold shell their daughter had built.

Then, Tony Miracolo dribbled into Jo's life, and her shell crumbled like the walls of Jericho.

Unlike girls like Kathleen Collins and Delores DePalma, Jo didn't know how to put on makeup to make her eyes pop or lips look kissable. She understood why Tony would be more interested in a rapidly developing girl like Delores DePalma than a skinny tomboy like her. She could live with that.

Jo smiled for the first time that morning. *We're just going to be friends.* She held that thought firmly in mind as Tony hurried out his front door and down the walk toward her.

"Sorry I'm late. My mom had a list of chores as long as my arm. C'mon." Tony pointed toward the church. "I heard Monsignor Hanrahan say once, if you arrive at Mass before the gospel, it still counts."

"Tony Miracolo, playing all the angles. I'm

shocked," Jo said, falling into step beside him.

Tony smiled. "Yeah, hard to believe. Sorry you couldn't come yesterday. You feeling better?"

"Yeah, thanks." Jo blushed, hating having lied to Tony and embarrassed she'd let her emotions get the best of her. "And sorry I wasn't there with you."

"That's okay, but I wish you could've seen it." Tony's hands flew like a symphony conductor's, his emotions running high as he retold yesterday's events with the dog. "I reread *White Fang*. It helped a lot with trying to imagine what Caesar's life might have been like before we got him away from Al Ridgeway and why he acts the way he does around people. But then, in the morning, I looked at the book you picked out."

"*The Little Prince*," Jo said tentatively.

"Yeah," Tony said with a nod. "At first, I wasn't sure." He shrugged. "You know, with all the drawings and everything. But the more I read, the more it made sense and how it all connected back to Caesar."

Tony's brow furrowed, as it did when he was deep in thought. "You know, how the fox tells the little prince if he wants to tame him, he'll have to be patient and not sit too close and only move close slowly."

"Exactly," Jo said. "And then, over time, the boy becomes the most special boy in the world for the fox, and the fox becomes the most special fox in the world to the boy. The whole journey helps the little prince grow. But I think the love he chooses to invest in the rose changes him most. I think what you're doing for Caesar will be good for you too."

Jo stopped short, afraid she may have said too much. But Tony, excitedly wrapped in telling her about his success, seemed not to notice or understand her point.

"Yeah, well, so anyway, that's what I did. Yesterday morning, I went to the bakery with a couple of thick roast beef sandwiches, and I plopped myself down on a milk crate a ways from Caesar." The two were walking again, and the excitement in Tony's voice only increased. "You know, acting calm as can be, just two old friends sitting in the sun. And I'd throw Caesar a juicy bit every few minutes and move my crate closer."

They stopped to let a car pass as they navigated through the crowded church parking lot.

"Nice and slow," Jo said, wishing she'd been there and cursing herself for the overreaction that had caused her to miss the small victory.

"Yeah," Tony said, his smile brighter than the snow-covered rooftops. "And you'll never guess what happened next. Caesar took the last piece right out of my hand."

"Wow." Jo's smile matched Tony's, and she almost reached out to take his hand but stopped, burying her hand in her coat pocket instead as she fumbled to find a kerchief to cover her hair before entering the church. "C'mon, let's grab seats in the back so we can get out quickly and see Caesar," Jo said, her voice cracking.

What was I thinking? I committed to not mess up this friendship. Smarten up.

But the hollow feeling in her stomach from seeing Tony kiss Delores DePalma on the dance floor lingered, like a movie's sad ending frozen on the screen.

Caesar's nose signaled first, but soon, his ears perked. The boy was near. The dog rose from where he'd been lying, getting up a bit easier each time now. He bowed, stretching out his back as he stood in the corner, his eyes on the door, waiting.

He didn't understand the changes happening to him, but for the first time since he was a pup sleeping next to his mother, he felt the need to be touched by another.

"Did you see the posters?" Rico sat on a milk crate behind the bakery with Tony and Jo.

"What posters?" Tony said before quickly pointing at Caesar, wiggling on his back in the fast-melting snow and acting momentarily like a regular dog. "Look at him. He's growing stronger every day."

"Posters are hangin' all over town, offerin' a reward for a missin' dog," the baker said. "Al Ridgeway's been very busy."

"Haven't seen 'em." Tony continued watching Caesar as Rico and Jo exchanged glances. She raised her shoulders in a *What can I say?* shrug.

"They're on every telephone pole in the neighborhood," Rico said. "Ridgeway ain't gonna let go on this."

"I don't care." Tony stood up, refusing to look at the baker.

"The dog is *legally* his."

"Don't care. The man doesn't deserve Caesar." Tony was pacing now, and the dog, sensing the tension, sat up warily. "Why is he such a miserable person, anyway?" Tony said as he continued to pace.

Rico shook his head. "He wasn't always. As a kid, he was just lonely and a little odd. Al Ridgeway was a seed planted in bad soil, and he grew ugly and twisted."

"What are you talking about, lousy soil? He's just a miserable excuse of a human being."

"Oh, that's right, you don't know his story. Ridgeway is Alistair Prescott's grandson, and that wasn't the easiest of lives."

"That's bull," Tony said. "I lived next door to the Prescotts all my life. They were both old maids."

"Yeah, but Ridgeway is Alistair Junior's son. After Junior killed himself, the Prescott sisters kicked their brother's widow and young Al out of the house. The widow took back her maiden name, moved into a triple-decker down by the marsh, and slowly drank herself to death, leavin' young Al to raise himself."

"Ridgeway grew up in my house?" Jo said.

"Till he was about ten years old."

"So all those scratchings my father painted over in the pantry that looked like the initials AP with a year beside each line were of Ridgeway, and the box of old toys in the attic must have been his, too."

"Probably." Rico nodded. "Some of us kids, Tony's father included, used to go over and play with the toys. Al was big, even then, but didn't know how to play with other kids. He just sorta stood there while the others played with the fancy toys or ran through the rocky woods behind the house, playin' cowboys and Indians and pretendin' that big old carriage house in the backyard was a fort." The baker stared at the shifting clouds and shook his head. "We were just kids, but we coulda tried harder. He was so quiet, and after his father died, he just got mean. I don't think I've said more than a coupla words to him in the last thirty years."

"So he's had a tough life. That's still no excuse for how he treated Caesar," Tony said.

"No, that's true. But like I said, growin' straight and tall is tough, and it's near impossible if you're planted in lousy soil. It's not surprisin' Ridgeway ended up the way he did. I know you don't wanna hear this." Rico tried to put his hand on Tony's shoulder but pulled away as Caesar rose, emitting a low, protective growl. The baker pointed at Caesar, who stood warily, watching the exchange. "That's what I mean. The dog's filled with hate and mistrust. I'm sorry, kid, but he was planted in bad soil, too. It's a shame and not his fault, but I don't know if you can undo all that."

Tony shook his head. "You say lots of stuff. You told me life's complicated, and the things that happen along the way change us. Our job is to make those experiences change us for the better. Last week, you told me to be more like my father and find the good in life. Well, that's what I'm doing.

My father looks for the good in people, and I see the good in Caesar."

Rico raised his hands in surrender as Tony used his own words against him. The kid could always argue a point. And who knows, maybe Tony and his immense heart could save the dog. But the animal's low growl and bared teeth, poised to attack at the first sign of danger to him or the boy, warned otherwise.

XVIII

Jo and Tony stood a few feet apart, each holding wet washcloths as they wiped down the blackboard at the front of the classroom.

Tony had once again offended Sister Agnes Helen's sensibilities, this time with a series of questions about original sin and how God made Eve out of Adam's rib. Jo had almost jumped out of her chair, trying to signal Tony to halt his nonstop questioning, but to no avail. Tony hypothesized that many Old Testament stories should be viewed as lessons to leading a good life and not some recounting of precise historical events.

"C'mon, Adam didn't really live to be nine hundred and thirty years old."

Jo finally gave up when she saw the firm set of his jaw. Tony Miracolo had a point to make, an argument to win, and there'd be no stopping him. So, Jo sat, stewing in silence, as Tony's debate drove headlong toward the inevitable cliff.

It ended with the nun spewing about the audacity of an uncouth eighth-grade boy trying to discern God's word and telling him he could contemplate his inappropriate behavior by staying after school and cleaning the blackboard.

"Great job, Perry Mason."

"What?" Tony said, a look of sanctimonious innocence on his face. "It wasn't my fault."

"It never is with you."

"As if you don't argue all the time."

"Yes," Jo said, "but I pick my battles. I argue about important stuff and with the people whose opinions matter to me. I care what you think, but I figure nothing I say will ever change the mind of someone like Sister Agnes Helen."

"Well, aren't you special?" Tony said. "Probably cuz you're such a *genius*. Why would you even want to hang around with a dope like me?"

"Oh, grow up," Jo said, bristling at the mention of her IQ. "But you're right, for once. There's no reason for me to hang out with a dope like you." Then she twisted the knife. "Hitchcock, hah. You're just an angry dreamer. And if you don't grow up, the stories you tell will be filled with ugliness because that's all you'll have learned from life."

"Oh yeah? Well, you're just a bitter little girl who, if she isn't careful, will end up a lonely old maid just like the crazy old bats who lived in your house before you."

Jo wound up and fired the washcloth at Tony's head with the speed of a fastball that would have pleased Sandy Koufax, forcing Tony to duck as the wet rag splatted against blackboard.

"I don't need to be here. I just wanted to help and be with you." Embarrassed at saying that part out loud, she spun away and raced out of the classroom.

What am I doing? It should have been Delores who stayed after school to help him anyway.

"Where's your friend?" Rico smiled at Tony, who sat across the counter on one of the bakery stools, the scowl on the boy's face a sure sign of another blowout between the two.

"She had lots of homework," Tony said, staring at the floor.

"Anthony, who you think you're talkin' to?"

"All right, we got in a fight."

"What was this one about?"

"I don't know, but wow, she can get me mad."

"Do you think she riles you up because she calls you out when you act stubborn or bullheaded?"

Tony laced his fingers, bringing the tips of his thumbs to his mouth to bite on them as he thought. "Maybe," Tony finally said with a smile.

"She's a sharp kid, and I figure bein' 'round her is good for you."

"Yeah."

"And she's prettier than a sunrise," Rico said with a wink.

"Please don't give me that look. She doesn't think of me that way." Tony jumped off the stool. "I'm going to check on Caesar."

Rico watched Tony walk to the back room and shook his head, wondering how two smart kids could be so dumb.

When Tony opened the door, Caesar's tail swished slowly across the floor. He rose, ears perked and head held high. But as Tony came closer, the dog froze, and his tail curled back between his legs. A lifetime of abuse kept him locked in place.

Reacting to the dog's tense posture, Tony dropped to his knees to be the same height. Then, avoiding direct eye contact, he said, "Hey, buddy, sorry I'm late. I messed up at school again and had to stay after."

Tony crept toward the dog as he spoke, showing his open palms for Caesar to sniff. Then, when close enough, Tony placed his hand on Caesar's chest and slowly ran his fingers through the dog's thick winter coat.

As he had each time, Caesar stiffened at the initial intimacy and crouched, as if to escape, but every day, the boy's gentle presence calmed him more. Today, Caesar held his head high, not dipping his shoulders to escape the contact. The dog relaxed and surrendered, letting the boy's hand explore his body, scratching his broad chest and back and then under his ears. Caesar leaned in to accentuate his touch, and the dog's back paw began to thump in rhythm to the scratches.

"That's right, buddy. I'm going to give you lots of pets."

Tony continued to speak, his gentle voice lulling Caesar into a sense of calm that seemed to grow with each passing day.

Tony rose early, unsure if Jo would even walk with him to school after yesterday's argument. He sat by the window, his coat on and bookbag on his shoulder, watching Jo's front door. She appeared on her porch and walked toward Tony's house, her head down, as if the ground held some incredible fascination.

Tony bounced out of his chair and almost knocked her over as he flew onto the sidewalk. The girl acknowledged his arrival with a noncommittal nod but didn't speak.

"I had a great day with Caesar yesterday," Tony said, falling into step beside her. "Wish you coulda been there." Tony stopped and bit his lip. "I mean, I wish you were there, too. I know it was my fault."

"I know what you meant."

Tony took a deep breath and exhaled slowly. "I don't know why I do it. But sometimes, I like to stir the pot. You know, raise the flame, let people slowly stew, and sit back smiling watching it all bubble over. Especially when it's someone as pigheaded as Sister Agnes Helen."

"I told you yesterday. It's not a competition. No one's keeping score. Pick your battles and know when to let go. Otherwise, you're acting like a child trying to win some silly game."

"You're right. It's just hard for me." Tony

squinted into the morning sun, wanting to feel even that tiny pain. "My Uncle Rico told me this story about a monkey in the jungle who comes across a cage filled with ripe bananas. Well, this monkey's a little hungry, so he reaches into the cage and wraps his hand around a banana. But the monkey can't get his hand back out from between the cage bars after he closes his fist. Now, this is the jungle, and he coulda found plenty of other food, but this monkey is stubborn. He won't let go, and he's willing to risk starving to death instead of letting go of that damn banana."

"Sounds like someone I know," Jo said.

Tony dropped his head. "I guess Uncle Rico's right. Sometimes I'm like that monkey."

"You don't have to be," Jo said with a sideways glance. "For one thing, you're probably smarter than that monkey."

"Probably," Tony said, trying to suppress a smile.

"*Probably.*"

"Listen, I really am sorry. I didn't mean anything I said about you being bitter. I just got mad because I knew you were right."

"Forget it."

"I'll try if you will." They stopped to let several cars drive into the school parking lot and Tony turned to face Jo. "But forgetting about mistakes is even harder than saying I'm sorry or admitting I was wrong."

"Work on it because I suspect you'll get a lot of practice in life."

"Ouch," Tony said, miming pulling an arrow

from his chest. "But I guess I deserved that."

"I'm sorry. That was mean, and I guess I owe you an apology, too."

"For what?"

"For calling you an angry dreamer."

"No," Tony said, shaking his head. "You're right."

"Only partly. You are angry sometimes, but you have beautiful dreams, and it'd be a shame not to share them."

"So, you figure you know all there is to know about me."

"Not even close, monkey boy," Jo said, giggling, "but I know enough."

Tony grabbed her by the shoulders, giving her a friendly shake. "Hah, hah, Trocki. So funny."

He swallowed hard as Jo bit her lower lip. Still holding Jo by the shoulders he froze, remembering her discomfort at the library. Tony quickly released his grip and looked away. When he glanced back, Jo's face was as red as it had been that night. Her embarrassment for him once again plain to see.

"We better hurry. The bell's gonna ring."

"Here," Jo said, fumbling in her pocket before pulling out a hairbrush. "For Caesar. It's an old one of mine, but I figured . . ."

"Thanks. But aren't you gonna come?"

"I wasn't sure you still wanted me to."

"Of course I do, and listen, about that night at the library—" The final bell interrupted Tony, and Jo turned away, her face flushed.

Tony dropped his head as he followed, hurrying into school. *Just let it go.*

XIX

The boy had arrived. Caesar anxiously paced, his tail slowly swishing as the murmured conversations continued outside the room. Finally, the door swung open, and Caesar hurried to greet a visitor for the first time since he was a young puppy. His slowly wagging tail grew to a spontaneous whippet of joy as he dropped in front of the boy he now knew as Tony.

Tony fell to his knees, hugging Caesar as the dog stiffened. "Hi, buddy, I missed you."

But the fear melted away, and the dog buried his head into Tony's body. He ran his hands across Caesar's chest and up to his ears, a spot that could set the dog's hind paw to thumping. Caesar snorted with pleasure and trustingly lifted his head, exposing his throat, allowing the boy's hand greater access across his body.

"Look what I . . . what Jo brought for you."

The rubbing stopped, and a disappointed Caesar looked at the boy, who held something in his hand and pointed it at the girl. The dog pulled his head back and growled. He'd been hit too many times by things humans clutched in their hands to like the presence of this thing the boy held.

"Tony, he's afraid of the brush." The girl's voice was calm and gentle.

"That's okay, Caesar. I promised I'd never hurt you." He returned to scratching Caesar's chest with one hand as the other slipped out of the dog's view.

Caesar flinched when he felt something high on his back. He started to pull away but stopped at the reassuring sound of the boy's voice.

"It's just a brush."

The bristles trailed pleasantly across the dog's back. And Caesar's shoulders relaxed as he slowly arched his spine to meet the next stroke.

"That's right, buddy. It feels good, doesn't it?"

For the next half hour, Caesar let Tony and then the girl take turns running the brush across his back, chest, and shoulders, undoing the matted snarls in his fur. Relaxed in a way he'd never known, he closed his eyes, slipping into an almost dream state. He snorted contentedly, letting them turn him into various positions so the brush could find new spots to work its magic touch. Then, with Caesar's head resting drowsily in his lap, the boy guided the dog onto his back. With his forepaws splayed, the dog exposed his entire vulnerable underbelly.

But Caesar's eyes flew open in sudden panic. He twisted, attempting to rise, but the dog calmed as the tantalizing bristles of the brush trailed against his furry chest. Then it traveled down to the soft fur of his bell. He chuffed as the boy spoke again.

"Oh yeah. Doesn't that feel good?"

Caesar wiggled on his back like a worm. Loving the touch of the brush, he surrendered to a relaxed, trusting calm.

"What do you say?" Tony paced in front of the baker.

Day seven, and Rico stood in the doorway of the storage room to discuss the dog's future with Tony and Jo.

It had been a roller coaster of emotions for everyone as the glacial sameness in the dog mixed with moments of promise and setbacks. The baker had silently watched the ebbs and flows of progress, his emotions swinging from hopeful, child-like optimism to one of doomed resignation. Despite his attempt to maintain an objective view, the drama drew him in. One minute, the baker could convince himself Tony was right. The dog might have a chance at life as a domesticated family pet. But then he'd worry the animal would forever prove a danger to anyone around him.

The other day had produced perfect examples of those highs and lows. Rico stood in the storage room doorway, watching, awe-struck, as the dog submitted like a puppy to the ministrations of the two kids brushing him. He exposed his underbelly, letting them both push and prod him into various positions to better brush his long, tangled fur. In that moment, the animal acted exactly like the domesticated lap dog Tony insisted he could be.

But less than an hour later, the dog reared back on his haunches, snarling like a wolf at the sight of Tony firing a snowball that hit a tree with a thudding explosion of white powder. Even Tony tensed momentarily at the sight of the dog's eyes on fire and teeth bared in a fierce display of power. The splat of the snowball touched some primal nerve in Caesar, only to be quelled by Tony's calming voice. They didn't discuss it, but the memory lingered in Rico's mind, heightening his sense of impending doom.

"C'mon, Uncle Rico, what do you say? Will you go with me to talk to my parents about keeping Caesar?"

The baker blinked, refocusing his attention on Tony, who'd stopped pacing and dropped cross-legged on the floor, with the dog benignly dropping his big head in the boy's lap.

"I'm sorry, kid. I just don't know."

"What do you mean, you don't know? You've seen how good Caesar can be."

"I won't deny he's better physically, but socially, except for you and maybe Jo, I don't know if it's safe for him to be 'round people. You saw how crazy he got the other day. Jeez, Tony, a damn snowball. He went nuts. I'm sorry, but you just don't know what could trigger him to go off and harm someone."

Tony lowered his head, unsuccessfully trying to keep from crying. The dog, still lying next to Tony, reached up, licking away the tears slowly running down his cheeks.

Rico sighed, nearly as heartbroken as the boy. "I'm sorry, Tony, but I'm gonna call animal rescue tomorrow mornin'. If nothin' else, maybe we can keep him from bein' given back to Al Ridgeway."

"Rico, I need two dozen rolls." A woman's voice followed the tinkling of the front door's bell.

"Customer." Rico couldn't look at Tony, the heartbreak on the boy's face more gut-wrenching than his own. "I gotta go."

"Let's take Caesar for a walk." Jo held the chain they'd used to pull the dog on the sled a week earlier. "We can use this as a leash. No one will see us if we head down toward the marsh and stay away from the park."

Tony followed in numb silence as Jo tied a loop around the collar he'd bought for the dog and, with a gentle prod, she induced Caesar to rise. The dog stretched before calmly following her out the back door of the storage room.

It was a long time before they spoke. The shared failure weighed heavily on both kids until Tony could no longer remain silent.

"You heard him say he planned to call animal rescue. There never was any friend with a farm."

"I know." Jo flicked Caesar's leash, directing the dog to follow the muddy path through the marsh. "I guess he wanted to make it easier on you if you had to . . . well, you know."

"I hate when grown-ups lie like that."

Jo tied Caesar's leash to a tree stump and walked down to the water, picking up flat rocks along the riverbank. Tony followed, and the two soon stood next to the river, skipping rocks across the slow-flowing water.

"Six, seven, eight, I win again," Jo said as she did a little celebratory dance, her clearly forced gaiety doing nothing to take Tony's mind off their failure.

Tony turned away from the river and walked back, searching for stones beneath the fast-melting snow before picking one up near Caesar. A low growl escaped the dog's chest as the frightened animal pulled on his leash, trying to escape.

Tony dropped the stone and looked at Jo as she watched, wide-eyed. "You see that?"

Jo nodded and pointed to a stick on the ground at Tony's feet. "Pick it up."

He bent to grab the stick, and Caesar tensed again, backing away, his eyes locked on the weapon in the boy's hand. Tony immediately let go and fell to his knees while showing his open palms to the wary dog. "I told you I'd never hurt you."

Jo hurried over to the stump and untied the chain, letting the dog walk cautiously toward Tony. After a tentative touch, the animal pressed his head against Tony's chest, demanding the boy's embrace. Tony wrapped his arms around the dog's neck as Caesar burrowed to get closer.

"It all makes sense," Jo said excitedly. "The snowball, the hairbrush, the way he tensed the other day when your uncle stood in the doorway with the broom in his hand. Caesar's afraid of them. He thinks he's going to get beaten. That's why he acted so aggressively. Caesar's just protecting himself, warning us not to hit him."

"Yeah," Tony said, excited about the discovery. But the excitement quickly faded, and he pulled Caesar closer to him, burying his face in the dog's fury chest.

Jo sat beside Tony and joined him in petting the dog. "I go crazy thinking about the cruel things people have done to him."

"Yeah, but if Al Ridgeway and others like him taught Caesar to fear and strike out, we can teach him to trust." Tony stood, grabbed the leash, and gave Caesar a gentle tug. "Come on. We have to talk to my uncle."

The baker sat quietly on a stack of bags of flour in the storage room as Tony and Jo explained what they'd discovered about the triggers to Caesar's aggressive behavior. Tony described his conviction that if Caesar's difficult life taught him to mistrust and strike out in self-defense, he could help the dog unlearn those behaviors. With Jo nodding in agreement, Tony excitedly detailed the positive effect a loving, safe home would have on a dog who'd never experienced a danger-free, nurturing life.

"Look," Tony said, "I'm not blind. I know Caesar's still skittish, and in the wrong situation, he could panic and strike out to protect himself. And I know Caesar's not ready to wander around town."

"That's right. We know it's going to take time." Jo got up to stand beside Tony. "But Caesar was great on the leash. He didn't pull and followed our directions with just a slight tug left or right. We figure we just need to keep Caesar on a leash until he grows more comfortable around strangers."

"Oh, so now it's *we*?" The baker smiled, his gaze going from the boy to the girl, each blushing brightly.

"Well, sure," Jo said with shrug. "Tony knows I'll do whatever I can to help with Caesar."

Rico's smile grew as the two kids exchanged embarrassed glances. "Listen. I can't deny I've seen some remarkable changes in the dog this past week. He's like a different animal in some ways. And I'm willin' to admit there's a chance Tony managed to touch a part of him that was locked away and nearly destroyed by the pain he experienced." The baker shook his head. "But he still has so far to go, and I just don't know if your parents are up for having the house turned upside down."

"It's not my parents," Tony said between clenched teeth. "You're like everyone else. Afraid of my *mother*."

"Damn right, I'm afraid of your mother," the baker said without a hint of embarrassment. "You'd have to be a fool not to be."

Caesar, who'd been sleeping, looked up at Tony. The dog might have snarled at the excited voices a week ago or backed into a corner to guard against a perceived danger. But instead, he stood up and stretched, his nose low to the ground, made several small circles, and dropped back down at the boy's feet. Then he exhaled deeply and closed his eyes, ready to return to sleep.

Rico watched with wide-eyed awe as Tony sat on the floor cross-legged and the dog lifted its massive head to rest in the boy's lap as Tony scratched behind his ear. The changes in the animal from one day to the next continued to amaze him. Maybe he was wrong. Maybe the dog could lead a life as an ordinary family pet. He didn't know, but he owed Tony—owed both of them—the chance to find out.

He cleared his throat. "Listen and listen good 'cause I'm only gonna say this once. That dog still scares the hell out of me, and my instincts tell me it's unsafe for him to be around people he doesn't trust. Think of the danger. You'd have to be on guard all the time. An old guy walkin' down the street with a cane. A neighbor holding a wrench or rake in his hand. Jeez, Tony, the animal could take your father's arm off if he didn't like the way he picked up a hammer."

Tony tried to interrupt, but the baker silenced him with a look. "Let me finish. Okay, I told you all the reasons I think it's a bad idea." Rico stopped and shook his head at the sight of the dog lying peacefully next to Tony. "But I've been watchin' you with the dog. I've seen the changes in Caesar. He's like a different animal when he's with you. But it's not just that. You're different around him."

"That's the first time you've ever called him Caesar. It's always been *the dog* or *that animal*." Tony stopped petting Caesar, who rolled onto his back, showing his belly, hoping for more attention. "Are you saying what I think you're saying?"

Rico raised his hands. "I give up. You're a

natural with Caesar, and like I said, I think he brings somethin' out in you. I figure alls your father's gotta do is see you with the dog, and he'll be on board. Now, your mother . . ." Rico's ran his fingers across the stubble of his chin. "Your mother's a different story."

"But you'll talk to her? To both of them?"

"I'll try."

Tony slipped out from under the resting Caesar and threw his arms around his uncle. The older man, filled with pride, ran a hand through the boy's thick curls, hoping he wasn't setting Tony up for a bigger heartbreak down the road. Jo joined the two, excitedly pounding Tony on the back as she repeatedly shouted a celebratory "Yesss!"

Initially startled by all the activity, Caesar jumped up, the fur high on his back, and moved protectively toward Tony but he relaxed as the joyful celebration continued. Seeing the boy was safe, the dog got pulled into the excitement and joined them—bouncing from side to side, his head bobbing, showing playfulness foreign until now—adding his throaty bark to the celebration.

But Rico had noticed the dog's initial reaction: a taunt body, ready to attack. He held Tony tighter and turned his face away from the kids, silently praying this wasn't a huge mistake.

Tony couldn't stop talking on the way home. He repeatedly thanked Jo for all her help and outlined his plans for Caesar. He had a dog of his very own, and he wasn't going to let anything change that.

They stopped at an intersection halfway up the hill, and Tony fell silent as a dark scowl appeared on his face. He grabbed a flyer nailed to the telephone pole beside them, crumpled it into a tight ball, and threw it into a nearby trashcan.

"Screw Al Ridgeway."

XX

Caesar woke, the fur bristling on his back at the sound of footsteps from above. He rose, as a snarl formed in his throat. Then he remembered: Several days earlier, under cover of darkness, Tony tied a rope to the collar he now wore and led him out of the bakery and onto the dimly lit street. Together with the girl who stood so often by the boy's side, the three walked up the hill, back to the place where Caesar stayed that first night, when he'd escaped from the giant and the muddy river.

Returning to the boy's home, he saw the others who lived there. All three had come down the stairs cautiously, keeping their distance as the boy talked nonstop.

The dog sensed Tony's anxiety, but he saw no immediate danger as the three stood back. And

Caesar grew less wary any time one of them came down the stairs to where he slept. He smelled the fear of the little girl but learned to ignore her quick gestures and chirping voice. The man—although powerfully built and clearly able to inflict great pain if he wished—seemed to always be smiling, and his voice resonated with calm whenever he spoke. The woman stared at the dog with intense dark eyes. But Caesar could see she loved the boy, so he detected no danger when she came near. He rarely saw the woman, but he sensed she would not be displeased to see him gone.

The woman needn't worry. He'd be leaving soon enough because Caesar had found a way out. Last night, while the rest of the house slept, the dog explored every corner of the basement, and he discovered if he walked up the back stairs of the cellar and jumped up on the door to hit the latch with his paw, the door would pop open.

Once outside, the dog stood in the backyard, staring up at the moon, his tongue lolling and nose in the air. He breathed in the freedom awaiting him in the rocky woods behind the house.

He'd stayed that way for a long time, the smell of freedom tempting. But a cold wind cut across his chest, and he remembered the comfort of lying by the boy's side, Tony's hands gently rubbing his fur. Caesar warmed at the memory. He'd grown accustomed to the boy, and the others presented little danger. Maybe he'd stay a while. The dog turned away from the woods, heading back into the house and down the stairs as the door caught in the wind and slammed shut behind him.

Caesar curled up on the blankets Tony had brought him and closed his eyes to rest. Not tonight, but soon. The weather was getting warmer, the snow all but gone as he grew stronger every day.

Soon. He'd leave soon.

Ridgeway sat in his truck, the pistol in his lap and an empty pint bottle of whiskey on the seat beside him. The big man stared up at the moon, hands trembling. His bottle had been empty for nearly an hour, and he needed another drink, badly. But he felt the need to hurt someone, to leave them beaten and bleeding, even more.

Someone had been tearing down his signs offering a reward for info on the dog that he'd hung on telephone poles and the sides of buildings all around town. Ridgeway had spent the night wandering the neighborhood's darkened streets searching for the offender. But as the night grew late, the big man's morose drunkenness became a hunger-filled demon, demanding to be fed.

Ridgeway was mean and violent, but he was no fool. Whenever this urge overtook him, he knew what he must do. Ridgeway drove for twenty minutes to Fields Corner, a neighborhood where he wouldn't be recognized, and parked on a side street off Dorchester Avenue. With bars on every corner, it wouldn't be long before he found his prey. He'd learned long ago to seek out this kind of pleasure far from home, leaving no trail for cops or friends of his victim seeking revenge.

He stepped out of the truck and walked toward the avenue. Closing time—the last remnants of drunken patrons staggering out of the bars in ones and twos. Ridgeway leaned against a mailbox in the shadows of a distant, dimly lit streetlight and pulled the pistol out from under his belt. He caressed the gun like a treasured piece of jewelry, imagining himself a great hunter—hidden patiently by a water hole, knowing his prey must come.

His body tingled, wondering what it must be like to pull the trigger and have the bullet tear into flesh. Ridgeway smiled, imagining the wounded man's hands covered in blood, writhing in agony as he slowly bled out, leaving Ridgeway towering over his victim, staring into the lifeless eyes he'd created. Burning with excitement, the big man shook his head, not tonight. He wanted his first kill to have meaning—vengeance, and punishment for a wrong done to him.

He'd been thinking about killing a lot since he'd gotten the gun, but it would not be tonight. The risk was too great to waste on some stranger. Tonight, to hurt and maim would have to suffice. The big man pushed the gun under his waistband and waited as images of hunting prey inflamed his mind.

A lone figure walked unsteadily toward him. The drunk stumbled forward, staring at the ground, as if worried it might disappear beneath his feet.

"Hey, pal, you got a light?" Ridgeway stood shrouded in darkness, an unlit cigarette dangling from the corner of his mouth.

The drunk looked up at the giant and offered a glassy-eyed grin before nodding and looking down again as he fumbled, reaching into his pocket. He never saw the ham-sized fist that caught him square on the chin, shattering his jaw.

The drunk fell to the ground in a clump, disappointing Ridgeway. He'd planned to pin his prey against the mailbox, pummeling away while seeing the man's battered face morph with each blow into an unrecognizable bloody pulp. But the guy dropped like a stone.

So instead, with the drunk curled in the fetal position, Ridgeway delivered a series of vicious kicks to the man's ribcage with his steel-toed boots. But the kicks didn't satisfy his bloodlust. Ridgeway spat on the fallen man and cursed him for dropping so quickly. He'd been denied the feel of flesh and bone crushing under his fist that he loved so much.

Ridgeway bent over to pick the drunk up and pinned him against the mailbox, poised to give a proper beating. But the sound of laughter, as a noisy group left the bar and walked toward them, ruined his plan. Ridgeway released his grip, and the drunk pitched forward, his head slamming off the side-walk with a crack. The big man sneered at the crumbled mass at his feet, delivered one final kick to the ribcage, and disappeared into the shadows.

As he walked, Ridgeway cursed, and his hand traced the pistol handle tucked under his belt. These beatings weren't as rewarding as they'd once been, and his churning gut told him he needed much more. He owed others a payback for besting him, embarrassing him.

The big man started the truck, his trembling hands tightening around the steering wheel as he drove through the dark city streets—his burning rage unfulfilled

Yes, there were others Al Ridgeway needed to hurt.

XXI

Tony feared his time may be running out. Despite all the cajoling from the baker and Tony's father, his mother initially had remained adamantly opposed to letting the dog stay with them. Carla Miracolo didn't relent until she heard the details of how badly Ridgeway treated the animal and how desperately the man wanted the dog back. Tony watched silently, letting the baker take the lead as his mother's jaw tightened, her eyes taking on the smoldering look that could put fear in the bravest souls. Tony knew, as hard as his mother could be, she couldn't let a bully mistreat a helpless animal.

Finally, his mother had conceded to let him "temporarily" keep the dog, but with a seemingly endless list of conditions. The dog was not permitted anywhere in the house but in the cellar. Tony's sister, Rosa, was not allowed near the dog.

The dog was not allowed anywhere outside except in their backyard, and then only after dark.

His mother said, with matriarchal finality, "We don't need the police or a drunken Al Ridgeway showing up at our door, demanding the dog back."

Tony nodded in agreement to each demand, barely listening through his excitement and deaf to the word *temporary* that his mother continually repeated.

He had a dog, his dog.

But with each passing day, his mother's mood grew more foreboding. She barely looked at Caesar, and Tony worried it was only a matter of time before she followed through on her threat and forced Tony "to find the dog a permanent home."

Tony and Jo met in the cellar that night, as they had every night since Caesar's arrival. The weather had turned, early spring offering a teasing hint of the coming summer months. Tony grabbed the length of rope he'd been using as a leash, tied it to Caesar's collar, and they set off into the woods.

"Are you sure this is a good idea?" Jo asked. "You know what your mother said about him not leaving the yard."

"My mom and dad went over to my Aunt Flavia's to play cards, and they took Rosa with them. They won't be back for hours." Tony looked up at the tree branches, popping with buds as they swayed in the gentle breeze, and exhaled deeply. Who knew how long he had with the dog? "Caesar's been locked up or chained his whole life. He deserves to get out a bit. Besides, no one's in the woods at night except older kids drinking beer.

We'll turn back if we hear anybody."

Tony lengthened his hold, giving Caesar additional rope, and the dog raced ahead, darting left and right, sniffing, as he excitedly marked spots.

"Well, he sure is enjoying himself, and I guess he needs to exercise that leg." Jo studied the dog, outlined against the moonlight, as he ran ahead, his left hind leg not fully extending, causing an awkward three-quarter stride. "He's moving better, and he's gained weight. I can't see his ribs anymore, but his leg's still not quite right."

"He's perfect," Tony said, his angry voice carrying through the woods.

"There you go again."

"What? Where am I going?" Tony tugged on the leash, reigning Caesar in as he turned to glare at Jo.

"You see everything as black and white. There's never any gray or room to compromise, and you're ready to turn any difference of opinion into a reason to fight."

"That's not true."

Jo frowned. "Look at yourself. Hands clenched, chin stuck out, and you've got those scary eyes, just like your mother's."

Tony pulled in his chin as he looked down at his hands, clenched by his side. He blinked several times, hoping to wash away the crazy eyes as his lips slowly turned up into a sad smile of surrender.

"I guess you're right. I never thought much about any of this until I started hanging out with you. But now I'm trying not to get in fights where even if I win, I lose." Tony looked away, giving

Caesars's leash another gentle tug. "I try, but I can't be like you."

"You don't want to be like me," Jo said. "Believe me."

"Oh, but I do. You're smart, diplomatic, and patient. Now *me*, I guess I've got some smarts. You showed me that. But I come up a little empty in the patience and diplomacy departments."

"Well, that's all true, but you make up for it by being the most stubborn boy I've ever met," Jo said with a giggle as she turned to run back toward the house.

Tony laughed, the conversation and sight of his friend racing through woods taking his mind off his fears about his mother's mistrust of Caesar. He flicked the dog's leash again, signaling the dog to follow them. But Caesar stopped, squaring his shoulders, the fur rising on his back as he stared off into the distance. Tony tugged harder.

"Come on, boy, there's nothing there."

That afternoon, unable to finish rebuilding an already two-day overdue truck transmission, Ridgeway argued with the truck owner—a barrel-chested bricklayer with two big-boned sons. Badly needing a drink, he turned his back on the three, promising to finish the job by noon the next day.

Ridgeway woke several hours later with a brain-searing headache and an empty bottle by his side. Stumbling from his couch, Ridgeway cracked open a fresh pint bottle and headed toward his truck. He drove around town, the bottle by his side, cursing and drinking, looking for anyone tearing down his flyers. After over an hour, he found himself at the far end of the church parking lot and stopped next to the entrance to a winding, wooded trail that led to the rocky heights overlooking the neighborhood. He grabbed his bottle and hiked for ten minutes before arriving at the base of a large rock formation at the high point of the woods.

Ridgeway pulled out the pint bottle from his back pocket, staring at the near empty bottle, and took a short tug. He should have smashed the bricklayer's face when the bastard got mouthy. But something held him back. The old AL Ridgeway would have hauled off and cold-cocked the SOB, then turned to the sons before they could move and said, "Who's next?" But he'd lost his edge and begun overthinking things. *What if the bricklayer didn't go down on the first punch? What if the sons didn't back down and both came after me?*

He turned to climb up the largest rock that looked down on his childhood home. As a teenager, he'd sit alone on the rocks, late at night, with a six-pack of beer, remembering what life had been like when he lived in the fancy house with its fancy lace curtains. When drunk enough, the young Ridgeway would sneak down from the hillside to set the trash cans on fire or bust a few of the house's ornate stained-glass windows before disappearing back up the hill into the woods. The teenager would giggle with childish delight over the high-pitched shrieks of his old-maid aunts, as they woke in a panic at his latest stunt.

Ridgeway lit a cigarette and held the burning match until it flamed out refusing to surrender to the searing pain in his fingers. He had few memories of his father, but he had one clear recollection of the man sternly chastising him for crying when he'd fallen as a boy and scraped his knee. Staring disdainfully, his father slapped him across the face, telling young Al to stop bawling. His father said if the boy learned nothing else in life, he must remember if something doesn't kill you, it only makes you stronger. Remembering that day— Ridgeway trailed his scorched fingers across his cheek, as if to feel the sting of the long-ago slap. When the business went sour, his coward father had swallowed his own gun before the boy's tenth birthday.

Ridgeway closed his eyes, trying to chase away the demons. After being outsmarted by competitors and bankers, Ridgeway's father left his family to the mercy of those same bankers and the hated aunts, who threw young Al and his mother out on the street.

Well, he wouldn't take the coward's way out. He was nothing like his father. He would use the pain in his life, and unlike his weakling fool of an old man, it would make him stronger. Ridgeway had vowed to remember all those who'd ever hurt him and to get even with them all.

As a teenager, he'd fantasized about burning the old house to the ground. But he was younger then, and hate hadn't settled in his bones like the old friend that now followed him everywhere. Ridgeway took another drag on the cigarette and exhaled, making small smoke rings he poked at with his finger. His aunts were lucky they were gone because the thought of setting the house ablaze to leave the selfish old hags crying in the dark as they vainly searched for a way out didn't seem so unimaginable anymore.

He lit a fresh cigarette off the one he was smoking and flicked the butt into the woods, where it hissed on a clump of wet leaves.

"Sons of bitches, I'll get 'em."

Ridgeway didn't realize he'd spoken the words out loud, and if asked, he couldn't say whom he meant by *them*. The loudmouthed bricklayer? The bankers and lawyers who had forced him and his mother to move out of his childhood home? The kids and that damn dog who'd bested him, causing this haunting self-doubt?

All of them. He'd get even with all of them.

Ridgeway reached into his pocket and lifted his head to empty the bottle. As the whiskey burned in his belly, three dark shadows moved below in the yard next to his childhood home, but they were gone when he looked back down. He rubbed his eyes. He could have sworn he saw something moving across the lawn in the moonlight.

The big man stood with a growl and threw the bottle, watching as it shattered on the rocks below. That damn dog and those punk kids had stolen his edge, and the embarrassing memory of that day burned in his gut hotter than the whiskey. He nodded as an anger-fueled resolution warmed him. He had to find the kids. Administering the pain would begin with them.

Only then could Ridgeway be whole again—invincible and feared by all.

XXII

"**W**ell, hello, strangers." Rico De Santo pointed a rolling pin back and forth, threatening Tony and Jo in mock anger. "What, you get a dog and forget about your old friends?"

Tony, looking embarrassed, said, "Sorry, Zio, I really have been very busy with Caesar. We got out of school an hour early to go to confession because Easter's on Sunday. So, we figured we'd stop off for a quick visit before heading home."

The baker noticed a subtle exchange between the two young people, and Tony gave Jo a quick *Don't go there* shake of the head.

"Problems?"

Tony stared down at the ground, but a sharp elbow in the ribs from Jo brought him upright.

"Go ahead and tell him."

"It's nothing," Tony said, his eyes back on the

ground. "It's just that Caesar still gets all squirrelly when people go down to the cellar, and he won't let anyone near him other than me or sometimes Jo." Tony shook his head. "My mother keeps saying spending twenty-three hours a day locked up in a dark basement is no fit life for a dog."

"She's not wrong. Is she talkin' 'bout callin' animal rescue?"

"Not yet, but she keeps mumbling about needing to find a permanent home for him. But he's got a permanent home."

"And what about your father?"

"Pop's Pop. Patient, as always. He lets my mom talk, but Caesar still scares him, and he won't let Rosa near the dog. He caught her trying to sneak down to the basement early one morning and went crazy. You know he's never raised a hand to either of us, but he grabbed Rosa's by the ear and hauled her upstairs, swearing if he caught her down there again, she'd get the beating of a lifetime. And my mother stood there in the kitchen, her arms folded across her chest, with that *I told you so* look of hers. Pop got mad and said, 'Not a word, Carla. We told the boy we'd give him some time, and that's what we're gonna do.'"

"Wow."

"Yeah. I'd never seen Pop get mad at my mom like that before. She didn't say a word the rest of the morning, and now Pop's being extra nice to her."

"Wise man, your father," the baker said with a wry smile.

"I guess," Tony said, seeming unable to see the humor. "Alls I know is, she won't give up, and if I can't find a way to get through to Caesar."

"Relax," the baker said. "Don't let your mind get ahead of you. You two," Rico gave a generous nod toward Jo, "have accomplished a lot with Caesar. A lot more than I ever imagined possible, and your father sees it, too."

"You've been talking to my father?"

The baker smiled. "Let's say we've been checkin' in with each other a bit. But Anthony didn't tell me about his little conversation with your mother. He probably surprised himself with that one." Rico's smile grew wider, imagining the easygoing Anthony Miracolo drawing a line against his indomitable wife. "Just know, your father's in your corner with this, and he'll help with your mother. We both will."

Tony looked ready to jump over the counter and hug his uncle. "I don't know what to say."

"There's nothin' to say. You and Jo did a wonderful thing, savin' that dog. But I'm afraid you still have a tough road ahead."

"I know," Tony said, turning away and pacing as he spoke. "I'm just not sure what to do. Caesar is still anxious around my family and goes all weird whenever someone picks up anything that looks like they could hit him with. Ridgeway treated him so cruelly that now I can't get him to trust or relax around other people."

"You're makin' more progress than you think, and your father's spendin' more time with Caesar than you know. He said he got up the other night and went down to the cellar to sit with Caesar for over an hour. He didn't try to pet the dog. I don't think either of 'em is ready for that." The baker snickered, picturing his friend sitting anxiously with the animal. "But he told me he senses somethin' in the dog. Gentleness, and a desire to trust that's achin' to find a way out."

"So, Pop sees it, too," Tony said. "I just worry being around Ridgway and living the ugly life he's led has scarred Caesar in places I can't reach."

"Ridgway beat Caesar, but he never broke the dog's spirit. Tony, I see a spark in him whenever he's near you, and now you have to help Caesar make that the difference between him and Al Ridgway. That man had a tough life, but he let it rot him from the inside. Don't let the ugly things that happened to Caesar define what he can be."

The baker paused. "He can't do it alone. It's gonna get harder, and I can't guarantee a happy endin'. But if you two are up for the challenge, I think, between your father and me, we can buy you enough time with your mom to give Caesar a fightin' chance at a normal life."

"I'll do *whatever* it takes."

"I know you will, kid. . . . Now, I made some cannoli for Easter," Rico said, trying to lighten the mood in the room as he reached into the display case and pushed two sausage-shaped pastries across the counter at the kids. "Here. Taste."

"What's cannoli?" Jo craned her neck, eyeing the treats.

"It's an Italian pastry," Tony said, seeming happy for the distraction, "and one of Uncle Rico's specialties."

"Technically, it's Sicilian," the baker said, taking

on his *lesson time* professorial voice. "But nowadays, every Neapolitan and Calabrese bakery in the city sells 'em, and the sons of bitches act like they invented the goddamn things." He threw a hand over his mouth. "Sorry, gotta watch my language."

Tony laughed. "Zio Rico always says we're Sicilian first, then Italian. But today, around here, if your name ends in a vowel and you look like I do, we all get lumped in the same basket."

Jo grabbed the pastry, appearing more interested in tasting the treat than the history of the amalgamation of Italian immigrants in America, and took a small bite.

"Delicious," she mumbled, then greedily took a bigger bite. Using her free hand, she caught a bit of the flaky hard shell before it fell to the ground, bringing it back to her already full mouth.

Tony and the baker nodded their approval as they took generous bites of their pastries. The cannoli tasted sweet but not cloyingly, the filling rich, creamy, and smooth, with a slight cheesy flavor. The hard crust's subtly sweet taste tickled Rico's tongue before the crispy tube broke away, releasing more of the ricotta filling.

After a second bite, Rico swallowed hard and said, "Know what we need to wash this down?"

"Milk," Tony said, with his head bobbing in agreement as he eyed another bite.

The baker pointed toward a set of stairs across from the storage room. "Jo, can you grab some? Upstairs, the kitchen's down the end of the hall. I wanna talk to my nephew for a minute."

Jo hurried up the stairs, curious to see the apartment she'd only heard about until now. She pushed open the door and walked down the hall to the kitchen of the baker's small place. Exactly like Tony had described, books lay everywhere, lining the shelves and windowsills. Jo smiled as her fingers traced the eclectic authors stacked on the counter beside the refrigerator: Tolstoy, Dostoevsky, Nietzsche, and Machiavelli. Now she understood how the self-taught man could speak intelligently on untold topics while still butchering the king's English.

Jo got a milk bottle from the refrigerator, set it on the countertop, and opened the cupboard to look for glasses. She laughed, finding the bottom two shelves filled with more books. She grabbed a stepstool from beneath the sink and, reaching in blindly, took several glasses from the top shelf. As Jo drew the last glass out, she knocked something off the shelf that fell to the ground with a crash, glass shattering as it hit the floor.

Cursing her clumsiness, she knelt to pick up a small picture frame with fresh, jagged cracks across the front. She studied the yellowing picture, her thumb carefully tracing the face of a young man, smiling as if he had a great secret he wanted to share. He leaned against a vintage car, his foot raised casually on the running board in front of the De Santo Bakery. His right arm rested comfortably around a pretty girl about the same age, who wore an expression much too severe for someone so young. The boy had a bushy mop of curly dark hair, a devilishly crooked smile, and eyes that seemed to stare right back at Jo through the camera's lens.

Jo grinned. She knew those eyes and the crooked smile. It was amazing. Tony looked exactly like his father did at that age. Then, cursing her clumsiness, Jo walked over to a garbage bin, removed the photo from the shattered frame, and placed the glass shards safely into the trash.

With the frame gone, Jo noticed writing on the back of the picture. She squinted, trying to read the faded inscription, wondering how old Mr. and Mrs. Miracolo were in the photo.

Jo's hands trembled, and her breath came short as she saw the writing on the back of the photo:

RICO AND CARLA, 1942

"I thought I'd give you a hand. Everythin' okay?" Rico De Santo stood in the doorway to the kitchen, his smile quickly disappearing.

"What's that?" Rico said, pointing at the photograph in Jo's hand. "You goin' through my personal things?"

"No. . . . I mean . . . It just . . . fell."

"You had no right!" The mild-mannered baker was shouting now.

"It's just a picture." But even as she said the words, the panicked look on the baker's face told Jo it was much more. Why else would he be so upset? She looked at the photograph again, the boy's face so much like Tony's, then into Rico's fiery eyes. *Those eyes.*

It all made sense. The special bond between

Tony and the baker. The way Tony said his mother would listen to Rico De Santo when no one else could get through to her.

Rico stood there, his look of anger replaced by one of creeping panic. "Please . . ."

"Please, what? Does Tony know?" Even as Jo said the words, she thought she must be crazy, but the baker's look of complete surrender told a different story.

"No, and he never can." Rico reached out, but Jo, clutching the photo, rushed past him and down the stairs.

"Where's the milk?" Tony said, looking up from his cannoli.

"I gotta go."

"Okay," Tony said, jumping off the stool to follow.

"No, you stay. I just forgot I'm supposed to watch Frank Junior. I'm gonna be too busy to hang out anyway."

She grabbed her coat from a hook on the wall and sped past him out the door as a flustered Rico came down the stairs holding two glasses of milk.

"What's wrong with Jo?" Tony said, turning from the baker to glimpse the fast-disappearing girl as she flew out the bakery door. "I thought I heard shouting."

"Nothin'." Trying to steady his trembling hand, Rico placed a glass of milk on the counter in front of Tony. "She just broke a piece of china, and she's embarrassed."

Tony pushed himself away from the counter. "Well, that's dumb, but I better catch up with her. She might wanna talk."

Rico grabbed Tony's arm, holding him back. "No, I think she needs to be alone."

Tony shrugged. After a lifetime of living with his mother, the boy probably understood that a woman needed to be alone at times. "You're sure she's okay?"

"She's fine. Everythin's fine," the baker said as he turned away, looking out onto the busy street.

But everything wasn't fine. Jo had discovered a secret that could destroy the boy they all loved.

XXIII

MIRIAM

I heard a yelp and looked down at my feet to see a sleeping Jules, his paws twitching, as if running from some imagined predator.

AJ reached down to run his hand along the dog's side, and Jules slipped back to sleep with a slow harrumph.

"Wow, that would be a gut punch," I said, thinking of young Tony Miracolo and imagining what a discovery like that could do to a fourteen-year-old kid's psyche. "So, I guess no one's life is quite what it seems, and everyone fails you sooner or later. I always thought my father loved me, but in the end, he left when my mother's nagging got to be too much for him."

"Did he?"

"What?"

"Your father, did he leave you?"

"Well, we're twenty-five hundred miles apart," I said, my voice rising. "So yeah, I'd say he left me."

"Close your eyes."

I hesitated.

"Go ahead, close your eyes." AJ placed a calloused hand on mine.

Conceding, I sighed and closed my eyes.

"Imagine a happy time, a time when you are at peace, safe, and loved. . . . Okay, who's there?"

I sat there as memories of happier times flashed through my mind and lowered my head as a solitary tear ran down my cheek. "My father. He's in every happy memory I have."

AJ nodded. "So, he never left you. He's with you now. That's how it is for all of us."

I wiped away the tear, not sure I believed him but too sad to argue and not ready to explore the pain in my own life. "So, what happens to our hero?"

"Oh, you're right. Life's no fairy tale. He and Caesar have some rough times ahead. Now sit back and listen."

XXIV

The boy had been gone a long time, and Caesar prowled the basement uneasily. Being locked in this dark space made him fretful, and Tony's long absence only heightened those feelings.

Maybe it was time to go. To set out on his own, away from all humans. Caesar might miss the boy, but he'd be safe in the open and able to protect himself against any aggressor. He'd grown stronger each day, and the ugly sore on his hindquarters had healed. Caesar could no longer smell the sickness in his leg. But he felt anxious now as thoughts of the boy's kindness—mixed with his distrust of humans and his drive to be free—left him confused and no closer to a decision.

The door opened, and the little girl stood on the stairs, holding a shiny stick in her hand. Memories of being beaten by the giant with his thick club came rushing back to the dog, making his heart race, and he stood up, backing into the corner.

"Hi, Caesar. Mom's busy gabbin' on the phone with Mrs. Trocki and didn't see me sneak down here, so we can hang out awhile." The girl walked down the stairs to stand a few feet from the dog and smiled nervously. "Mom and Dad don't want me coming down here, but if you're gonna be a part of the family, we need to get to know each other."

Caesars squared his shoulders, intently watching the girl. He hadn't spent much time around her, but he liked how the little girl smelled and how her voice always sounded so happy. But her rapid movements and nervous energy could make him uneasy. He held his head high, not liking the stick she clutched in her hand.

The girl seemed to notice. "Oh, don't worry about this. It's just my baton. Look what I can do."

She stepped back and spun the stick between her fingers, then threw it in the air before dropping to one knee to catch it. But the baton hit the ceiling and clattered to the floor in front of Caesar, who jumped back, panicked, and snarled at the stick.

"Get away from her!"

Caesar looked up to find the girl's mother standing on the stairs, waving a long stick with bristles on the end. The stick looked like one the dog had seen the baker pushing across the floor of his shop. The baker never came near Caesar when he held it and always moved cautiously, but the animal had learned long ago, humans could use almost anything as a weapon.

A low growl formed in the dog's throat, and his

ears lay flat against his head, waiting for the inevitable blow. He wouldn't attack, but he arched his shoulder, fur up on his back, ready to defend.

"Mommy don't hurt him. I scared him with the baton."

Caesar recognized the little girl's fear and looked at the woman, holding the stick out as if to defend the child. He stared into the woman's eyes and saw only a desire to protect her loved one.

The fur on his shoulders relaxed. He'd never hurt ones such as these.

But he made his decision.

The dog spun away and ran up the stairs at the back of the house. He jumped up, his paw hitting the latch several times until the door popped open. Pushing through, he raced across the yard and into the rocky wooded hillside behind the house.

As he ran, he heard the mournful callings of the little girl. "Caesar, come back!"

He ignored the cries. It was time to go.

In the woods, he stopped and marked several trees, enjoying the freedom and sense of power.

He might miss Tony and his gentle touch, but it was best to be away from humans. The painful memories of the giant and the men who'd cheered and screamed as the dog fought in the cage too hauntingly vivid to forget. The kindness of one young boy hadn't washed away the ugly scars.

Caesar moved deeper into the woods, his nostrils flaring with the scent of freedom.

When Jo arrived home from the bakery she took a deep breath, relieved to find her mother on the phone and not sitting in the kitchen drinking coffee with Mrs. Miracolo, as they often did. The last thing she needed was to see Tony's mother.

"I don't blame you, Carla, for hating having that animal in the house. You're right, that dog just can't be trusted around kids—Oh, hi, honey. You're back early."

Jo mumbled a hello and ran upstairs to hide the picture. She returned and grabbed Frank Junior from his highchair, where he sat, pushing Cheerios into his mouth. She picked up her brother and, without making eye contact with her mother, offered to take the baby for a walk.

"Thanks, hon. . . . Okay, Carla, I'll let you go check on Rosa. We'll talk later." Her mother hung up from her conversation as Jo hurried out of the house, pushing Frank Junior in his carriage.

It was a beautiful early spring afternoon, with high white clouds and temperatures topping sixty, but Jo couldn't enjoy the warm sun and clear blue skies. With her hands tightly clutching the handle, she pushed the carriage down the street, eyes wide, alert for Tony's arrival. She didn't have a clue what to do. Could she keep this secret to herself? Didn't he deserve to know the truth?

Cries came from Tony's house, and Jo, pushing the baby carriage, rushed into her neighbor's backyard where Rosa stood, franticly calling into the woods for the dog.

"Caesar," Jo said, the name catching in her throat.

"We scared him." Rosa stood crying staring into the woods. "It's all my fault. I was showing off and spinning my baton, and he thought I was gonna hit him." Rosa stopped and wiped away her tears before turning an accusatory eye toward her mother. "And then *she* started waving that broom, and Caesar just freaked out. He broke out through the back door and took off."

Tony ran into the backyard, out of breath. "What happened? I heard all the shouting from down the street." He listened anxiously as Rosa retold her story. He hugged his sister, telling her it was all right, but refused to look at his mother, who stood a few feet away, the broom still in her hand.

"He's only been gone a couple of minutes," Jo said. "Let me bring Frank Junior home, and we can look for him."

"I'm heading out now," Tony said, pointing toward the woods. "Catch up with me." He turned away and ran, still refusing to look at his mother and ignoring his sister's repeated cries of "I'm sorry."

"Save your apologies for your father when we tell him what you did. You know you weren't allowed downstairs with that dog." Carla Miracolo walked past her daughter to place her hand on Jo's shoulder. "I'll take the baby home. Help my boy, please."

Jo's body tensed at the women's touch, unable to look at her, and spun away, racing after Tony.

The kids searched the woods and worked their

way down the Heights, past rows of houses to the factory and playground, and finally down to the riverbank, where they'd saved Caesar only a few weeks earlier.

"My mother never wanted him in the first place. I bet she did it on purpose. Scared him and made him run away."

"We'll find him. I know we will," Jo said as panicked memories of Caesar nearly drowning in the river rushed back to her.

They headed back from the marsh and stopped in front of the stone entrance to the park.

"Let's check with Uncle Rico. Caesar spent a week there. Maybe he went back," Tony said, pointing farther down the street at the bakery.

"Nah." Jo struggled to control her nerves. She hadn't decided if she had the right to keep his parents' secret from Tony, but she needed to be alone when she returned to face the man who'd been lying to her friend all his life. "Let's check out the back of the diner. I bet the trash is filled with food. If he's hungry, he might've gone there."

"Good idea, and we go right past the bakery on the way."

"I really think that's a waste of time," Jo said, stammering.

Tony stopped and stared at her, a quizzical look on his face. "That doesn't make sense. We go *right past* the bakery."

The sound of a faint whistle saved her. "Your father."

"I know," Tony said, choking on the words.

"You better go. I'll stop off at the bakery. I can

check out the diner after that. My dad won't be home from work for another hour, so I have time. I'll call and let you know if I find anything."

Jo watched Tony walk away, his hands buried in his pockets, and head hung low. She waited until he turned the corner before heading toward the bakery. Jo found the front door to the shop locked, and a closed sign hung in the window. After knocking several times, she stepped back and looked up. A dim light glimmered softly from the window of the second-floor apartment. But no one stirred.

Tony had told her the baker rarely went out and spent his free time reading after work in his small apartment. She returned to knocking loudly on the door until Mr. Caputo, the old cobbler, shuffled by on his way back to his shop. Embarrassed, Jo shrugged, saying, "I guess he went shopping."

She tucked her head and turned, walking toward the diner. Maybe it was her imagination, but as she looked back, Jo could have sworn she saw the curtains in the second-floor apartment flutter.

XXV

Caesar's stomach growled. He knew that feeling. Hunger. His nostrils flared as he lifted his snout in the air. Food nearby. The rising sun glistening on the slow-flowing river signaled the start of a new day. Caesar turned from the riverbank and headed toward the narrow alleys separating the shops. He had to find food quickly before the men came out to start their day. The dog had barely seen a human since last night's sunset, and experience taught him to stay out of sight. No humans meant no beatings, no rocks, no sticks, and no pain. After running away from the frightened woman waving the stick, he'd kept off the streets, hidden in the woods near Tony's house. Then, when it got dark, he moved down the hill and drank from the river before lying in the tall grass to sleep along the riverbank.

Yesterday, he'd heard the boy and the girl calling

for him, and his tail wagged at the welcoming sound. But he moved away from them, deeper into the woods. He'd made up his mind.

Now, his nostrils quivered as his nose led him toward an alley with trash cans lined up behind a building. Caesar jumped up, landing on a barrel with his front paws, and it toppled with a clatter. The dog jumped back, startled, and checked to see if the noise attracted anyone before approaching the spilled contents. He pawed at the pile, tearing open a bag finding tiny bits of meat and much larger chunks of vegetables jumbled together. With another quick check to ensure he was alone, Caesar lowered his head, devouring the food. His stomach full, the dog walked to the back of the alley to drink from a large puddle formed from the last remnants of a fast-shrinking snow pile.

He heard footsteps on the street and smelled the city coming to life. An old woman hobbled by, pushing a small cart. Time to get away. He trotted out of the alley and up the hill, back toward the woods and safety.

With the ache in his stomach gone and his thirst quenched, Caesar should have been content. But he felt an emptiness. Something was missing. Near the top of the hill, he raised his snout, sniffing the early morning air as his body imagined an unseen touch.

The dog followed the scent to the front of a large building, where a flag rippled in the wind on a pole high above his head. Tony's scent was strong here, and Caesar wondered if he would ever see him again. The dog didn't know what brought the boy here, but Caesar could tell he'd come often and had been to this place recently. With his nose trailing along the ground the dog climbed up the stairs at the front of the building where he could smell many different visitors. But Tony's scent was distinct.

Caesar paused, looking around. Instinct told him to go and hide, but something kept him frozen. He dropped down on all fours and lay on the large stone landing at the top of the stairs. With his head resting on his paws, he closed his eyes and slept, dreaming of the boy.

The ringing pulled Ridgeway out of a fitful sleep. He stumbled from the couch, sending an empty whiskey bottle skittering across the floor as he grabbed the phone from the kitchen wall.

"What?!"

"Al, it's me, Charley."

"What do you want?" Ridgeway shook his head, trying to clear his clouded brain. "I fired your ass weeks ago."

"Yeah, well, we can talk about that, but first, are ya still innerested in findin' that dog?"

"Wait a minute." The big man put the phone on the counter and stuck his head under the kitchen faucet. Wiping his face on a dirty towel, he picked the phone back up. "You saw the mutt?"

"Yeah, and listen, ya can keep the fifty bucks. I just need my job back. Whata'ya say?"

"If the info's good, we can talk about the job. Now, where'd you see it?"

"Deal, and the info's rock-solid. I was just

drivin' from my girl's place, and I spotted him sittin' on the front steps of the school, like he was waitin' for the mornin' bell. I was gonna try and get 'em but figured you'd wanna grab 'em yourself. Listen, 'bout the job—"

Ridgeway hung up and grabbed his keys, his head suddenly clear with visions of the beating he'd give the dog when he got his hands on him.

Tony and Jo walked toward the school. He kept looking over his shoulder back at his house. Last night's dinner had been tense. Rosa kept crying, even though she'd avoided her mother's promised punishment. Tony's father brooded silently, poking at his food, while his mother came as close as she could to apologizing for scaring Caesar into running away. But she remained firm in her position. The animal could never be a family pet, and his escape, although unfortunate, had probably been for the best. Tony barely said two words, listening in sullen silence as his mother warned him to not even think about trying to sneak out or skip school to search for the dog, but she'd agreed he could head out early in the morning, as long as he got to school on time.

"She's still watching," Tony said, burying his hands in his pockets.

"Yeah," Jo said, peeking back at the Miracolo's kitchen window.

"She's never trusted me." Tony sighed, looking at Jo, who quickly averted her eyes. "Thanks for getting up early. I told my mom we're gonna leave our book bags at school before we go looking for Caesar, but there she is at the window, checking on me. Jeez, we only got a half day cause it's Good Friday. I promised her I wouldn't skip school, and she still's there checking on me."

"Forget about your mother. If we hurry, we can make it down to the marsh and still have time to check the trash cans in the alleys behind the diner and the movie theater and get back up to school before they ring the bell."

Jo's voice sounded strained, and Tony patted her on the shoulder, touched by how hard she'd taken Caesar's disappearance. "He'll be fine. I know he will," Tony said, trying to mask his own panicked doubts. "And my father said he'd finish work early today so he could drive me around looking after school."

Jo stared at the ground as Tony, deep in thought, walked by her side. A truck sped by, but neither noticed the big man behind the wheel.

Ridgeway slowed as he approached the school and pulled his truck into the parking lot behind the building. He didn't need some dog lover calling the cops on him. The big man intended to grab the dog quickly and get out of there. Once he had the mutt back at his shop, he could take his sweet time teaching the animal the lesson of a lifetime.

As he drove into the school parking lot, Ridgeway spotted a sour-faced old nun clapping erasers together, the chalk powder making her alabaster skin even whiter. He smiled a cruel smile. The pasty-white nun looked like one of the bloodless corpses from his fantasies.

Ridgeway reached toward his belt and cursed, remembering in his haste, he'd left his gun at the shop. No problem. He didn't plan on killing the mutt. At least not right away. The big man reached under the seat and pulled out a sawed-off baseball bat and a length of rope with a wide noose, perfect for choking the dog out. All it would take was one solid whack on the side of the head to stun the dog and then cut off his oxygen with the noose. By the time the bastard woke, he'd have the mutt chained and muzzled at the shop. Ridgeway's heart pounded in his chest. This was gonna be fun.

XXVI

"Caesar!"

The dog raised his head, squinting into the bright sun, and his tail swished wildly. He jumped up to run to the boy who raced toward him.

The dog flew across the ground. The only flaw in the powerful animal's body was a slight hitch in his stride from a hind leg that would never be entirely right. That hitch and the scars on Caesar's face and shoulders were haunting vestiges of the painful life he'd led. But something had changed in Caesar. His time with Tony had opened the door to another world. A world of goodness and love.

With one final bound, Caesar jumped on Tony, knocking the boy over, pinning him to the ground and madly licking his face. Then, closing his eyes, he pressed his head against Tony's chest as the dog's long torso wiggled back and forth like a salmon swimming upstream.

"I found you. I found you."

Caesar got lost in Tony's arms, pressing against the boy's chest, demanding the embrace he'd missed—the embrace he'd grown to love. Tony tried to rise, but Caesar grabbed the boy's sleeve with his powerful jaw and pulled him to the ground to play as Tony buried his face in the dense fur of the dog's neck. He lay on top of Tony, his broad chest and heavy forelegs keeping the giggling boy pinned to the ground as the girl knelt beside them to wrap her arms around the dog's muscled shoulders.

Caesar tensed for a moment, then relaxed. Jo had been there since the beginning, helping him escape from the giant and saving him from the muddy river. Tony had taught him that other humans could be kind, too. Caesar licked Tony's face as the girl held the dog tighter, brushing her cheek against his chest.

"Hey, you punks, get away from the dog."

Startled, Caesar jumped off Tony and growled, his forepaws spread wide, hackles spiked, and head held high as the giant lumbered toward them, the familiar scent of the man—alcohol, tobacco, and sour sweat—bringing all the scar-filled memories of his past life rushing back to him. But Caesar smelled something more, the evil in the man, trying to separate Caesar from the boy he'd learned to love.

The dog's trained-fighter mind cautioned him to be patient and not run headlong at the man who'd caused him so much pain. But Caesar's bloodlust tempted him to attack. A heavy growl grew in his chest as he fought to suppress his rage. With his body tensed, the dog considered the distance, preparing for any trick as his foe moved closer.

"You can't have him. He's mine!" Tony ran straight at Ridgeway, only to be swatted away by a massive backhand that sent the boy sprawling. Stunned, with blood smeared across his nose and mouth, Tony lay face first on the ground.

Jo screamed, a sound of fear and anger, as she rushed to Tony and the dog let out a beastly howl. Blind with fury, he bounded toward Ridgeway, but Caesar veered away at the last moment. He circled behind the big man and pulled up ten feet from him, forcing his foe to pivot.

Yes, Caesar had learned his lessons well, none more clearly than the ones administered daily at the hands of the giant. Moments before leaping to mindlessly attack, Caesar realized Ridgeway was holding a hand behind his back. And he smelled no fear in the man, just a hunger to strike.

Such confidence could mean only one thing. The man had a weapon.

When Caesar was a young pup, Ridgeway would cuff him with an open hand and later, as the dog grew, a closed fist. But Caesar soon became too big for slaps or punches, and the big man graduated to carrying a short, fat stick. Through practice, Ridgeway discovered just how hard to hit to avoid a mortal blow but severe enough to stun the dog, leaving the helpless animal twitching on the ground, unable to rise.

Now, the positioning of the big man's feet, the hidden hand, and the smell of confidence all registered. Caesar calmed his rage to let the life-threatening battle play out, using all the brutal lessons he'd learned.

The dog circled the man. Ridgeway turned in unison with Caesar, now revealing the weapon and slapping his open palm with the deadly club.

Caesar crouched, his body compact and ready to pounce, waiting for Ridgeway to make a mistake.

"Caesar, don't! He'll kill you!" Tony staggered to his feet with the girl standing beside him, trying to keep her friend from falling.

The dog froze at the sound of the boy's voice, and Ridgeway used the moment to close on him, taking a massive swing with his club that could have split the dog's head open like a ripe melon. Caesar saw the club at the last moment and turned away, dipping his head as a blow landed on his shoulder, shooting a scorching pain through his leg.

Caesar pivoted quickly on his now flat-footed attacker. The dog slipped under a poorly directed protective backhand swing and tore into the giant's leg, dragging the off-balanced man to the ground.

Ridgeway screamed in pain as razor-sharp canines sunk into his leg, piercing flesh and muscles. As the big man flailed, trying to grab the club that now lay by his side, Caesar pulled away and spun around, landing on top of Ridgeway, his forepaws pinning the man's shoulders to the ground.

With his broad chest pounding and his throat quivering in a deadly snarl, Caesar lowered his massive head, white canines glistening in the sunlight.

Prepared to deliver the kill, Caesar hesitated. Despite the giant's helpless panic, Caesar could still see the smoldering rage in the man's eyes and smell the hungering thirst for blood pouring from the big man's pores. The dog hated the man for all the pain he'd caused him, and hesitating to finish a wounded foe was contrary to every lesson beaten into him by fist and club.

Yet he didn't finish it. Caesar had escaped that world. He still reviled this man, who'd beaten him so cruelly. But the burning desire to maim and hurt had been replaced by the memory of the gentle touch of the boy and the loyal girl.

"Please, Caesar. He's not worth it. C'mon, boy." Tony stood unsteadily, begging the dog to turn away and follow him.

Caesar looked down at the giant and then at the wounded boy. The dog stepped off the big man's chest and trotted after Tony, who stumbled up the hill toward the woods.

The boy's gait grew steadier. And Caesar, also limping from the blow to his shoulder, whoofed at the sight of Tony running free with the girl called Jo lovingly watching to ensure the boy didn't fall. Caesar snorted, ignoring the tightness in his shoulder, and caught up with the two in a handful of space-gobbling bounds.

He thought to look back at the giant, but that man had nothing Caesar needed. He brushed his flank against the boy's leg, and Tony's hand grazed against him. This was his world now. He belonged to the boy as Tony belonged to him. Old pains were a thing of the past. His future rested with the two young people running by his side. Together, they flew past a woman in a long black dress, who shouted at them as they ran toward the woods, away from the giant and all the horror he represented.

"Mister Mi-ra-co-lo, come back here!"

Ridgeway pulled himself into a sitting position as the dog ran into the woods with the two kids. He winced as he rolled up his pant leg, looking at the gash in his calf. Not like he could catch them on two good legs. But that was okay. His lips curled, showing large, yellow teeth as wolfish as the fighting dogs he loved to watch. He'd heard the nun call out the boy's name, and he knew now why the kid looked familiar. Ridgeway had seen him before. The boy had been playing in the yard next door when Ridgeway sat drinking, high up on the rocks, looking down at the house he grew up in.

The big man hobbled back to his truck, ignoring the shrewish crowing of the old nun storming toward him.

"What is the meaning of that disgusting display? You are on church property, not the back alley of some cheap saloon."

"Piss off, Sister." Ridgeway smiled an evil sneer, enjoying the shocked look on the nun's face, reminiscent of the old hags he'd hated so many years ago.

He ignored the pain in his leg as he limped toward the street. The man had all the time in the world now. Ridgeway could be patient when the patience brought him sweeter revenge. He knew where to find the dog, and he'd bide his time to make sure the mutt and the boy suffered.

But he needed to be sure no trail led back to him because Ridgeway had plans. Slow and painful plans.

XXVII

Claws tearing at the fresh spring grass, Caesar flew across the path, leading Tony and Jo deep into the woods. He looked back to discover the boy struggling to keep up and waited. He lifted his nose to confirm the giant hadn't followed. They were safe.

"Good boy." Tony dropped to his knees to wrap his arms around the dog's neck, and Caesar leaned in, molding his body to the caress. "I missed you."

"He looks good." Jo knelt beside the two and gently ran her hand across the dog's flank, and like with the boy's touch, the dog welcomed her closeness. "But what do we do now?"

They'd stopped at a dry, open area where several fallen trees created a private spot splashed with sun and protected from the cool early morning breeze. Jo helped clean the boy's bloody face with a scarf she'd worn while they talked.

Caesar settled in at their feet, letting both freely run their hands through his fur in a way that would have been unimaginable just weeks earlier. He closed his eyes, listening to their murmuring voices, head resting on his forepaws as the breeze rustled his fur.

Everything about being with these two differed from his life with the giant. His lips curled at memories of being forced to fight, his paws twitching, reliving an earlier battle. Tony, perhaps noticing the change, leaned closer, whispering tender words and pulling Caesar to him. The dog jerked his head, chasing away the demons of his old life, and looked up at the boy's loving face.

Caesar sighed contentedly and dropped his head to rest on Tony's lap. Those painful days were over.

He would live with the boy now. The boy and this gentle girl were his to trust. He warmed at the ancient memories of belonging to something bigger than himself, to the instinctive urge that drives all dogs—the need to love someone more than they love themselves.

Tony stopped petting Caesar for a moment as he checked to see if his nose had stopped bleeding. The dog reached out with his paw, nudging the boy to continue petting him, and Tony laughed, pulling the dog closer. Caesar nuzzled against the boy— appreciating everything he'd been missing.

The dog's eyes flickered and then closed, thinking of life with the boy and his family. Yes, good people surrounded the boy. People unlike any Caesar had known before, each of whom the dog now accepted as members of his pack. The first man with his hidden sadness, the family Tony lived with, and the fiercely loyal girl sitting by Tony's side. Caesar accepted them all.

He'd lay down his life to defend them as he'd once fought only to protect himself. He'd found a purpose, and the loving boy had brought him to this new life.

Ridgeway hated doctors. The big man returned to his shop and opened a new bottle of Four Roses. He winced, pouring some onto his bleeding leg before binding the wound with strips cut from an old t-shirt. After limping to the lot entrance, he locked the gate and hurried back to the couch in his office. Over the next several hours, he emptied the quart bottle of whiskey before passing out on the couch, reveling in bloody images of what he would do to the SOB dog and pissant kids when he got ahold of them.

The empty bottle fell from his hand and crashed onto the concrete floor. Ridgeway jumped up, surrounded by darkness, shivering, and covered in sweat. He'd been dreaming a frightening, twisted nightmare, filled with jumbled images that changed before his eyes. He'd been running through the woods, his heart pounding and arms flailing, struggling to escape the demon wolf chasing him. He moved in slow motion as the hellhound's cries drew closer with each step. Panic-stricken, he felt the beast's hot breath on his neck, and he fell to his knees, a pleading coward, begging the demon to spare him. Ridgeway looked into the wolf's malevolent yellow eyes, and the beast's lips arched, flashing life-taking canines. But the creature didn't attack. The wolf lifted its head and laughed at him.

Ridgeway struck out, filled with rage and shame, but his meaty fist passed through the demon's body like a brick thrown through a puff of smoke. And the beast laughed even harder as its face morphed from the wolf's to that of the hated dog, then into the boy who stole him, finally becoming the image of Ridgeway's father. The father hovered over him, laughing at his impotence, his cowardice, his every failure.

Ridgeway shook off the dream. Covered in sweat, he limped to his desk, pulled out a fresh bottle, and took a gurgling tug. His father lay rotting in a grave, but there were others he could punish, others he could make suffer. The big man took another drink, less urgent, the alcohol and the thought of how near the dog and boy were warming him. He plopped down in a chair and tore open a fresh pack of Lucky Strikes. He'd show them. He'd show everyone. You can't mess with Al Ridgeway.

But he'd be clever. Just like with the beatings he doled out to hapless drunks—Ridgeway would ensure nothing could point back to him when he got his revenge against the mutt and the punk kids.

Ashes dropped from his cigarette and smoldered in his lap. Ridgeway beat at the spark with his massive paw. But the burning sensation awoke something in him. He puffed on the cigarette, returning it to a glowing red, and pressed it against his open palm until he could smell his burning flesh. The pain felt good and right, a symbol of all he was. He'd show his father. The coward swallowed his gun. Ridgeway was twice the man his father was. He'd never turn a gun on himself. He'd hurt others, and soon.

Tony's mother paced in the kitchen, hands on her hips, shaking her head disapprovingly as her eyes shifted from Tony to Jo to the dog. Jo's parents and Tony's father sat at the kitchen table, waiting to speak, but since the kids' arrival, Carla Miracolo held center stage.

The kids had spent the rest of the day in the woods. As darkness approached, they retraced their steps to pick up their book bags in the hedges, where they'd thrown them that morning. Then they arrived home to find Jo's parents sitting in the Miracolo's kitchen.

Both homes had received a call from the school advising them of the early morning sighting and subsequent absence. The parents' initial anger slowly abated, replaced by a deepening fear as the day grew long and darkness set in. So, when the kids finally arrived home, with Caesar walking docilely by their side, they faced a much less hostile environment.

"So you see, we didn't have a choice. Ridgeway had a club, and he was going to kill Caesar," Tony said, looking toward his father, hoping for the intersession that so often saved him from his mother's heated interrogations. But he was met with nothing but silence and his father's furrowed brow.

"Sister Agnes Helen said you ignored her when she called for you to stop, and you ran right past her." Tony's mother wasn't letting up.

"We had to, Mrs. Miracolo." Jo put her hand out to stop Tony. "You see, we knew we had to get Caesar as far away from that man as possible. Sister Agnes Helen sure is scary, but we figured even she wasn't scary enough to stop *Al Ridgeway*."

Tony saw the other adults look away, hiding smiles at Jo's description, as his mother bit her lower lip.

"We know we were wrong not to go back to school," Jo said, "but we thought the safest thing to do was to keep Caesar out of sight until dark."

Anthony Miracolo took his wife's hand and pulled her toward the empty seat beside him. She fell into the chair as the anger on her face faded, replaced by a look of relief she'd successfully masked until then.

"Well everyone's safe now. That's the important thing," Tony's father said as he continued to squeeze his wife's hand. "Jo, I know your parents will have a separate conversation with you, as we will with Tony. And there will be consequences." He nodded at the Trockis. "But there's one thing I'd like to say to the two of you."

Tony lowered his head, waiting for the scolding: the lecture that was sure to come about being responsible, thinking about consequences, and doing the right thing.

But it didn't come.

Anthony Miracolo walked over to the two kids as Caesar sat by their feet, taking in all the activity in the crowded room with a newfound calmness. Tony's father smiled down at the dog before placing a gentle hand on the kids' shoulders. "I won't speak for anyone else, but I'm proud of both of you."

Tony looked up, stunned.

"Loyalty is a rare thing in the world today. And friendship, true friendship, is even rarer." He squeezed their shoulders. "You two showed me something—the way you stood up to a bully like Al Ridgeway and having each other's back. I hope you both know how lucky you are to find a friend like that. You're blessed if you find one or two people you can trust your entire life. You two are lucky to have found one so young." Anthony Miracolo looked back, smiled at his wife, and said, "Believe me, I know."

Tony stared at the TV, mindless to the antics of Red Skelton, as the rest of the family roared at Skelton's Freddie the Freeloader's lamenting. "People say money talks, but all mine ever says is goodbye." Tony felt terrible about lying to his father, telling him he bruised his face falling when he ran from the schoolyard. But the boy understood the one thing that could send his gentle, even-tempered father into a white-hot rage was to have someone raise their hand against one of his kids.

Tony's father still wanted to talk to Ridgeway, but his wife convinced him nothing good could come of it. She didn't like or trust the man and insisted every family member stay clear of the junkyard. She said, with any luck, they wouldn't cross paths with the troubled Al Ridgeway.

Anthony Miracolo nodded begrudgingly to his wife's wishes, while Tony shifted uncomfortably, wondering if they'd heard the last from the dangerous man. But he'd brushed his doubts aside. Caesar waited in the basement. Tony still couldn't convince his parents to let the dog sleep upstairs in the house, but he'd noticed a change in their attitudes. His father relaxed and smiled when Caesar sat at Tony's feet during supper, and even his mother seemed less rigid around the dog. Tony suspected his sister's tears—detailing how their mother frightened Caesar and how the dog ran instead of attacking them in self-defense—had put a chink in his mother's usually impenetrable armor. Even the punishment she doled out failed to come with the usual judgmental scolding.

Tony excused himself and went downstairs to let Caesar out and say good night. He sat on the top step as Caesar traversed the backyard, making himself at home, happily marking trees. The dog came over and lay beside Tony, dropping his head in the boy's lap. Tony pressed his head against the dog's and kissed his snout. His dog was back where he belonged, but Tony sighed uneasily.

His father said Tony was lucky to have found a friend like Jo. He agreed, but something was wrong. She'd been acting strange. At first, he thought it was out of worry for Caesar, but it only got worse after they found the dog. That entire day in the woods, their conversations were stilted, and Tony swore if it hadn't been for protecting Caesar, Jo would have found any excuse she could to get as far away from him as possible. And tonight, when she left with her parents, she wouldn't even look at him. What had changed to make the girl who always seemed so at ease in his company start acting so strange?

Tony blushed as the answer came to him.

He stood up and clapped his hands, signaling Caesar to follow him into the house. It wouldn't be easy, but his father always told him a gentleman should never make a lady feel uncomfortable, and if they did, they needed to apologize. And that's precisely what he planned to do.

XXVIII

Jo sat alone in the diner, barely touching the hot chocolate she'd ordered. She opened her copy of *David Copperfield* and took out the photograph, staring at the yellowing image of the two young people.

She'd seen Tony's look of admiration when Mr. Miracolo talked to them earlier that night and remembered the many times Tony spoke about his special relationship with his father. Tony would shrug, embarrassed by his inability to connect with his demanding mother, and then smile, admitting he'd be lost without the rare connection shared with his father.

Jo closed the book with a sighed. Tony's entire life had been built on a lie, and she didn't know what to do with the terrible secret. The clock on the wall read eight forty-five. Her parents would be expecting her back from the library soon. She pushed the cocoa away, walked out into the street, and headed toward the bakery.

The baker must have seen her coming because he met her at the front door.

"Been expectin' you," he said, stepping aside to let Jo in as he locked the door behind them.

"We need to talk," Jo said, opening the book and handing the baker the photograph.

Rico took the photo and stared at it for the longest time, a sad smile outlining his face. "Yeah, we do." He gestured for Jo to sit on one of the stools at the counter and pulled a second close to face her. "Sorry, I've been avoidin' you."

Jo sat silently, her hands clenched in her lap.

"I was here the other day when you stopped by." The baker looked down again at the photo. "I didn't know what to tell you."

"And now?"

Rico sighed. "I guess all I can do is tell you the truth. So what do you wanna know?"

She took the photo back, staring again at the twenty-five-year-old picture with the young boy's face so much like Tony's. Then she flipped the image over and read aloud:

"Rico and Carla 1942…. Does Tony know?"

"God no!"

"Mister Miracolo?"

"Anthony?" Rico cracked the saddest smile. "God bless him. Yes, Anthony knows everythin'."

"Anyone else?"

Rico shook his head. "And we swore to keep it that way. I shoulda thrown the picture away years ago."

"There must be other pictures or older people in town who remember you two as kids."

"Nah, not a lotta picture-takin' back then. And the old-timers around here used to confuse me and Anthony all the time. Our families came from the same small village in Sicily, so we're probably related somewhere way back when. And we sure looked alike as kids. They used to call us the De Miracolo brothers." The baker laughed, the memory seeming to momentarily lift his sadness.

"But the picture," Jo said, looking back at the photo. "Tony doesn't look *similar* to you at that age. You look like twins."

"Yeah, I recognized the uncanny resemblance in the photo 'bout a year ago. I shoulda destroyed it but couldn't. No one's ever in my apartment. I thought the secret would be safe stuffed away in the cupboard."

"Hidden away or not, Tony's whole life is based on a lie. He thinks the sun sets and rises on his father. . . . I mean Mister Miracolo. And he's spent his life trying to satisfy his mother, trying to meet her impossible expectations for him, when she's nothing but a—"

"Don't!" The baker slammed his hand on the counter, stunning Jo. "You heard the stories of how tough her life was. It damaged Carla and made her difficult to be with sometimes. But at her core, she's one of the most decent people you'll ever know, and she loves Tony with all her heart."

"Okay." Jo put her hands on her hips. "Then how can you justify what she . . . what you both did?"

"You're young," Rico said, sounding very tired. "It's easy to judge when you're young. As you grow older, you learn. Life ain't black and white. There's no perfect people, and even your heroes fall short of who you think they are. But they never stop lovin' you, and you never stop needin' them. Now, I'm gonna treat you like an adult. So, no justification, but if you're willin' to listen, I'll tell you what happened."

Jo nodded. "Please."

"Okay, I told you what Carla was like before her mother died and how she had to grow up overnight. She changed, but the sweet girl was still there, where the people who really knew her could still see. Anthony Miracolo recognized how special she could be, and so did I.

"Anthony waited patiently for years, and then when Flavia, the youngest, graduated high school, Carla finally agreed to marry him. But a month before the weddin', Carla's father was killed. He tried breakin' up a fight between two strangers arguin' over a seat on the subway."

The baker shook his head. "What a waste. I'd never seen Carla in worse shape. She called off the weddin' and shut herself off from everyone. And then . . ."

The baker stopped, the pain from those old memories etched on his face.

"Go on. And then?"

"Ya gotta understand, she loved him, and he loved her. Me?" Rico shrugged. "I loved them both. But they were soulmates, and even *that* night, deep down, I knew it.

"A few weeks after the breakup, she came to my apartment, heartbroken, her life and future stolen from her. That evenin', we shared a bottle of wine, laughed and cried, and told stories about her mother and father, celebratin' their lives. At the end of the night . . ."

Rico looked away. "I'd wanted to be with her my whole life, but Anthony was my friend." The baker hung his head. "I have no excuse. But you know the sad part? Despite my shame, deep in my heart, I knew I'd do it again.

"Carla went to see Anthony the next day. She told him everythin' and said she'd marry him if he still wanted her. They got married later that month, and six weeks later, I found out Carla was pregnant. She refused to discuss what happened that night but, as surely as summer follows spring, I knew the baby was mine. As the years passed, I watched Tony grow, and my conviction grew. I didn't need no picture of me at fifteen to prove it."

"What about Mister Miracolo?"

"Like I said, she told him everythin'. Carla could never lie or keep a secret from the man she loved. The woman's too honorable to ever do that. Anthony somehow found it in his giant heart to forgive us both. I think he believed I helped Carla find her way back to him. Who knows, maybe he's right." The baker stopped, unable to go on.

"And you three have carried this silently all these years?"

The baker nodded. "It is the greatest shame of my life, and from that shame came my most profound source of pride. Tony's an exceptional young man, and I believe it took the three of us to make him who he is today.

"But let me make one thing clear. Anthony Miracolo is Tony's father. Has been since the day the boy was born. I've never seen that man look at Tony with even a single moment of doubt or disappointment in his eyes. He'd give up his life for that boy."

Rico took a deep breath and slowly exhaled, his shoulders dropping like a pricked balloon. "So, now you know. Are you gonna tell him?"

"It's not my place, but he deserves to know."

"What does that mean?"

"It's a part of who he is. It's wrong to keep the truth from him."

"It would crush him."

"Tony's much stronger than you think. Stronger than his parents think." Jo put the picture back in her book and got up. "I have to go. My parents will be expecting me."

She turned and walked out of the bakery, the stars sparkling in the clear night sky. Was the baker right? Maybe Tony couldn't handle the truth. But could she be a part of keeping such a secret from him?

A truck stopped at a red light as Jo crossed the street. Lifting her eyes, she stared up at the starry skies, never more unsure of the right thing to do.

Ridgeway saw the girl. He took a long drag on his cigarette, exhaled through his nose, and flicked the butt out the window, where it sparked and skittered toward her. Ridgeway's hands tightened on the steering wheel as his lips parted to show an ugly smile. He'd be paying the girl's friend a visit very soon. Who knew, maybe with luck, the burning pain he brought might spread to the house next door.

The girl passed directly in front of his truck. His smile turned to a sneer as he eased his foot off the brake. The car began to roll. It would be so easy: floor the gas pedal and crush her young body. He could say he'd dropped his cigarette in his lap and hadn't seen the light change. It would be over in an instant.

Ridgeway blinked, and the girl stepped onto the sidewalk. But no problem. There were better, more imaginative ways that would never point back to him. Besides, hurting the girl and her family would be nice, but it was the boy and the dog who must suffer first. If in reaping his revenge against them, he could also destroy the happy, loving family living in the house that held only ugly memories for him, all the better.

The light changed, and he drove slowly past the girl. She could wait. He'd been in the woods, looking down at the Miracolo's house, and seen everything he needed to see. The time had come to ruin those who had defied him.

XXIX

Tony poured more turpentine onto the rag and tried to rub the last bits of paint from his hand as Caesar lay basking in the warm spring sun in a nearby pile of leaves. After getting caught skipping school, his father failed to give the boy the dreaded *You're better than that* look that cut so deeply and his mother remained oddly silent. But his parents never failed to take advantage of any transgression. Their kids were bound to find a long list of chores to perform as penance if one of them disappointed Carla or Anthony Miracolo. And that's how Tony spent his weekend.

After working all Saturday morning raking leaves into a huge mound and piling them next to the Trockis' old barn, Tony spent the rest of the day painting the Miracolo house. Sunday morning after Mass with the family, he was back at work painting, only allowed to break for a massive Easter lunch of baked ham, lasagna, and stuffed artichokes.

He'd seen Jo in front of church, talking to Danny Walsh after Mass. She slipped away and apologized to Tony for not visiting Caesar on Saturday before promising to come help paint, but she never came. He'd barely seen her all weekend. Further proof of how uncomfortable he'd made her. He vowed today would be the day. He'd set things straight.

"Look at Caesar. I bet that's the softest bed he's ever been on." Tony's sister dropped to her knees in the backyard and clapped her hands. The dog rose from the pile of leaves, shook himself, and walked toward the girl, his tail wagging. "That's right, we're friends now."

"Careful." Tony cautioned, afraid for anything to go wrong now that the dog finally seemed to be settling in.

"Nah, it took Caesar a while to figure out we're family, but he's home now." Rosa giggled. "Don't tell Ma I told you, but I caught her sneaking him a couple of slices of ham in the kitchen earlier when she thought I was still at the Trockis'."

Tony smiled. At least his mother had begun to come around, and Caesar seemed more relaxed with his family. There was only one thing left to resolve. "You were next door?"

"Yep. Mrs. Trocki wanted me to eat something, but I'm still stuffed." Rosa stopped and reached into her pocket. "But look what Jo gave me." She held out a colorfully decorated egg with finely detailed etchings on its shell. "It's called a *pisanki*. Isn't it beautiful?"

Tony glanced at the egg. *Still avoiding me, and what's her excuse? Making fancy Easter eggs?*

"Oh, and Jo said you should stop over after supper if you wanted to." Rosa wore that same sly grin everybody had when they talked to Tony about Jo.

Tony looked away, unwilling to take the bait. "Thanks." At least he'd clear the air tonight.

"Oh, and I already told Ma," Rosa said in a teasing sing-song voice. Then she stopped, affecting a newfound interest in the egg while keeping a watchful eye on Tony. "And she said, under no circumstance are you allowed to go upstairs at the Trockis'."

"Get outta here!"

Tony threw the paint-stained rag at Rosa, who dodged it and ran into the house as she sang, "Tony and Jo Jo, sittin' in a tree . . ."

Even Rosa could see how foolishly he'd been acting.

Tony gathered the soiled rags, turpentine, and half-filled paint cans, placing everything next to the house with the additional paint supplies before covering it with a large burlap sheet. With his head down, he headed inside.

"C'mon, Caesar, let's go. I gotta clean-up for supper."

Caesar stood near the back of the lot, fur up high on his shoulders, nose in the air as he stared into the wooded hillside. Tony called again, and the dog slowly turned away, galloping to catch up. Tony reached down to run his hand through the fur of the dog's powerful neck, and Caesar brushed his side against the boy's leg.

"Rosa was right about one thing. We're a family. I don't know what I'd do without you."

Tony pushed the cellar door open and headed down the stairs but stopped, waiting impatiently as Caesar turned to look up into the hills.

Ridgeway sat on the highest rock, looking through the trees to the houses below. His hands trembled as he reached into his pocket for a cigarette and matches. He hadn't had a drink for hours, and his body craved alcohol. But the big man had vowed not to touch a drop until he finished the job. Now was not the time to get sloppy.

It had been unseasonably warm the last few days, and tomorrow's weather report promised more of the same: clear blue skies with temperatures approaching seventy. Ridgeway fumbled, lighting a cigarette, his trembling fingers betraying the calm efficiency he struggled to maintain. With the cigarette lit, he carefully blew out the match. He didn't want a premature fire in the woods to ruin his plan. Ridgeway smiled. Another day under the hot sun would turn the leaf piles near the boy's house and against the old barn into a dangerous tinder box.

He lifted his pant leg. Purple and red scabs shone over the still raw wound. But there was no infection, and the dog hadn't damaged any tendons. His meaty calf had protected him against permanent damage from the animal's powerful jaw and razor-sharp teeth. His fingers traced the wound, and he ground his teeth.

Until the scene in the schoolyard, he'd wanted the dog back to punish it. But all that had changed. Ridgeway no longer needed the dog in his garage to secure the revenge his hate-filled ego demanded he collect.

Jo sat in her room, holding the photograph, tracing the face of the young Rico De Santo with her fingers. *If you squint, you'd swear it's Tony standing there.*

"Jo Jo, we're leaving," her father called. "Come down so we can talk a second before we go."

"Coming." Jo slipped the picture between the pages of her paperback and headed downstairs.

"I already fed Frank Junior, so all you have to do is get him in his PJs and put him down by seven thirty." Jo's mother put her hands on her hips. "And no spoiling him. We let you cry yourself to sleep when you were a baby, and you turned out just fine. He's going to have to learn as well."

"Come on, we need to go," Jo's father said, taking his wife's hand and leading her away. "We'll be home by ten thirty."

Jo lifted her brother from the highchair and followed her parents to the front door. She wanted one of them to ask her if everything was okay. To say they noticed she seemed anxious lately and ask if anything was troubling her. But no one did anymore. She'd gotten lost in the rush of daily life.

Now, only Tony seemed to have time for her. But with the secret she'd discovered, Jo was afraid to talk with her one true friend.

Jo waved as her parents drove away. After setting the baby on the carpet with some blocks. She ran upstairs, grabbed her book with the photograph inside, and hurried down to place it on the mantle above the fireplace. Tony should be there soon, and she still didn't know what to do.

Caesar lay on the floor in the Trockis' living room with Frank Junior. sleeping on a blanket beside him. He'd arrived with Tony, much to the delight of the excitable child. Tony and Jo watched intently as the dog patiently withstood the pokes and prods of Jo's energetic baby brother until the boy drifted off to sleep with Caesar by his side. The dog's eyelids began to flutter as he, too, slipped into a peaceful slumber.

"He's come a long way," Tony said, his voice filled with pride. "It's like we managed to tap into gentleness hidden there all along. I don't even worry about him snapping or hurting someone unless, of course . . ." Tony didn't finish. He didn't have to.

"Yes, he's changed a lot, and I think he's helped you change, too."

"How have I changed?" Tony asked, his voice tinged with his old defensiveness.

"I've been thinking about that," Jo said. "You haven't always been the easiest person to be around.

But Caesar changed you. Just like how I told you the rose changed the little prince. In caring for Caesar, you've placed someone else above your wants and needs for the first time."

Tony nodded. "I guess you're right, but I couldn't have gotten here without you." He paused. *Time to clear the air.* "You're right. I'm not the easiest person to be around, and I know I've made you uncomfortable by trying to turn a great friendship into something more."

Jo's eyebrows arched, confusion outlining her young face. "Not sure what you mean."

"Please, Jo, just let me finish." Tony stood up and began to pace. "I saw the way you looked at me that night at the library. I could see how uncomfortable you got whenever I thought about holding your hand or kissing you, and I pulled back because I didn't want to ruin our friendship."

"So, you think I acted like that because I didn't want you to try anything?" Jo stared at Tony. "Did you ever think it was because of Delores?"

"Delores? Delores DePalma? What's she got to do with anything?"

"I saw you kiss her at the dance."

"I didn't kiss her. She kissed me."

"I think you need to tell your tongue that. It seemed like a mutual kiss to me. She said you asked her to go steady." Jo folded her arms across her chest. "*And* she told me all about you two on the Ferris wheel last summer."

"Last summer? Going steady? I'm not going anywhere with Delores DePalma." Tony stiffened. "Okay, so what about you and Danny Walsh? You let him walk you home, and I saw you two together whispering all week during recess and again in front of church this morning." Tony paused. "I don't blame you. You're smart and pretty and nice. It only makes sense you'd want to be with someone like—"

"You think I'm interested in Danny?!" Jo held her sides, suppressing her laughter as her eyes met Tony's. "You actually believe I like self-absorbed, pretty-boy Danny Walsh?"

"Why else would you two be talking so intently all the time?"

"Well, our class president can't seem to take a hint. I think his ego took a shot when I wouldn't let him kiss me after he walked me home from the dance. He keeps asking me to go ice skating or to the movies." Jo shook her head. "I don't think he even likes me. Mr. Walsh just can't stand the idea that even one girl in class doesn't fall all over him. I finally admitted I like someone else, but he still wouldn't . . ." Jo stopped, her face turning a crimson red.

"Wait. You didn't let him kiss you?" Tony said, smiling triumphantly. "Because you like someone else? But you held back with this person because you thought he was interested in another girl. When all the while this guy thinks you're about the greatest girl in the world. Smart, pretty, kind, and so far out of his league you'd never be interested in a hot-tempered, moody dope like—"

Jo rushed across the room and pushed Tony hard, knocking him back onto the recliner. "Anthony Miracolo, for once in your life, shut up."

Tony looked up as Jo held him by his shoulders and brought her face close to his. "You talk too much."

Jo grabbed Tony's shirt, pulling him closer, and kissed him long and gently.

Surprised, Tony accepted the kiss in numb disbelief before slowly warming to the idea. *Wow, can she kiss!* Tony's mind raced, thinking what a fool he'd been. How he'd held back for so long, thinking Jo couldn't possibly be interested in him while he'd screwed up at the dance, leaving her hurt and confused.

Jo stopped, looked at him, and smiled. "Stop thinking and kiss me back."

And he did.

"You want to know what I like about you?" Tony sat beside Jo on the couch with her hand resting comfortably in his.

"Well, considering that until a few minutes ago, I wasn't sure you even liked me, yes, I very much want to hear what you like about me." Jo teasingly nudged Tony with her shoulder and was rewarded with one of his beaming smiles.

"Here goes." Tony cleared his throat. "I like how you bite your low lip when you think. I like the *way* you think. So logical and precise. I like how you brush the hair off your face with the back of your hand, like you're the queen of England waving at a crowd. I like the way your nose twitches like something smells whenever anyone says something stupid, and the sideway look you give me as you try not to giggle." Tony shrugged. "The truth is, I like just about everything about you, but nothing more than your sense of loyalty. I know I could trust you with anything, and that you'd never betray our friendship."

Jo squeezed his hand, kissing him on the cheek as she got up and walked over to the fireplace. She took a deep breath and grabbed her book from the mantle.

"There's something I have to show you."

Carla Miracolo walked into the living room and turned off the Bruins game. Rosa was in her room listening to records, and Tony was next door at the Trockis'. "We need to talk."

Her husband ground out his cigarette and placed his beer on the coffee table in front of him. "You've been acting strange all day. I figured you'd tell me what's up when you were ready."

Carla sat beside Anthony and placed her hand on his. "Rico called yesterday when you were at the hardware store."

"Okay."

She swallowed hard. "Rico's afraid Tony may know."

"Know what?"

"About Rico and—"

"There's nothing to know. We agreed about this

a long a time ago."

"Please, listen." Carla squeezed his hand. "I know that's how you feel, and I love you for it, more than you'll ever know, but Tony may disagree." Her throat grew tight. "Jo saw a picture of Rico as a kid the other day, and he looked just like Tony. She confronted Rico, and he told her the truth."

"Tony's *my* son," Anthony said, banging his fist on the coffee table. "There's nothing to know. He's been my son since the moment I held him in my arms."

"I'm so ashamed." Carla dropped her face in her hands as she wept, her moment of weakness from so long ago returning to haunt them all. "I don't deserve you."

"You made my life worth living and gave me the two most incredible kids I could ever ask for. I can't imagine life without the three of you." Anthony placed his hand under Carla's chin and lifted her face as he stared into her tear-filled eyes. "I told you long ago, I don't care how we became a family. I just thank God we are, and that's always been enough for me. Now, this is the last I will say about this: I love you. I love my life with you, and I love *our children*. There is nothing more to discuss."

Carla wrapped her arms around Anthony, burying her face against his chest. After so many years of marriage, she knew he meant every word. What had she done to deserve the love of such a good man? But what about Tony? Would he feel the same?

"It's okay, we'll face this together," Anthony

said as he tried to pull back and look at her.

But Carla clung to him more fiercely. She didn't want her husband to see the doubt and fear etched across her face.

Tony held the yellowing photograph, staring at the grainy images of the boy and girl. He recognized the young woman as his mother from a picture of her in her confirmation dress that hung on the wall in his parents' bedroom with half a dozen other family photos. The young man looked like a slightly older version of himself, dressed up for a school play.

"Where'd you get this?" he asked, his eyebrow raised. He'd never seen this photo of his parents before and didn't understand why Jo seemed so nervous about showing it to him.

"Rico De Santo." Jo's voice caught in her throat.

"Zio Rico?"

Jo nodded and leaned back against the fireplace, where she'd retreated after handing Tony the photo, arms folded across her chest.

"I look just like my father," Tony said, laughing. But his words turned a nervous Jo's face white as she refused to look at him. Confused, Tony looked back at the photo and turned it over, his eyes fixing on the faded writing on the back and said in a whisper, "Rico and Carla."

Tony's hands trembled, the photo flapping like a flag caught in the wind. He studied the boy's face— Rico De Santo's face. His face smiling back at him.

Mocking him.

"I look just like Zio Rico," Tony said, shaking his head in disbelief. "But that doesn't make sense …. I mean …. You talked to him?"

Jo nodded, swallowing hard.

"What did he say?"

Jo looked away. "I think you need to talk to your parents."

Tony arrived home, with Caesar trailing behind, to find his parents on the couch, holding hands, watching the end of the Bruins game. He shoved the photograph in his pocket, mumbled something about having homework, and took a book to the basement to settle Caesar for the night. He sat on the floor next to the dog, staring at the same page for an hour, his world as he knew it changed forever.

Caesar's nostrils widened, and his tail stiffened. The giant was out there. He could smell his presence coming closer through the woods—hovering around the house as he had for several days now. The dog bristled and looked at the boy, who was anxious about something but unaware of the looming danger. Upstairs, with the little girl sent to bed, the others talked in hushed tones, seemingly ignorant of the threat near their home.

Caesar waited for a reaction, but Tony's nose

didn't twitch. He didn't cock his head or perk his ears. Upstairs, the others didn't pace the floor nervously. Caesar's muscles tensed. The rest of the pack was dangerously unaware of the impending menace.

The dog rose, spreading his paws wide as he lifted his head and released a series of deep-chested barks into the black night. It was no mere *I know you're out there* warning. The primal howl stood as a threat, a promise to do whatever he must to protect the boy and his family if the menace approached.

"What is it, buddy? You smell a squirrel?" Tony came to the dog, wrapped his arms around Caesar, and buried his face in the dog's chest. "I don't know what I'd do without you."

Tony rose and walked up the cellar stairs to let him out for his last break of the night. Caesar followed and ran past Tony to the edge of the backyard, where he raced back and forth across the tree line as he stared up toward the rocks. The dog eventually calmed, and his hackles dropped as he proceeded to mark half a dozen trees at the entrance to the woods.

Caesar's raised snout noted the giant's slow disappearance. But he'd remain on guard, the giant's presence warning him of an imminent danger.

Ridgeway stepped carefully off the rocky peak and walked through the woods, away from the boy's house, toward his parked truck. He'd seen everything he needed and would return the next night while everyone slept.

The big man returned to his shop, fighting to control his drinking until his work was done. He sat on a crate in the back of the junkyard and pulled out his pistol, the cold steel glistening in the glow of the burning trash can. Smiling, Ridgeway stuck the gun back under his belt as he grabbed another stack of bound papers. He still limped a little, which pleased him. He found the pain a talisman, a perverse reminder of the debt the man intended to collect.

He threw the stack of papers into the barrel and moved closer as the fringes caught before shooting orange flames high into the sky to light his face. Ridgeway stared into the fire, reminded how the striking of a match could destroy something once solid and seemingly impermeable. The thought sent a visceral charge of excitement through his body.

His face flushed at the flames and the memory of how, once as a kid, he'd accidentally lit the woods behind his house on fire. That blaze came dangerously close, threatening the family home before the firefighters managed to control it. When his father found matches in young Al's room, he'd pulled off his belt and given the boy a savage beating, leaving raised, discolored welts on the boy's arms and bare legs.

But the beating revealed one thing to the desperately lonely child. His father's beating stood as proof the man knew his son existed, and perversely, the attention fed something dark in the impressionable boy. If people didn't see him for any other reason, they'd see him when he struck out and hurt others.

So now he'd light a flame and watch as fire consumed everything in its path.

Both of the kids' fathers smoked. It wouldn't take a lot for the fire marshal's investigation to point toward an errant cigarette butt dropped in the leaves as the starting point of the fire. Ridgeway's eyes glazed over, remembering the boy's father growing up. Anthony Miracolo, always smiling and surrounded by friends.

But not after tomorrow night.

Ridgeway sneered, thinking of the heartache and pain tomorrow would bring. His heart raced as images of burning destruction left him faint. He shook his head, struggling to concentrate—his trembling worse. Maybe a small drink to steady his nerves.

Squeezing his hands together to control the shaking, he closed his eyes, battling his need, but the cravings assaulting his core grew stronger.

One small drink. He limped into his office and grabbed the bottle from his top drawer. He took a long, slow draw, and then another. He raised the bottle to his lips a third time but stopped. Cursing, he threw the bottle against the cinderblock wall, where it shattered into a hundred pieces.

"I'll show all of them." He growled, relishing the alcohol-fueled pleasure awaiting him tomorrow night, his just reward for punishing those who'd wronged him.

XXXI

"**J**o, Tony's here."

Jo wiped her brother's mouth and put the empty jar of baby food in the trash as she stepped from the breakfast table.

"Thanks, Mom. I'll be right there." She hurried to the front door, where a sleep-deprived Tony waited. "You okay?"

"I can't go to school today. Can you cover for me?"

"What? How?"

"Just tell Sister Agnes Helen I got sick on the walk to school and went home. My mother's working at the rectory, so no one will be home if anyone calls to check. Maybe they'll think I'm sleeping." He looked away. "I don't care anyway."

"What are you going to do?"

"I don't know. I just need to be alone to think."

"Can I . . . ?"

Tony smiled sadly, shaking his head, and walked away, hurrying down the hill as an anxious Jo stood watching from the doorway until he was out of sight.

Tony sat on a log beside the river as smoke billowed from the bakery's chimney, the smell of freshly baked bread and his grumbling stomach reminding him of his skipped breakfast. Tony inhaled, thinking of simpler times. Sunday mornings—his father sitting at the kitchen table reading the sports page while his mother fried meatballs for breakfast. His father would walk over to the stove, kiss his wife as she slipped a flattened patty between thick-crusted rustica bread and handed it to him to place in front of a still sleepy Tony. His father would smile as he sat back down, mussing the boy's hair and then, humming some gentle tune, return to his newspaper.

Tony's jaw flexed, taking an imaginary bite, the bread snapping between his teeth, and he warmed, remembering the meatball's savory taste. Then he clenched his fists. Even his simplest of memories were tainted.

He took the photograph out of his back pocket and stared at it. Everything he thought to be true, all the touchstones, gone. He put the photo back, buried his hands in his pockets, and walked through the thickets toward the bakery.

Rico De Santo stood at the counter making change when he heard the back door to the shop open. He followed the customer to the exit, put the closed sign in the windowpane, and turned to face his son.

"You talked to Jo."

"So it's true?"

Rico nodded. "But it doesn't change anythin'."

"Doesn't change anything?" Tony's face twisted in anger. "It changes *everything*. My entire life's built on a lie."

"Tony, that's not true. Your mother loves you. You're father loves you. I—"

"My father?!" Tony shouted. "You mean the man I thought was my father."

"Anthony Miracolo is your father and has been from the moment you were born. He was by your mother's side when she rushed you to Mass General at two in the mornin' durin' the polio scare. He never missed a baseball game. He's been there to help with your homework and run interference like nobody else could when your mother got in one of her moods."

Tony looked away. "And what about you? Didn't you want me?"

"More than anythin' in the world." Rico tried to reach out, but Tony pushed him away. "Please understand, your mother and father were in love, and I respected that. For the longest time, we didn't know for sure, and even in the last few years . . ." The baker sighed. "It never mattered to Anthony. To any of us. None of us could love you more than we already do."

"And what about my mother?" Tony said, his rage building. "My mother's no better than a common whore!"

The baker's hand moved in a blur, catching Tony open-handed across the face. "Don't ever say that. Your mother's been with two men in her life, and she truly loves your father."

Tony's mouth flew open, and he touched his cheek. "Well, I *hate* her." His lips curled in an ugly snarl. "I hate all of you!" Then, staring into the baker's eyes, he said the words that cut the deepest. "But I hate *you* most of all. You're nothing but a coward who stood by and let another man raise his son."

Rico's face paled, anger gone, replaced by gut-wrenching pain. He closed his eyes, fighting back the heartache and guilt he'd carried for so long. "Tony, I'm so sorry. We're all sorry. We did what we thought was best."

But he was talking to himself. Tony had disappeared out the door, running deep into the marshland behind the bakery.

"It'll be okay. It's just a lot for him." Rico sat at the Miracolo's kitchen table as a distraught Carla paced back and forth, staring anxiously out the window.

"It's all my fault. God's punishing me for my sins."

"Don't say that. How could Tony ever be a punishment? He's the only worthwhile thing I've ever done."

"Well, we should have—"

"Should've what, Carla? There was no way for us to know, and God bless Anthony, none of it could ever change how he feels about you or the boy. You did what you hadda do."

Carla didn't answer. It was all true. Tony's birth had been a wonderful gift, and her husband never considered the boy anything but his son. If not for the undeniable physical resemblance that had revealed itself in the last few years, they'd all have gone to their graves with the secret.

The back door opened, and Anthony Miracolo appeared in the doorway. He looked at the two anxious faces. "So he knows?"

They both nodded.

"Where's Rosa?" Anthony looked past them into the living room.

"Next door, helping Donna with Frank Junior," Carla said. "She doesn't suspect anything. Just thinks Tony's in trouble again."

"Good, good," Anthony said, bobbing his head. "Okay, so, he knows. Doesn't matter," Anthony said firmly. "Never did."

Carla crossed the room and wrapped her arms around her husband. "I know, and I love you for it. But it matters to him. He didn't go to school today, and nobody's seen him since early this morning."

"So what now?" Anthony frowned as he looked at Rico De Santo across the room.

Ridgeway sat on the rock, looking down at the houses below. He took the pint bottle out of his pocket, promising to only take a sip to steady his nerves. But the sip became a swallow, then a second. He brought the bottle to his lips a third time and stopped. Grinding his teeth, he put the bottle away. It would all be over in a few hours, and then he could drink all he wanted.

He grabbed the gunnysack with his supplies and headed down the hill, through the woods toward the house. Ridgeway cursed, scratching his face on a branch. He'd decided not to use a flashlight, avoiding the risk of anyone spotting him or later recalling seeing a light in the woods. As he cleared a thicket of trees, he caught sight of the Victorian house next door and the barn on the side of the property. He looked away, trying to drive out painful childhood memories of life in the vast, unloving home. No time for that now. He had to take care of the dog and the boy's family.

The woods came alive as a strong gust cut through the trees, and he smiled. The wind would help. He stopped, hidden from view of either house by the large wooden barn. Any closer, the mutt would start yapping. He dropped the gunnysack and checked his supplies: an unopened can of turpentine and over a dozen rags already soaked with the accelerant. All to ensure the house would go up quickly while leaving the paint supplies as the presumed flashpoint for the cause of the blaze. All his handiwork would burn up in the inferno. And if the kid didn't fry, he'd blame himself for the rest of his life.

The big man's eyes grew wide, picturing the house consumed by flames as the wind whipped across his face.

But first, time to silence the dog.

He reached into his coat pocket to grab the paper bag with a half-pound of hamburger laced with antifreeze. The man had been studying the family's movements in the house for several days and knew they let the dog out each night around ten o'clock.

Ridgeway snorted, wiping his nose against his sleeve, and leaned back to hurl the meat into the backyard. He laughed—a mean, humorless sound—and retraced his steps into the woods. There was no sense in risking the dog smelling him. His hands trembled as he fumbled, trying to pull his pack of Lucky Strikes from his pocket. Maybe he'd have a small drink back at the garage while he waited. The mutt would be dead in two hours, and the rest of the house asleep. That's when the real fun would start.

XXXII

The boy's mother signaled Caesar to follow her outside. Their relationship had changed since Caesar ran, rather than confronting her as she waved the broom. He was allowed upstairs to rest at Tony's feet as the boy sat eating, doing his homework, and watching TV. Caesar no longer smelled fear in the woman, and she'd drop scraps for him on the floor of what she'd cooked while ensuring the dog's water bowl remained full.

But this morning had been different. The boy left early and was gone all day. Something was wrong. The man Caesar stayed with when Tony first freed him from the giant knocked on the door. The little girl was sent next door, and the two sat talking in anxious tones. Then the boy's father came home, and the tense conversation continued.

As darkness set in, the sad man finally left—his

eyes filled with worry.

The family ate in strained discomfort. The girl's chirping voice met with atypical, muted responses.

Time to sleep, but still no sign of his boy.

"Come on, Caesar, let's go." The woman stood by the back door, calling.

Caesar jumped up to follow. When he entered the backyard, the woman dropped to her knees, wrapping her arms around the dog to fiercely hug him. Startled, Caesar tried to pull back, shocked by the woman's embrace. She'd never touched him until now. But the dog relaxed and pressed against her when he felt the woman's trembling need.

"Tell me our boy's going be okay."

She stood, allowing Caesar to pass. But he waited and rubbed his head under her hand until she reached down to mindlessly scratched behind his ear. The dog wanted to do more to ease her pain, but the anguish ran too deep. He licked her hand before lowering his head to run past her and into the backyard.

The woman watched, wiping away tears, as Caesar marked various spots along the tree line, the scent of the giant signaling his recent presence, adding to the dog's anxiousness. Caesar's nostrils flared, and he raised his snout as drool formed on his lips. The smell of the fresh meat overpowered his senses. His nose twitched, and Caesar followed the scent. Since coming to live with the boy's family, the dog no longer suffered the constant hunger that had been his life, but he never let dropped or found food go unclaimed. He lowered his head, ready to gobble up his find.

He hesitated. Along with the scent of the meat, he could smell the giant. The man Caesar hated and once feared had never given him meat like this. Why would he now? Since smelling the giant's presence in recent days, Caesar had remained alert as the big man prowled the woods behind the house. Maybe the man accidentally dropped the meat.

Caesar's mouth closed on the beef, and he tossed his head back, prepared to swallow his prize in one chugging gulp.

"Tony! Honey, you're back."

The woman's cry of delight startled the dog, who turned and raced to greet the boy. The boy dropped to his knees, wrapping his arms around the dog as his mother hovered over them.

Tony stood to face his mother. "Please, I can't," he said, his voice flat. "I'm not ready."

Turning his back on his mother, he signaled for Caesar to follow him, and the two walked down the stairs to the cellar.

The moon hung high in the sky as Ridgeway slipped behind the barn and grabbed the gunnysack with his supplies, where he'd left it. He moved slowly toward the house, still wary of a potential warning howl from the dog. But an evil smile slowly lined his face as he came closer. The house sat in silence. His antifreeze-laced hamburger had done the trick. The mutt was dead, and with it, the first step in his act of revenge. Now, the big man could move around freely without having the boy's family alerted.

He reached down and patted the gun at his hip. With the dog out of the way, the need for the pistol seemed less likely. But he found the feel of the cold steel comforting.

Ridgeway crept across the yard, dropped to his knees at the back of the barn, and pulled his supplies out of the gunnysack. He opened the can of turpentine and soaked the leaves piled against the barn before hurrying to the paint supplies the boy had stored beside the family's wood-framed house. Then, scattering presoaked rags on top of the burlap-covered supplies, he emptied the rest of the can.

He stuffed the empty can back into the gunnysack and tossed the evidence into the woods, where he could grab it when he made his escape. Satisfied, Ridgeway crept back toward the barn. He planned to set the accelerant-soaked leaves ablaze there before lighting the paint supplies piled against the house. By the time the fire engines arrived, both the boy's home and the old wooden carriage house where he'd played as a kid would be aflame.

The firefighters' immediate priority would be to try and save the boy's house. With luck and a strong wind, the fiery inferno might spread from the neglected barn and hopefully destroy his childhood home.

But he intended to be long gone by then. And the best part: The intense flames would consume any trace of his presence. Whatever they found in the rubble—rags or traces of turpentine—would all point back to the negligence of a stupid, careless kid.

His head bobbed in satisfaction. This was going to be far more rewarding than his fist splattering some nameless wino's nose. In just a few minutes, he'd be high up on the rocks, looking down at the inferno of his destructive creation. The revenge that belonged to him.

Ridgeway reached into his pocket and pulled out a book of matches. He struck one, tossed it, and stepped back as the turpentine-soaked leaves burst into flames, catching the barn ablaze.

He struck another match and took several long strides toward the back of the boy's house.

Caesar lay on his side, retching, a green bile puddle beside his snout, and he struggled to control his bowels. He trembled, and his stomach churned as his entire body battled with the strange sickness attacking him.

After coming in from outside, he'd jumped all over the boy, excited to have him back, but soon Caesar felt dizzy and lay on the basement floor. He could smell the anxiousness on the boy and wanted to help him, but he just lay there panting as Tony sat next to him, staring into the dark corners of the basement. After Tony went upstairs, Caesar's pain grew worse. Panicked and confused, he rose and, struggling, managed to nervously wander the basement for several minutes until he vomited and collapsed by the back door. He lay there on his side, panting, his heart pounding and gut twisting in unimaginable agony.

Then, through the blinding fog of pain, his nose twitched—a stranger outside the house. No, not a stranger. The giant had returned, and memories of the strange, sweet-smelling meat rushed back. He'd dropped most of the meat at the sight of Tony, but the taste lingered as he grew sicker and sicker.

Caesar attempted to snarl, and he tried to rise, only to fall back, his head dropping to the floor. His chest heaved again as more bile spilled to the ground. He couldn't move, the contraction in his stomach tightening while the scent of the giant grew stronger. The dog tried to bark at the evil presence outside, but his burning throat failed him. A series of hacks brought more poison from his system, and as the man's looming danger came closer, he forced himself up.

Caesar stood in wobbly uncertainty with his paws splayed wide. He hacked, his chest again clenching in mind-numbing pain, and his stomach contracted like prey caught in the jaws of death.

The baker stuffed his hands in his pockets as he walked up the hill toward the Heights.

Anthony Miracolo had called Rico several hours earlier to tell him Tony had returned. The baker's "I love you all" was met with silence. There was nothing more to say. The boy they all cared for so deeply was safe.

Rico tried to sleep. But he'd tossed and turned, thinking of the pain his weakness had caused so many good people. Finally, unable to quiet his mind, he dressed and walked out of his apartment and into the balmy spring night. Since his wife's passing, the baker frequently rose late at night and wandered the streets of the neighborhood, often ending in the shadows across the street from the Miracolo home. He'd stand in the darkness, staring at the sleeping house, thinking of all he'd lost. All he'd never have.

But tonight, he simply needed to be near.

Rico hoped Tony knew . . . No, not just the boy. The baker prayed the whole family knew the love he felt for them, the love he'd always carry.

XXXIII

The fur on Caesar's back rose, and he slowly lifted his head with a snarl. He knew that smell. The giant stood outside. Danger crept toward the house, and Caesar must stop it. Summoning the last of his strength, the dog struggled up the stairs and jumped against the door, causing the latch to pop free. He staggered out to find the giant standing there.

The big man took something out of his pocket, and a spark appeared in his hand. He tossed it on a pile of leaves, and they burst into flames. Then the man turned from the fire and struck his hands together again as another spark appeared. With a glow appearing from the tips of his fingers, Caesar's enemy rushed toward the house.

The dog didn't understand how the giant did it, but the foul-smelling man had created this danger. Blinded by rage and filled with adrenaline, Caesar growled, took several bounds, and jumped, catching the big man in the chest and knocking him to the ground. The match fell from the man's hand. But the effort had exhausted the last of the dog's power, and he collapsed to the ground.

Blindsided, a stunned Ridgeway recovered quickly, scrambling to stand over Caesar, staring with hate-filled eyes down at the dog.

"You should be dead." Ridgeway raised his leg, a massive steel-toed boot hovering over the dog's head. "That's all right. Oh, so much better this way."

Rico leaned against a mailbox across the street from the Miracolo house. He sighed as he reached for a cigarette but froze as the backyard burst into flames. He dropped his cigarettes and ran toward the light.

A hulking man stood in the yard, one leg raised over a prone form. The baker caught Ridgeway waist-high, his shoulder burying into the big man's gut in perfect tackling form. With the wind knocked out of him, Ridgeway rolled onto his knees, trying to rise. But Rico, enraged and aware of his foe's physical power, didn't give him time to recover. He spun around and as he rose caught the much bigger man with a vicious uppercut, knocking Ridgway onto his back. Rico jumped on top of him, pummeling the big man with a string of punishing lefts and rights.

The giant wailed, trying to break free as his hand fumbled at his belt.

Several loud bangs exploded in the night, and Rico De Santo cried out as he fell to the ground, hands clutching his stomach.

Lights flew on throughout the neighborhood as people poured out of their homes.

Tony jumped from his bed at the sound of the shots, his backyard lit up like the middle of the day.

He ran outside to find his father shouting orders as he unfurled a garden hose and turned to battle the spreading fire with its spiraling pile of fiery leaves.

"Rosa, fast as you can, the fire alarm on the corner! Frank, get the hose from your house!"

Tony's father continued shouting order as others sprinted to help him fight the fire.

But Tony hurried past them toward the sound of a painful groan to find a man curled up on the ground.

He gasped and dropped to his knees next to Rico.

The baker tried to rise but fell back as blood spread across his broad chest. "Ridgeway... It was Ridgeway."

Tony spotted his mother rushing out the back door.

"Mom! Call an ambulance!"

He pulled off his t-shirt and pressed it against the baker's wounds, attempting to staunch the bleeding.

"Don't move. Help's coming."

"Tony . . ."

"Don't talk. Plenty of time later."

But the sight of the blood soaking his shirt and

spreading across the boy's hands told a different story.

The baker shook his head. "No. Things you gotta hear." He grimaced in pain. "You're a good man. I couldn't be prouder of you."

"I know that, and I'm sorry about everything I said. It's just—"

The baker coughed up blood, struggling to talk. "Tony, there's one thing you gotta know. We all love you. Nothin' could change that." He shivered, and his eyes grew glassy. "It's awful cold."

As the sirens drew near. Rico grabbed the boy's hand and pulled him closer to whisper, "You're the best of us."

Crying, Tony lowered his head to hear above the clamor all around them.

"Promise me. . . . Don't . . . let it . . . Don't let any of this define you. People will fail you but learn to forgive and hold on to the good." The words came harder now. "Do this for me. . . . You have beautiful stories. . . . Tell them. . . . Promise me."

Strong hands dragged Tony away as two uniformed men dropped to their knees to hover over Rico. The boy struggled to his feet in stunned silence and, stumbling to keep up, followed as they loaded the wounded baker into the ambulance.

Tony stood sobbing as the doors slammed shut. Red lights flashed, lighting the skyline as the ambulance raced down the street to be lost in the darkness.

"I promise."

The siren faded, and Tony looked back to find his soot-covered mother holding a garden hose against the flames as his father helped firefighters drag a thick fire hose into position.

He placed his hand on his mother's shoulder, surprised to discover how much taller he was than her. "Let me," he said gently, taking the hose from her trembling hands. He pointed at his sister, who stood nearby crying as she clutched her favorite doll. "Go check on Rosa."

Rico De Santo was right. He had people who loved him and would sacrifice anything for him. And he'd been blessed to have each of them.

Tony lifted his eyes to the starlit sky. "I do. I promise."

The lawn around him turned a mottled black, and a gray mist rose off the defeated flames. Tony shivered as a breeze whipped across his shirtless chest. Weeping, he dragged the hose to join the others in the ongoing battle. Water from multiple fire hoses crisscrossed in the night sky and battered the barn, where the fire still burned brightly. The flames licked their way up the side of the building, but when he looked toward his house, he saw only burnt grass now soaked by the hoses.

Rico De Santo had saved them. Tony felt like his heart had been pulled from his chest and couldn't imagine a more unbearable pain. Then he saw Jo bent over a form outlined by the glow of the burning barn. He dropped the hose, rushing to the sobbing girl, and fell to the ground beside her.

Jo cradled Caesar's massive head in her lap as she rocked back and forth, murmuring in numbed prayer.

Rico De Santo had not fought alone.

Tony ran his hand across the dog's scarred face and released an anguished scream into the night sky. Hands pulled on his shoulders, trying to lead him away. But he fought back, wrapping his arms around the dog's neck and burying his face in Caesar's thick fur.

XXXIV

MIRIAM

"Code Blue."

The buzz of hospital staff in full action mode jolted me out of the story. I turned as several nurses dashed from their station, and a doctor rushed past us, following the others down the hall.

AJ wiped away a tear, pressed his hands against the arms of the chair, and pushed himself up to stand. "It's time. I have to go."

I reached out to keep him from walking away, but it was like trying to grab a ray of sunlight. "Wait, you can't leave yet," I said, my voice rising above the buzz of activity. "I've been listening to you for hours. I have to know how the story ends. Rico, Caesar. Do they live? And what becomes of

Tony and Jo?"

AJ smiled. "Some people love to tell you stories about all the pains in their lives or all the times they've been offended by this person or that one. Others like to share some angst-ridden secret from their childhood or just complain about the simplest of pains. My head hurts. My knee hurts. My ass hurts." He laughed, covering his mouth like a small child caught being naughty. "Sorry, you get the point. Ultimately, it's all a waste of time. Life's too short to spend precious time rehashing the ugliness."

"Okay, I get it. Roberto Benigni in *Life is Beautiful*. Love conquers all, blah blah blah," I said, frustrated by this naïve, homespun sermon. "But I need to know how *this* story ends."

"Haven't you learned anything from what I've told you?" AJ's eyes grew bright, and he leaned forward, giving me an avuncular kiss on the forehead. His wisp of a touch felt like the butterfly kisses my father gave me as a little girl. "Miriam, you are a storyteller. Write your own ending."

He smiled that smile of his, then turned and walked away. I called after him, but he didn't stop. With a brisk backward wave of his hand, he said, "I'm predicting a beautiful life for you, Miriam Singer. Come on, Jules. She'll be expecting us."

I watched as the dog loped after him, tail disappearing around the corner of the lobby.

A golden moon now hung high in the sky outside the hospital windows as California palms swayed gently in the breeze. I checked my phone: 7:40. My shift ended hours ago, and I'd missed the interview with my mother's plastic surgeon. I had over a half dozen more texts from my mother, each angrier than the last. I deleted her numerous voicemails to spare myself the pain of her shrill lecturing. The text messages would suffice:

> *What was I thinking?*
> *Time to grow up.*
> *I'd disappointed her, yet again.*
> *Too much like my father.*

I got up, but the thought of being alone or facing my mother left me cold. My stomach growled, so I rode the elevator to the cafeteria. I sat, dazed, nibbling on a sandwich, rehashing AJ's story and his sudden departure with the parting words, "Write your own ending."

Good advice for a would-be novelist, but what about real life? What happened to Tony? Or was the tale of the boy's life with Rico, Caesar, and Jo all a fantasy fashioned by a kind stranger to help an unhappy teenager escape for a few hours from her well-crafted sorrows?

With my tasteless sandwich barely touched, I sat as cafeteria staff worked around me, bussing tables and preparing to close for the night. I'm not sure why I lingered. I could find plenty of places to grab something better to eat or take a short drive and walk in the sand at the Santa Monica Pier. Maybe, in the back of my mind, I hoped AJ might reappear to tell me the end of his tale.

He said I should write my own, but I had no need for some concocted fairy-tale ending.

If Tony Miracolo's story wasn't simply some fanciful tale, I needed to know how it ended and bristled at advice that sounded like it came from a greeting card. I pushed my sandwich away. AJ had more to tell me and left before he could.

I sat, silent with my thoughts, when a man came in to be met with a "Sorry, the register's closed."

He nodded, stopped to buy coffee from a vending machine, and sat one table over from me. My eyes followed him. It looked like he'd been crying, but he appeared oddly at peace.

"You okay?" I guess it was my day to talk to strangers, and the guy had a familiar, welcoming face.

He smiled weakly and said, "It's been a tough few weeks."

"I'm sorry."

"Thanks, but in a way, she's been gone for nearly a month. . . . Life support." He shrugged. "But it's over. She's with my father now."

"Belief is a powerful thing."

"My father always said that." The man fixed his eyes on me as he straightened in his chair. "It's odd. I've been feeling his presence all day."

A chill ran up my spine as I studied the man— his kind eyes, warm smile, and broad shoulders. Could it be? The resemblance was undeniable.

"My name's Miriam."

"Rico," he said.

My jaw clamped shut, and I swallowed hard. "Family name?" I finally managed to ask.

"Yes, after my great-uncle. I never met him, but my father talked about him so much, it felt like he was always with us."

"I'm sure he was."

"You do sound like my father," the man said.

"Thank you." I smiled, feeling I'd never received a greater compliment.

"Rico." A man stood at the entrance to the cafeteria, signaling. "The family's waiting."

Rico gave him a half-wave and turned back to me. "My brother Anthony," Rico said as he stood up. "Well, thanks for listening. It helped."

Trembling, I mumbled a polite goodbye. Rico left the cafeteria to be met by half a dozen family members, and I sighed, warmed by the love enveloping him.

With unsteady hands, I grabbed my phone and did a Google search of AJ Miracolo. The images I found confirmed it.

My man was famous. Well, behind-the-scenes famous, anyway. He'd taught film at several prestigious universities and was known around Hollywood for decades as the "Screenplay Doctor," brought on to projects hundreds of times to save a floundering script. A small excerpt of the article read:

> *Throughout his long career, the unassuming Miracolo, whose journey began as a teenager making short films with a second-hand eight-millimeter camera, gained industry fame for bringing a Capraesque feel to the projects he worked on. His stories celebrated the unique goodness Miracolo saw in people and the nobility he found in a*

simple life well-lived. His most common advice: "Write your own ending."

A few years before his sudden death from a heart attack, Miracolo wrote a successful, heartwarming memoir about his childhood: "So Many Kinds of Love"

I clicked on a link that brought me to the book and read the opening lines.

Jules died in my arms, with my wife Jo by our side. My son, Rico, slept in the room next door. Never able to get his young tongue wrapped around the words Caesar or Julius, my son gave the dog the diminutive Jules, and so our loyal friend became Jules for all of us.

Heartbreak failed to describe the pain I bore as I tried to imagine my life without the dog who had always been there for me. But belief is a powerful thing, and I knew this was not the end of our story. What we had would not, could not, end with a passing breath. Moments before he died, Jules flicked out his tongue to lick my hand. Then he closed his eyes as my mind took me back to the road we'd traveled, knowing that journey was only the first step in what lay ahead for both of us. My Caesar would never leave me, never stop loving me.

Our journey had just begun.

I wiped away the tears that wouldn't stop flowing. AJ had told me loving someone made life worth living, and Rico told Jo there are no perfect people. Even your heroes fall short of who you think they are. But they never stop loving you. And you never stop needing them.

AJ's story proved that, and I knew what I must do. I needed to return to the people I loved, the people who made me whole. I grabbed my phone and sent a cryptic text to my father.

♥ *Coming home. Kiss Bubbe for me. I'll see you soon.*

But first, I had to go back to Santa Monica, face my mother, and tell her I didn't want to be an actress. I had a different dream.

I left the hospital and caught my reflection in the window. I saw the gentlest eyes looking back at me. My father's eyes, and they *were* beautiful. I smiled, and the pretty face smiled back at me. The wide-set eyes and strong jaw framed perfectly by a lovely aquiline nose. What was my mother thinking? AJ was right. I'm perfect, just the way I am.

A warm ocean breeze caressed my face, and I looked at the starlit sky, more at peace than I had been in a long time.

My friend told me to write my ending, and that's what I planned to do, just as AJ had written his. But my stories would differ from those I thought I wanted to write just a few hours earlier. AJ had taught me about the power of love.

My journey had begun, and it was time to write my story.

Through the Dog's Eyes

Jake has a dream to get away from his working-class town, but fate may have a different plan for him. Through heartache and loss, his dog Bull is by his side as Jake searches for meaning in this heartfelt coming-of-age story.

~ ~ ~ ~

He held me close and walked out of the house into an icy-cold clear daylight. Shocked by the biting cold, I nuzzled against his warm body as he carried me away from the only life I'd ever known. Something roared high above us, and he stopped. My Boy stared up into the sky as a giant shiny bird raced across the clouds. His chest beat faster, matching my pounding heart, and his eyes flashed in excitement, like he'd found his favorite toy to chew. His eyes grew wider, and he held me closer, our hearts now beating as one.

"That's gonna be me someday, buddy. Just you wait and see."

I would see that look and hear the excitement in his voice a lot in the years to come whenever he stared into the sun-streaked sky. My Boy wanted something special out of life, and I was to be by his side as he chased his elusive dreams.

Made in the USA
Las Vegas, NV
01 December 2025

35476157R00174